An Imperfect

Perception

Ruby Ridgeway

To my family

For your endless support

Contents

One

There are a few moments every day that are mine and mine alone. Moments in which the noise wanes, the chaos clears and the muscles in my neck begin to gently unfurl. A hiatus from the usual bedlam that I cherish –

'Good day, love?'

Oh God. You're back.

That's not what I say. That's just what I want to say, along with *if you mean did I enjoy spending the last nine hours picking up pants and wiping wee off the bathroom walls, then yes, it was a highlight compared to Sharon hacking up a massive hairball and looking at me like it was my fault. Oh, and Beasley ate the prawns I left out to defrost so look forward to more of that later and yes, before you mention it, the boys haven't stopped bickering all day so I said they could go on their tablets even though you keep insinuating that I let them watch too much, you condescending twat.*

I don't say that. I say 'Just the usual.'

'Mmm. Something smells nice. What's for dinner?'

Really? Must we go through this every day?

7

That's not what I say. I say 'Fish pie,' and I don't even flinch when Ben says 'Mmm' again. I manage a terse smile and then sensing terse smiles are probably worse than no smile at all, I hide my face in the freezer and rummage around the frozen veg drawer looking for peas. He hovers there despite the inconceivable lengths I go to putting it all back neatly until finally I'm forced to stand or lose a finger to frostbite.

'Glass of wine? Oh, you've already got one.'

Yes, I've got one. Well done for making your point though.

'I'll just go and say hello to the boys then. If they can drag themselves away from YouTube, that is.'

And there it is.

I take a deep breath and exhale slowly through my mouth but it's no good. My teeth snap back together with the force of a bear trap and I can't help but roll my eyes, supposedly at the glacier of peas standing majestically in the pan among the marine life. A peaberg, as Jacob would call it if he weren't upstairs lost in a game of Fortnite or Forza or whatever he's into these days, his headphones on, the door shut tight. Avoiding us.

Zac and Oscar's voices are raised now. Singsong and overexcited as though they haven't seen Ben in weeks and he comes bearing gifts. He probably does. He's probably snuck them both a Kinder Egg. And right before dinner. Bloody typical.

'Come on, lads.' His voice rings out from the sitting room as he swings the double doors open too quickly, smacking the handles against the walls with a crunch that'll leave another dent. 'Turn off that rubbish and let's help lay the table.'

Great. Thank you. That's just what I need.

'I don't really —' It's too late. Here they come, shoulders slumped like they're off to the gallows.

'Right, you two. Clear this mess up, then Zac, you're in charge of knives, forks and carving the carrots into roses. Ozzie, you're plates and napkins. Swans this time, not aeroplanes. I'm going to have a quick shower and this place had better look like a five star restaurant by the time I get down.' He laughs and ruffles Oscar's hair. Gives Zac a kiss on the top of his head.

They both pull away giggling and I'm struck, not for the first time, by their likeness - all three of them ludicrously fair and blue-eyed as though joined in an alliance against Jacob and me. A spotlight reflects off Ben's forehead and I notice the hair on his temples is thinning cruelly in contrast to the rest of his body. My lip curls instinctively at the traces of fur sprouting from his collar like an invasive species of moss. A thick wiry cloak rising over his shoulders and descending down his back, still ash blonde but destined to grey soon. Was there ever a time I thought that was attractive? I bash the last of the ice off the peaberg and grind my teeth.

'You okay?' he asks in a pleading tone. The one that leaves no room for anything but confirmation.

'Yep.'

He returns my tight smile with his own and then, my serenity in tatters, he finally leaves.

Thanks a lot, dear. I'll deal with the kids then.

'How do I make a swan, Mummy?'

'I don't know. There's probably a tutorial about it on YouTube. Why don't you look it up?'

Oscar's eyebrows arch enthusiastically and he marches over to the sideboard where the tablets are enjoying a well-earned break. 'I was only –'

'Awww, it stinks!' Zac flings the cutlery at the table and barrels into the sitting room again, his hands plastered over his nose as though a blackbird has threatened to peck it.

Yes, stay there.

The sofa screeches against the floorboards as he hurls himself at it. Quite unnecessarily.

'Beasley's farted! Bad dog. You stink!! Farty, stinker poo boy!!!!'

To be fair, there is something in the air but I'm not sure it warrants breaking the furniture. I'm also not a hundred per cent sure it's not the haddock until Beasley lifts his hangdog eyes and stares woefully at Oscar as though mildly disgusted.

Nice try.

'Eufff.' Ben's back. 'Is that you, Zac?' *Oh God.* The only thing worse than Dad Jokes is the false accusations of trumping in public.

'Noooooo!!!!' Zac squeals utterly bloody delighted. 'It was Oscar!!'

'Maaaate! You're back on your tablet.'

'Mum told me to find out how to fold napkins –'

Ben looks at me as though I can't be reasoned with.

'I was joking. Obviously. Oscar.' I take a large swig of wine.

'Alright. I forgot my phone. Be as quick as I can.' Ben leans in to kiss me and then he's off again. My cheek smarts where his stubble grazed it and I instinctively wipe away the light trace of sweat he's left there.

He never used to be this sweaty, let alone deposit it all over me. Not unless we were both sweaty and had good reason to be. Nowadays, he has the air of a menopausal fanatic only instead of burning up and getting irritated, he's obsessed with road bikes and Fitbits. Was this always a thing? I don't remember my dad trotting into the house every night wearing Lycra, though to be fair, I barely remember my dad at all, which isn't a bad thing. Especially if he did wear cycling shorts, but I'm sure he didn't.

Ben certainly never used to be into fitness like this either. The most we used to do on a Saturday morning was brush flakes of French pastries off the duvet, our soft fleshy legs entwined (or more latterly, stick Cbeebies on). Now he's out racing over the Surrey Hills by 8am – waking me in the process – supposedly so he can be back here by eleven to help out with the boys. Nice for some.

Of course, we're usually back from football practice by then, which is a shame because it was his suggestion they join in the first place because – and I quote – it would get them out from under my feet for a few hours every weekend. Yet somehow now my feet always seem to be planted firmly at the sidelines

11

hoping the inevitable drizzle turns into a downpour so at least we can all go home.

'How long's dinner going to be?' Oscar's brow is furrowed with concentration as he massacres his third sheet of kitchen towel with a level of focus he has failed to ever apply to his schoolwork.

'At least half an hour. I haven't even put it in the oven yet. I don't know why Daddy called you in so early.'

Zac shuffles over, gasping for breath and gagging dramatically through the splayed fingers stuffed into his nostrils. He brushes past me and my skin crawls, shrinking away from his touch.

'Can I have something to eat?'

'I've just said dinner's going to be ready in half an hour. You'll have to wait.'

'What is it?'

I sigh. Take another swig of wine. 'Fish pie.'

'I don't like fish.'

'You do like fish. You threw a tantrum yesterday because you couldn't have fish fingers.'

'I don't like that fish. It smells like Beasley's f –'

'Yes, alright.'

'Do I have to have fish pie, Mummy?' Oscar's given up on the swans and is putting his efforts into raising a fleet of aeroplanes to accompany dinner.

I give him a look. We all know what that looks means. All apart from Zac who is climbing onto the workbench, presumably

12

to scavenge for food in the crisp cupboard (which sounds a bit irresponsible, I know. Not the six-year-old crawling all over the surfaces with bare feet, but the fact we have a whole cupboard dedicated to crisps. Although, maybe everyone's got a crisp cupboard. How would I know? Who would ever admit it? In my defence, it didn't start off that way, but what can I say? Everyone likes crisps and naturally no one likes the same flavour. Except for my crisps. Everyone seems to like mine.)

'Get down. Zac. Get down.' I'm certain I screeched it loud enough. I've woken the dog up. Briefly. 'Zac.'

He stares at me defiantly and swings the door open.

That's it. 'Get down. Now.'

He grabs a packet of Wotsits (not my Thai Chilli Sensations at least) and I grab him.

'I said no.'

'Ah-ah-arghhhh.' Zac wrenches himself away, slamming the door back and pinging it on its hinges.

'Be careful.' I'm pulling at his shirt now, half to hold him up, half to drag him down.

'Get off.'

'Put those back and get down. You're going to fall and hurt yourself.'

'Get off.' Zac thrashes his arms about, pushing me away.

'Mate.' Ben, still damp and underdressed, strides towards us as Zac strikes out one last time and I spin away, bent double and blinded by a searing pain.

I stumble back a few feet while Ben gently lifts Zac down from the worktop but he pulls out of his grasp wailing hot angry tears and barges past me, hurtling out the kitchen on his way to throw himself back on the sofa. It's never had such a battering in its life, that poor thing. DFS have better have a bloody sale on. It'll be the one time…

'Are you okay?' Ben bends down to me, tenderly lifting my chin. Concern scars his forehead and I blink furiously at the salty puddle pooling in my eye.

'He caught me with the crisp packet.'

'The crisp packet?'

I blink again. I think he's scratched the cornea. Ben pulls my eyelids apart and angles my face towards the light.

'I can't see anything.' And then he snickers. 'I thought he'd punched you.'

I break away and press my palm against my eyeball. It really bloody hurts.

'A crisp packet. What are you like?' And then he shakes his head as though we're both in on the same joke, squeezes my shoulder and goes off to console Zac in the next room.

'Are you alright, Mummy?' Oscar ventures tentatively.

I mutter, 'Fine' and shuffle off to the downstairs loo to check out the damage and am almost disappointed (quite disappointed in fact) to discover there is none. It seems like quite a lot of fuss to go through only to have nothing to show for it. I know it was only a bit of a silvery plastic, mustn't grumble and all that, but it must have been the angle or something. It was a lot sharper than you might expect and feels like a paper cut, but in the eye. *The eye* and yes, it was an accident (I assume if Zac had the forethought to hurt me, he'd have armed himself better than that) but it's the principle.

Anyway, by the time I get back, Zac is eating an apple (There really will be hell to pay if he doesn't finish everything on his plate now), Oscar has destroyed an entire roll of kitchen towels and the fish sauce has burnt to bottom of the pan. And it's still only Monday.

Ben sidles back into the kitchen with a hesitant grin. 'At least the schools go back tomorrow.'

Much as I want to pour the remnants of dinner over his shiny balding head, I have to admit that occasionally he knows just what to say.

Two

It's actually only the primary schools that are reopening after six glorious weeks of fun-filled family activities (or screaming at the children and drinking too much, depending on who you talk to) which means Oscar and Jacob will be skulking around for two more days, but that's fine. More than fine, actually. It'll be nice to have some time to ourselves away from the constant backdrop of demands and hysterics that usually plague us.

They've been waiting all summer to see the latest Marvel movie. I forget which one, despite being forced to watch the trailer twenty-six times, usually while also trying to cook dinner, walk Beasley, feed Sharon, clear up and fix whatever Zac's broken and I'd like to say they've been patient, but they haven't. They been banging on about it for months but now finally we can spend the day doing what they want for a change. I might even treat them to Pizza Express afterwards so they can recount every scene to me in minute detail even though I've just sat through the whole ruddy thing. But first to get Zac up and out of the house.

He hasn't been to school since before the last lockdown and he's never been to this particular school at all so I'm surprised

17

when he seems up for it and not surprised when he has a meltdown in the playground at drop off. I can sense a eager blend of judgement and pity emanating from the sanctimonious parents skipping past me at the gate, heady with freedom and no doubt off to file their tax returns now they've finally got a minute to themselves (or other worthy plans they'll ditch for a cheeky glass of Chablis at lunch. '*Well, it's not like the kids go back to school everyday!*').

I'm just flaying strips of broiled skin from Zac's burning body (or so it would seem judging by his reaction to my attempts to mollify him) when a pair of brown brogues and tight trousers approaches, facilitated, in spite of the morning scrum, by the wide berth everyone else is giving us.

'Heeey.' The trousers scrunch at the knees and a young Lenny Kravitz crouches down. He's not a child or anything. I just mean *young* as in how he was in his heyday – although I'm sure he's aged well (no offence, Lenny).

This guy on the other hand is about thirty and he's not only wearing trousers, I should probably add. He has some sort of collarless shirt with rolled up sleeves buttoned up at the elbow but that's not really relevant. More significantly, he isn't glaring at me as though I'm wilfully creating a scene. Instead he winks. I don't wink back. I don't do anything at all. I have tears in the corners of my eyes and they will fall if I dare to close them.

He turns and points a finger at Zac's sparrow-like chest, hitching in fear and panic and says, 'You must be Zippity. Is that right?'

Zac heaves one last mighty breath and turns warily to the stranger who is beaming at him as though they're old friends. I have warned him about men like these and I can tell he is weighing up the odds of this one having puppies and me letting him pet them. At this point, so am I. If it gives me a few hours...

'Or is it Zaggerty?'

'It's Zachary!' I weigh in shrill with false rapture and Lenny 2.0 gasps.

'Nooo. I have a kid in my class called Zachary who's supposed to be starting today. Do you know him?'

The ends of Zac's mouth are unfurling as he stares out from behind a clump of damp eyelashes.

'Or... It couldn't be... It's not... you?'

Slowly, almost imperceptibly, Zac nods.

'No way! That's so lucky because Dolly, our guinea pig, is feeling a bit anxious about being back at school after such a long break and I was hoping you could give her a cuddle to settle her in.' Not a puppy then but whatever does the trick. 'Would that be alright? Do you think you could do that for me?'

Zac nods shyly again and his mouth twitches with the strain of holding back a smile.

'Atta boy. Come on then, let's not keep her waiting.'

Lenny pats him on the arm and springs up like a Duracell bunny. I, in contrast, wobble like a geriatric with a new hip and have to grab Zac's other arm for leverage.

'Easy does it,' Lenny laughs and then as if remembering his manners says, 'I'm Zac's teacher, Mr Matthews, by the way. I'm not kidnapping him.'

'Oh,' I titter. 'You're welcome to him. I've got more at home if you're interested…'

His smile falters and I sense we've probably had enough of the predatory paedophile jokes for one day.

'I did want to catch you actually,' he continues, clearing his throat – either causing or attempting to disguise the blush creeping up his neck. 'I've been briefed about the situation and was hoping to maybe meet up at some point after drop off this week, to sort of, go over any worries you and Zac might have or you know, well, anything at all.'

'Er. Sure. That would be great. I'll, erm…'

'Does Thursday work? I have an hour of admin duty first thing if that suits you?'

'Yep, nope, fine. Sounds good.'

'Fantastic. Mrs… Harrison, isn't it?'

'Lara. Lara's fine' I insist and immediately feel a bit silly. 'Bye, Zac. Have an amazing day, won't you? Give Dolly a squeeze from me. I mean a cuddle, not a squeeze. Zac, did you hear me?'

I don't get much in the way of acknowledgement from him, which doesn't bode well for the guinea pig but I do get another wink from Lenny (who winks these days?) and it's all I can do to contain a little side-skip and dance towards the gate.

I hold it in but there's nothing I can do to stop myself from bursting into a run and then regretting it but I'm nearly at the finish line. It's been nine months since I last had any space to breathe, any time to myself, a minute to think without being interrupted.

Greater London was put back on the high risk list weeks before the rest of the country so while everyone else was discussing whether or not to kill Granny at Christmas, we already knew we were screwed, but the truth is I really enjoyed lockdown. It must have been awful for anyone living on their own or with kids in a small flat but our set up was reasonably comfortable, the schools were pretty good at providing work and it was actually quite nice not having to worry about who would be spending what day with whom in the holidays and how offended that would make everyone else in the process.

Ben had already turned the box room into his office the first time around and once the rest of us got used to the multi-decibel Zoom calls shaking the walls and him bursting into the kitchen at all hours of the day, we all sort of slowed down and found each other again. Rediscovered family walks and board games, started eating lunch together. Prosecco o'clock got progressively earlier in celebration of getting through another day (or simply because we were becoming moderately alcohol dependent).

We didn't have to make laborious plans for the weekends or ferry the kids around to different clubs every night because it was illegal to do anything. At all. We were wonderfully

21

powerless, stripped of choice, relaxed and content in our own surreal bubble.

Life only became intolerable after Easter when everything changed and the schools re-opened. It had been over a year by then and the novelty of being at home all the time was becoming a challenge we were destined to fail. My head was no longer in the right place and I'd have given anything to get back to normality, picking up where I'd left off before anyone had ever heard of wet markets – setting up my new business, seeing to my own needs but instead of listening to the inner voice that wept and wailed inside me, we decided to keep Zac at home until the autumn term started.

And it's funny how in those days six and a half hours dragged like a coach journey from Kings Cross to Singapore (with none of the highlights or breaks) yet when the kids are at school there only seems to be time to make a quick coffee, lose it somewhere in the house, make another, take the washing out and hightail it back down the road for pick up and today is no exception.

Any ambitions I had of reintroducing Pizza Express's dough balls to the kid's palettes before the dreaded 'twenty-past-three' were abandoned as soon as I realised we'd only have three minutes to eat them after the film so we settled for a damp tray of nachos with weird cheese which brought on a plethora of *Nat Yo Cheese* jokes and an unsettling queasy sensation.

Now having rushed back to the house to pick up Beasley before he howled us into a court order, I find myself once again in a playground I thought I'd never have to see again, avoiding people I hoped never to meet and ignoring children I never seem to be able to get away from.

Beasley has finished his business and with no further pressing engagements scheduled, has resigned himself to sleeping on my foot, which is more than can be said for Jacob, who, having exhausted his daily quota of small talk, has stayed home in order to complete seven more challenges in Fortnite so as to 'earn another skin before the new season comes out'. Whatever that means.

The other two are less easy to entice back to the house. Zac's playing with some South-East Asian looking kid, screeching and squealing as Oscar gives chase in the same game of tag I've seen a hundred thousand times before. Please don't let me be *homie.* A stifled groan creeks up my throat at the thought of them both launching themselves at me, dragging my arms across their bodies like shields and screaming that they're safe. *Homiieeee!!!* My jaw clenches and I inhale laboriously, allowing my unseeing gaze to drift across the playground.

Bugger it. I made eye contact with someone. It was for less than a nanosecond and I looked away really bloody quickly, but my body and mind are suddenly alert to a silhouette creeping in from the left. *Jesus wept.* There's no ignoring her, even though I clearly am. She's right there in my periphery, inching towards me as if about to cry 'What's the time, Mr Wolf?' *Oh, for goodness sake.* I plug furiously at the passcode on my phone and scroll madly through my emails grasping at anything to read, grateful for once to hear that Wayfair is having a clearance sale. Again.

'Hi. I'm Kay. Theodore's mum.'

Kay leans into to my line of vision with an anxious grimace, her straight-cut bob swinging across her cheeks. I look up, startled with feigned surprise. Am I supposed to know who Theodore is? I mean, I'm guessing it's the screamer, but it's not like he introduced himself. I keep my phone poised standoffishly in front of me and smile as though slightly flustered and clearly in the middle of something, probably work related and possibly life-threatening, but as she lingers besides me expectantly, her own smile starts to falter and an old reflex kicks in.

'Oh, hi. Nice to meet you. I'm Lara.' *Bloody hell.*

She stands straight now and I'm forced to squint up at her shiny black hair, the porcelain skin, the small features I can barely make out against the glare of the sun glistening behind her. I raise my hand to shield my eyes, but she stretches her own out to shake it.

Oh God. I just can't be bothered. I am quite clearly radiating fuck off vibes. There must be someone else she can talk to. *Holy Mother.*

'They are in the same class, I think. Mr Matthews.'

'Oh, okay.'

'Yes. We moved here at the start of the summer so we don't know anyone yet. Theodore is desperate to make friends.'

He doesn't seem to be the only one and I want to say to her *Look, I'm sorry. You seem very nice but I've already been*

24

through this so many times and I just can't be arsed. But I don't. I say 'ahh' which she takes to mean *why don't you sit down?*

'May I?'

'Yes, of course.' I move my bag and place it reluctantly on the ground next to Beasley whose back leg is dancing, a sure sign that he's on the chase. *Well, you can try, old boy.*

'It's your dog,' Kay announces, leaning down to rub the top of his head. More fool her.

He opens one bloodshot eye, makes as if to rise, decides against it and slumps back down against my trainers (ancient hand-me-downs from Jacob that I had to wash twice to get the smell out).

'He's getting old.'

'Very cute.' He's not really. And he's not my dog. 'So pretty here.'

I glance around at the crumbling tarmac, the chewing gum fused to the flaking paint on the bench by her arm. '

In Kingston. So many trees. And the river.'

'Yeah, we're lucky having Richmond Park on our doorstep.'

'So beautiful. Are you from Kingston?'

Ohhh, please stop. 'Not originally, no. We were in Central London before and the south coast before that.'

It had been a tough decision to leave London after almost twelve years there. That is to say, a much discussed decision and one that I'd pushed through even though Ben would have been more than happy to stay put for another decade, feeding off the vibrancy and energy the city offered. Plus he only had a fifteen-minute commute to work, but he understood. The twenty-four hour bagel shops, nightclubs and bars on every corner were all well and good when we were single and childless but once Jacob and Oscar started calling the shots, it became apparent that every day when he buggered off to the office, so did everyone else who worked, leaving us behind with all the people who didn't. Not to judge but let's just say there seemed to be a direct correlation between having a job and a full set of teeth (and I don't mean the babies).

How we ever agreed on Kingston, I'll never know. We hadn't agreed on anywhere else but as soon as we found ourselves in a traffic diversion on the way back from Ben's mum and dad's and saw the John Lewis rising above us, we both knew.

Admittedly we seriously misjudged how much a fairly largish garden flat in zone 2 (zone 2!) would get us in zone 6 (6!) and were slightly unnerved to realise that according to Rightmove we'd be lucky to afford a three-bedroomed 1930s mock-Tudor semi-detached (as long as the owners had died recently) but it was too late. We were already committed mentally and emotionally to the place.

Within six months we'd taken advantage of a lovely family's grief, been shafted by the arseholes buying our flat, pulled at the heartstrings of the late owner's children again and were finally ensconced in our new life. And we never looked back (although we did add a kitchen extension and a master bedroom in the loft as soon as finances allowed).

I know I should ask Kay where she's from, but I can already guess. She's Japanese and married to some small English teacher who spent three years persuading her to come back home with him so he could open some sushi-fish and chip fusion bar or finally write that novel about a small English teacher navigating local etiquette and customs in some remote village near Nagasaki (no doubt with hilarious consequences).

But I don't care enough to ask. Everyone is from somewhere here. It was one of the reasons we loved it. I can remember boasting that twenty-eight out of thirty kids in Jacob's class had at least one parent or grandparent who wasn't British. It had seemed like the perfect melting pot – a veritable cauldron of diversity with all the cultural variety of Central London but on a more intimate scale. A global soup without the cliques and tensions, where difference was celebrated rather than mistrusted or derided. And it's still like that in my humble, white, middle-class opinion. I just do not give two shits about it anymore.

'Ahh. I love London… So big.'

Hmmm. I raise my phone again to check those outstanding emails. I don't mean to be rude, it's just I'm clearly very busy and important.

'How did you end up here?'

I make a bit of a show of dragging my eyes away from the screen and snapping my head as if to focus. 'Oh you know. We had to make the usual escape to the suburbs when my eldest got to school age.'

'It's your eldest?'

27

Oscar (who is not my eldest but I can't be bothered to explain) has Theodore in a headlock and Zac is pummelling him in the side trying to make him let go of his classmate. At least I presume that's Theodore. She still hasn't said.

'Both gorgeous boys. So much beautiful hair. Very blonde.'

'Yeah. They get it from my husband's side. Not that he's quite as blonde now. Or gorgeous.'

'Oh!' She hides her mouth behind a tier of tiny fingers and giggles like a child. 'Funny. Maybe gorgeousness is you. You are also very similar. Same eyes and nose.'

'Oh, the little one's not mine.'

'Ahh! Not your son...?'

'No. He's my nephew. He's staying with us for a while.'

'Holiday?'

Ohhhh. I could gloss everything like I usually do but I don't want to encourage any more conversation and if anything will see her off, this will. Besides I can't spend the next five years of drop offs, pickups, play-dates and school assemblies avoiding the subject. The rumours will spread soon enough.

'Not really. His mum – my sister-in-law, she died earlier this year.' Elena's face flashes through my mind. I cough and blink the image away.

'Died? Ah, I'm so sorry. Died?'

'Yeah.'

Her hand flies across her mouth again, her voice strangled with horror as though she's somehow responsible. 'So terrible.'

Beasley breaks wind. I don't hear him but the unmistakeable stench of prawns wafts through the air and I can't tell if Kay's eyes are watering on Zac's behalf or if she's just not used to dogs. Either way, I bet she wishes she'd never sat down here.

'I'm so sorry,' she says again lowering her hand and exposing one crooked front tooth. It's adorable. She's like a Disney caricature, or anime I guess. I feel bad for making her feel so uncomfortable and strain the corners of my mouth across my taut face.

'That's okay. We're taking it one day at a time. At least he's made a new friend.' I indicate towards Theodore just as Zac wrestles the poor kid's shoe off and throws it over the fence. Looks like that's our cue to leave. 'Annnnnyway, nice talking to you. I'm sure we'll bump into each other again. We'll probably be here most days.'

'Yes, nice talking to you too.'

So earnest. So awkward. She drags her eyes away from Zac (who is now sitting astride Theodore) and melts with relief as I haul Beasley away, still whimpering and chasing his dreams.

Three

It takes an ironclad effort to avoid the other parents on Thursday morning. I bow my head, absorbed once again in my phone but it's impossible to ignore all twenty-nine curious glances as twenty-nine other kids are dropped off.

I lurk outside the classroom until twenty-nine middle-aged women (twenty-seven and a couple of dads actually) have thrown their heads back, flicking their hair and tinkling with laughter at whatever rib-tickling observation Lenny has made and then I shuffle pseudo-patiently in front of the glass door as he reads the register. Thirty tiny hands shoot up in slow succession accompanied by tinny voices that would have once warmed my heart but now grate on my last stretched nerve. Zac, bored with flapping his hands at me is now intent on scuffing some chunky dark-haired child's shoes and the teaching assistant intervenes with a look that suggests it's not for the first time.

Eventually, thirty tiny creatures rise clumsily from the grimy floor mat, line up neatly and file into the corridor as well as they can with Zac clinging to the doorframe, gesticulating wildly as though lost at sea. I wave back grimly and finally he grins and allows the poor TA to lead him to the drama hall.

Lenny strides over to the door and swings it open, gesturing for me to enter.

'Sorry to keep you waiting. Come inside.'

I smile enigmatically and glance around the classroom. It's been a while since I've been in the infants' block and this is the same room Jacob had when he was in Year Two. My heart swells and I falter, taken aback by the memory of him sitting expectantly at his desk at 3.20 everyday, his coat on, bags ready to go, the huge beam on his face at the sight of me through the window stretching even further at the sound of his name. And inevitably his first words to me every afternoon;

'Have you got anything to eat?'

'Don't I even get a hello?'

My kiss on his soft cheek the moment before he hands me some piece of impractical artwork on its convoluted route towards my recycling bin.

It had all seemed so sweet then. That mat was new for a start. It all was and I took it for granted, never expecting anything to change until it was too late and those days were behind us. But now I'm back again.

'Take a seat.'

I catch my breath and scuttle across the room like a schoolgirl. Lenny is reclining at his desk, grimacing sheepishly towards the miniscule chair he's pulled across for me to sit on.

'Oh.'

'Sorry, we're not very well set up for adults in here.'

'That's okay,' I bat away the urge to remind him that I may need to be winched back up and instead do a masterful job of pretending the crunch of my knees going down is my bag rubbing against the floor. Even so, I feel ridiculous and at something of a disadvantage to say the least.

'So let me start off, first of all, by welcoming you both to Gold class. I know you're already familiar with the school.'

'You could say that.'

He smiles at me kindly, too kindly. I don't need anyone to look at me like that.

'Thought I'd finally be done with the school run when Oscar got to secondary. What do they say about the best laid plans?'

'It must be… very hard for you all. And I want you to know, I'm here to help in anyway I can.'

I reach down for my water bottle, grip it tightly and fiddle with the lid to disguise the tremor in my hands. He clears his throat.

'So, I know it can't have been a priority at all, understandably, but I wondered if you'd had a chance to look at any Key Stage One material with Zac over the last few months?'

'We did a bit.'

We did more than a bit truth be told. Keeping him close seemed like the right choice at the time and I threw myself into homeschooling like never before, blocking out everything but phonics, phonemes and chunking methods. Zac on the other hand, took to tearing the pages out of his workbooks but I forced him to continue all the same. The screaming, the shouting, the tears – it wasn't my finest hour and in hindsight the results were questionable if not destructive to us both.

'There's no right answer. It would just be helpful to have an idea about what sort of things he's been doing up until now. I know he missed out on quite a bit of school last year, but to be honest, compared to the gaps in knowledge that we're seeing in a lot of kids post-lockdown, there don't really seem to be any major issues. He's clearly very bright, or well, I'm sure you've just been doing a really good job at home.'

'We did try. I feel like I probably could have done better. It wasn't easy to...' I was going to say *not kill him* but I go for *keep him engaged* instead.

'No and that's to be expected, of course. Even kids who haven't been through the trauma Zac's experienced would struggle – have struggled with readjusting to the learning environment, not only the in terms of the classwork but with the social aspects of school too. And that would probably be my greatest concern at the moment as far as Zac is concerned.'

'The social aspects?'

'Yes.' He lifts his eyes from the report he's fixated on. 'Zac is obviously intelligent with above average dexterity, co-ordination and problem-solving skills. He has an excellent reading level for his age, but is –'

All I can focus on is the little gap between his front teeth. I mean he isn't unattractive and he could fix it so easily. What's stopping him? Is it cute? I mean, I guess he can get away with it.

'–understandably, displaying a number of behavioural issues and of course, it's early days and he may well settle down as soon as he feels more at home – here, in the classroom, I mean. So with that in mind, currently my main motivation is to integrate him more with his peers and to… address some of the more obvious traits of his… behaviour.'

The sociopathic traits? I don't say. I say 'Sounds good' because I suppose it does.

'I'm sorry to ask and of course, I would totally expect him to be affected by… everything he's been through, with his…' He looks back at his notes and flutters the page as if shaking off an ant. 'But would you describe his, let's say, lack of attention and… excitability as a recent phenomenon or has he always been fairly…'

'Highly strung?'

'Yes,' he cries, relieved not to have to come up with his own unloaded adjective.

'He's always been a handful. He's worse now, I'd say but yeah. His mum wasn't what you'd call strict and he's always been pretty boisterous.'

And by boisterous I mean he always seems to have just downed a bottle of coke with a triple espresso chaser. He's never met a wall he hasn't bounced off, a toy he hasn't broken or another parent who hasn't shuddered with dread, disapproval and relief that he's not their child.

It seems disloyal to dwell on any of that and to be fair, Elena did try to discipline him. It wasn't like she sat there chuckling

35

indulgently as he ripped wrapping paper off other children's presents and kicked them in the shins, but it was hard not to wish that she'd done more. She'd learned to pick her battles, she said, although I missed that process of elimination entirely. I did, however, understand.

Don't get me wrong. Zac could be sweet. Occasionally he'd catch me off guard with an impromptu cuddle or handmade card and he loved Jacob and Oscar – Oscar especially. He adoooored them, much to their distress and I must admit, I happily palmed him off them if it meant Elena and I could sit undisturbed at the kitchen table drinking wine and fending off the inevitable complaints about Zac messing up Jacob's hair or taking apart Oscar's Lego.

I can see it was easier to ignore his more spirited conduct so maybe his psychopathic tendencies are part of his make up, maybe it was his mother's lacklustre parenting or maybe a combination of both, but they aren't due entirely to everything he's been through in the last six months. It's irrelevant anyway. Whatever the cause, it's all down to me to deal with now.

'– plan moving forward –'

Sorry, I completely zoned out then.

'– is to set him up with three one-to-one sessions a week with Ms Conwell, our SEN co-ordinator. Not that's he's got special educational needs in the true sense, of course, but she's also our primary pastoral care provider.'

What is he talking about? I rack my brain back to when the other two were this age, but I never had to go through any of this. They were so blessedly normal. So perfectly average and unremarkable.

'Luckily, as I say, he appears to be bright and resilient. He's already made a few friends and this is a nice class. Most of the kids have been together since reception but we've had a few late joiners over the last two years and they've all settled in nicely so I don't think Zac will have any trouble fitting in. We'll just have to keep an eye on his tendency to get…over-enthusiastic at times. He's good kid, that's the main thing. Well, you know that, of course.'

Do I? 'Okay. That all seems…'

'And do you have any questions for me? Or anything you'd like to add?'

'No, no. It sounds like you've got it covered.' I'm immediately struck by a flickering concern that I should be expressing more interest but the relief flooding Lenny's face tells me I've made the right choice.

'Great.' He springs up, one hand outstretched towards me and it feels like I've reached the end of a job interview, but I have no idea how it went.

For Christ's sake, this chair. His arm droops a little and his eyes begin to cloud as he waits for me to hoist myself up, flustered and grappling with my water bottle, bag and the laws of physics. *Give me a minute, for goodness sake.*

'Well, thank you for seeing me. And for everything you're doing for Zac. He seems to like it here. I think it was time.'

He smiles his gappy smile. It's growing on me, I suppose.

37

'We'll keep a special eye on him, don't worry, Lara.'

And there I go, feeling foolish again.

My chin tilts towards the sun as I step into the light and there's a slight bounce in my walk that wasn't there a few days ago. Not only that but I finally find the coffee I lost yesterday when I go to reheat this morning's cup after it resurfaced in the bathroom. It was in the microwave! So I'm not going mad, although I may be suffering from early onset dementia. Besides, can you really be going mad if you know you're going mad? Because sometimes I feel like I'm losing it a little bit (all of the time). But if I know I'm losing it, surely that's okay?

'And wouldn't you? Wouldn't anyone in my position?' I ask the dog, who takes as much notice of me as the brush I'm using to sweep around his bed, but what does he know? Sharon gets it. Sharon feels the same way I do. Her feet have hardly touched the ground since Beasley joined us. Instead she navigates around the house with a series of complex parkour moves as though there's a chance in hell her usurper could raise more than an eyelid to reach her with his arthritic legs, rotund belly and general lack of being arsed.

I'd have been swatting her sweet derriere for climbing on the kitchen worktops a few months ago but if the downside to her not leaving home is the occasional hair in dinner (lunch and breakfast) so be it. I have enough on my plate, so to speak, without trying to reconstruct those affronted cat becomes friends with gnarly dog videos always doing the rounds on Facebook.

So she *has* gone a bit mad 'in my position', but as for anyone else, it's one of those questions I've learned not to delve into. The implications are too huge, the judgements too ready and I'm well aware the right answer is the polar opposite to how I feel and it doesn't change a thing. I already know how outrageous it sounds. I loved Elena, I really did, even if I'll never forgive her and though he might be a holy terror, my heart bleeds for her little boy. But it also bleeds for all of us, for everything we've lost but there's no option to wallow in despair. My grief is overshadowed by Zac, my strength sucked up in the task of staying strong for him. Easing his transition from happiness to this new upturned life. But just as his world has been turned upside down so has mine and not one single person has ever asked me how I feel about restructuring it all. Of course they haven't.

'What sort of monster would put their own feelings before a child, Beasley?' My remorse before his confusion, my misgivings before his pain? Ben and I are his legal guardians just as Elena would have been there for our kids. We'd had the hypothetical chat, hypothetically agreeing to each take on each other's children in the hypothetic event of our demise. 'Ha!'

We'd all been gushing and selfless and 99% confident it was never going to happen and the reality was, *we* haven't taken on Zac. '*I* have. And you, lazy stink bomb that you are. You're no help either. I mean, no offence. I probably shouldn't be moaning to you about it, but can you see where I'm coming from? Objectively at least.'

39

Beasley's always been cool and rational-minded. To the point of indifference.

'What was I thinking anyway? That because Oscar was finally at big school I could finally carve out a life of my own?' Put a stamp on the world before that world fell apart. And now the dust has cleared, I'm the one still picking up the pieces and I can never ever say that out loud. 'Oh, that's right. Ignore me. I'm almost done here anyway.'

I traipse up the stairs for the hundredth thousand time, rags in one hand, the cleaning caddy in the other, every step dragged down by the heavy sinking sensation of walking through sediment.

And *God.* I wish Ben would shut up. He's on another conference call but anyone would be forgiven for thinking he's trapped down a well. Worse still, he's got his headphones on so all I can hear are his contributions to this boring, *boring* conversation reverberating through the walls, making every outburst a volley of gunfire.

And the state of these bedrooms. Oscar's has always been a tip but since Zac moved into the top bunk, it looks more like the Randomz stall at a school fete (when all that's left are the one-legged robots, two dozen battered cars and half a Spiderman suit). It doesn't matter how many times I clear it up, it will all be strewn across the floor as soon as they get back home from school. I lift a discarded T-shirt off a lame dinosaur and the crunch it makes sends shivers down my spine. *G-ross.*

'COULDN'T AGREE WITH YOU MORE, MATT, BUT TRY GETTING THAT PAST ACCOUNTS.'

Mary, Mother of Christ. Someone tell that man how to use a microphone. I slam the window with a bang, fling a few books on the shelf and drown out the call with a thunderous crash of Lego smashing into its box (from a bit of a height). And then I stomp (a little more than necessary) towards Jacob's room, pausing only at the doorway to marvel at how tidy it still is – every object in its place just the way he left it. A row of Xbox games lined up next to the console, his headset curling neatly around the controller.

Why can't they all be like that? A little anal, a little OCD and so, so much easier to maintain. Why do the other two have to be so much like me? I can't even blame genetics. Elena was just as messy, some would say a slob (Ben, Ben's mum, Ben's Aunt Sue and anyone who'd ever been to her flat) and there was a time I was the same, but years of my husband fussing over the occasional piles of washing up left out until morning or a light layer of dust on the windowsills, has trained me to keep on top of the housework – not quite to his exacting standards but somewhere in between the squalor he likes to refer to me living in when we met and the M&S showroom he'd prefer.

And I've got to admit I prefer it this way too now although it entails me endlessly cleaning – the kitchen, the bathrooms, the toilets. Well, not the toilets per se. The toilets barely seem to get a look in. It's the walls, floors and toilet brushes that take up the time. The loo rolls that spin in the slightest breeze sending reams

41

of paper onto the urine-speckled tiles below. The pale yellow flecks splattered on every surface as far as the eye can see like residue spray from a fireman's hose.

But I stand corrected today. Today someone has managed to hit the bowl itself and sticky pools of orange tinkle have collected around the hinges. It doesn't look healthy. I must make sure they're drinking enough water.

And that's it. That's my day. Three half-drunk cups of coffee and a piece of toast. Three clean bogs, two shiny showers, seven gleaming taps. A disinterested nod at Ben on his way out to cycle around Richmond Park at lunchtime, a glare at the dregs of his protein shake curdling next to the sink. A word with Sharon to please stop grooming herself on the island while I'm cooking, a batch of sausage rolls for the boys to demolish when they let themselves in after school and a pasta sauce, ready to heat up when I stagger back from the playground on the brink of tears after hours of pleading and begging Zac to come home.

I check there's wine in the fridge. We're running low, but there should be enough to get through the evening and if not, I have an emergency bottle of almond liqueur from about nine years ago that no one can ever bring themselves to drink.

'No need to crack open the mouthwash yet, old boy.'

Beasley sighs. I made the same observation yesterday and the day before.

'Come on. It's that time again. Off we go, back to hell.'

I click the lead onto his collar and he jolts unsteadily to his feet. Sharon gives him a contemptible stare that would chill his bones if he could be bothered to look at her, but he can't. He merely ambles along besides me until we reach the school gates where a hundred exuberant kids cry out with joy at the sight of him – a sentiment that's clearly not reciprocated but he tolerates being fondled a hundred times anyway.

Zac, on the other hand, skids past us screaming 'Can I go to the playground?' without the slightest concern as to whether we can or not. He's already darted across the pedestrian crossing before I've had a chance to tell him nothing would please me more.

To think one of the reasons we chose Park View over the other equally excellent schools in the area was so I could let the kids play on the swings and slides on the way home, but what had once been a treat has become torture. A trial to be endured, not enjoyed.

For the love of God. Can we please just go home?

He's off with Theodore again and I have no excuse to ignore Kay, who bless her, is making a valiant effort to overcome the sheer awkwardness of our first encounter by beckoning furiously and it's not for want of friends. She's clearly made a few and it would be churlish of me not to head over to them and introduce myself even though I'd rather crack my kneecaps in two with a baseball bat.

'Well, hello!' the tallest, heaviest-set one exclaims. "You must be Zac's… I'm Stella, Lottie's mum. You might have heard of her. She's taken quite the shining to him.'

43

'Really?' It takes all sorts and no, he hasn't mentioned her or anything else about school at all apart from the flapjacks they get at break time which taste like dog's do. I suggested sawdust was probably more appropriate but he was adamant, though whatever knowledge he has about that, I'll have to attribute to Elena.

'I'm Lara. Zac's aunt.'

The convivial round of nodding and murmurs suggests Kay has already filled them in and more names follow, none of which I remember, but everyone is very nice. Very young. Still enthusiastic about reading levels and national averages. Spelling tests and who's going to volunteer to be class rep this year. Pretty much all of them as it turns out. *Sweet Jesus.*

'Are you putting your name in the hat, Lara?'

'No, that's okay. You go ahead. I've already done it a few times. Don't worry about me.' *Knock yourself out, suckers. Give it a few years and you'll give your wrinkle-free foreheads not to have to organise another Christmas Fair, parent helper rota or end-of-year present ever again.* 'In fact, I've just noticed the time. I need to give Zac a five-minute warning. It'll take about half an hour so I'd better start now.'

He's racing around the climbing frame, chasing another boy who doesn't look like he wants to be chased and has one arm tangled up inside his sweater, which I assume has something to do with Zac. I can tell which one is his mother by the way she twitches, desperate to intervene, but horribly conscious of me standing there.

44

I swing my bag over one shoulder and throw a few hasty goodbyes over the other, much to their relief, but Zac's prey leaps over the fence into the playing field with Zac in quick pursuit before I can reach them. Only the lure of a lukewarm sausage roll can draw him anywhere near me and Armless takes the opportunity to go running back to his mum.

This is where it pays to withhold food so I can to bait my nephew like a dog to get him home and it's only as I'm walking backwards dangling his snack in my outstretched arm that I see Lenny standing by the roadside. He has a pile of files in the crook of one arm and is wrestling his car door with the other, but he still makes time to take a lesson on parenting from me.

'That must be where I'm going wrong. Is that how you get kids to do what you want?'

'Bribery? Of course. How can you not know that by now?'

'Hello, Mr Matthews. Goodbye Mr Matthews,' Zac squeals making a dash for it.

'Not so fast," I grab his hood with a grin-ace and less grip than I'd normally use and he twists away, leaving his hair standing on end and me holding his coat. And then he pegs it back to the playground with the sausage roll. *Ah.*

'Sorry! I ruined your getaway. Hey, you've got a beagle. I love beagles!'

'What, this old thing? I've had it for years.' I haven't had it for years. What am I talking about?

'He's very cute. I'm considering getting one myself. Bit late, I know. I'm probably the only person in the UK who waited until lockdown was over to get a dog but better late than never.'

'Well, maybe the prices will have come down a bit at least.'

'I hope so. They were going for about three grand last time I checked.'

I suck air through my teeth, no doubt adding to my allure. 'We got this one for free actually. He was part of a two-for-one deal.'

'Really? Oh, you mean…' The colour creeping up his neck could be described as magenta.

'He's, I mean, he's lovely. It's fine. The cat's a bit put out but fortunately Beasley here's past caring about anything more than getting a good nap and any food scraps that fall on the floor.'

'Ahhh. He reminds me of the beagle my neighbours had when I was growing up.'

Can't have been long ago.

'I always wanted one of my own. I mean, if they still make them, that is. Seems like everything but French Bulldogs and Cockerpoos is on the endangered list these days.'

'I know! What's that about?' I laugh and am about to tell him what a nightmare Elena used to have with Beasley when he was a puppy, chewing up chair legs and chasing squirrels up trees and then I realise he probably doesn't want to stand there with an armful of papers that need marking when he has a home to get to, just like me. 'Well, good luck finding one. They're sweet dogs. Buggers to train and no recall whatsoever, but yeah, they're alright as long as you're not too keen on your furniture.'

'I will bear that in mind.' He flashes that little gappy smile of his and finally manages to wrangle the door open, dropping his files on the passenger side and straightening back up towards me. 'Good luck getting Zachary home.'

That's right. I'd forgotten all about him but a quick glance towards the playground reveals he's back on the disk swing with a bunch of older boys who probably won't be leaving for ages. *Bugger it.*

'Ohhh dear. Looks like I'll be needing it.'

He shakes his curly dreads as he grins and scoops into the driver's seat. 'See you tomorrow, Lara.'

And I say, 'See you tomorrow, Mr Matthews.'

And then I stand there for a bit after he's gone.

Four

'Mmmm, Lara, this is delicious. You must tell me what you put in it.'

That's my mother-in-law, Sylvia who has an excessive appreciation of my cooking and I have no idea if she wants me to tell her what I put in it or not.

Do you mean now or at some unspecified time in the future? Because you're going to forget anyway. 'Oh, good. I'm glad you like it. It's just shepherd's pie. I don't think I did anything different to it than usual.'

'You know she's got the magic touch, Mum. This woman can make Brussels sprout taste good.'

Oh, shut up, Ben.

'Talking of which, what's happening with that catering idea you were working on, Lara, dear?'

'Oh, I've put it on hold for now, Sylvia,' I reply deadpan. 'I've sort of had my hands full of late.'

'Shame. Martin and I were looking forward to becoming your official tasters.'

Ahhh, the old official tasters gag again.

'Still, at least you're getting plenty of practice in the meantime. These boys don't stop eating, do they? They've grown so much since we last saw them, haven't you, my darlings?'

Zac rears up from his chair and canters around the table, a broccoli head clenched between his teeth, gravy dripping down his chin.

Nice. 'Sit down, please,' I say evenly. 'We haven't finished eating.'

'Look how tall I am now, Nanny. I'm nearly taller than you.' He makes as if to decapitate her and at the last moment swings his hand back and forth to demonstrate how he towers over her now. Sylvia wipes the broccoli spittle from her cheek and smiles indulgently.

'You cheeky monkey. I'm sitting down.'

'I'm still taller than you. Stand up.'

'Zac,' I chide gently. 'You can measure yourself against Nanny after lunch. Please come and finish your food now.'

But Sylvia's shifted off her chair and Zac's guffawing at the sight of her standing besides him, knees bent comically like a troll. He continues to bash her in the forehead and her crow's feet crinkle with affection.

'Told you I was taller.'

Oscar pushes his own chair back ready to put Zac in his place.

I say, 'Don't,' in the menacing tone I usually reserve for cold callers and he lowers back down, his knife and fork abandoned pointedly, his expression contrite.

'Food's getting cold, chap,' Ben remarks and Sylvia raises herself stiffly, gripping the table in mock-rebuke.

She tweaks her grandson's nose playfully, her eyes dancing. Then she runs her fingers through his hair and bobs her head towards his plate. He groans and slithers back down the table, slumping into his chair where he remains slouched and chastised until Ben says, 'There's dessert for anyone who manages to finish everything on their plates.'

'Yeahhh!' Zac grabs a mound of mashed potato and shoves it in dry. He has to. Any gravy that hasn't soaked into his T-shirt is on the tablecloth.

'Ah-ha! That cheered you up,' Ben's dad exclaims stretching forwards. 'Looks like you need another spoonful, it's going down so quickly.'

'Noooo!'

That's right. Threaten him with the food I spent an hour cooking as though it's worms and cat's vomit. Thank you, Martin.

'I'll have some more, if there's any going,' Ben says and there goes my plan of giving the boys leftovers for tea tomorrow. He'll leave too much to finish off now, but not enough to feed them all without cooking up a whole new batch of extra veg. And then he'll moan that he's eaten too much. He's leaning across me with the serving spoon aloft and I can't help but recoil.

'Mum?'

'I couldn't, Ben.' She pats her flat stomach and puffs out her cheeks. 'Much as I'd love to. It really is delicious, Lara.'

'Thank you.'

'Elena always used to do a really tasty one with lentils and sweet potato.'

She did not. It was awful.

'Did you ever have it?'

'Mmm' I manage, balking at the memory of the undercooked filling and overcooked crust.

For a creative person, Elena was a remarkably terrible cook. She could take the most delicious ingredients and turn them into Play-Doh without even trying, which was a shame because she did try. It just never paid off. We used to eat a huge brunch before we went there, knowing lunch would be bland, lumpy, strange and three hours late. Suffice to say, Ben and I generally found ourselves hosting more than our fair share of family dos and that was the way we all preferred it.

'You're probably thinking of the one Lara used to make for Elena sometimes, Mum. You always said you liked it.'

'Oh, yes, of course.'

And with that Sylvia swallows and her eyes veil behind the sudden prick of tears. Martin reaches out taking her hand and together they sit in a deafening silence composing themselves. I know the same mask of pain will be etched on Ben's face and I avert my gaze, sending a clatter of cutlery against the plates.

'Right, is everyone done here?' I say and my chair screeches on the floorboards breaking the spell. 'Shall I get dessert? I think Nanny and Grandpa brought apple strudel.'

Sylvia clears her throat, Martin squeezes her hand one more time before he lets go and they both dab their napkins, smeared mashed potato and all, against their glassy eyes.

'Oh, it's only shop bought,' Sylvia simpers dismissively.

'Yayyy!' Zac punches his hand in the air because there's nothing better than a bit of dry pastry brimming with salt, sugar and preservatives. I flare my nostrils and hold back a retort. I don't like making desserts anyway.

Even so, you ungrateful little...

Ben scrapes the last of his veg onto his fork as I rip his plate away, piling it on top of the others and into the almost (but not quite) empty serving dish.

'I'll do that,' he says through a mouthful of red cabbage (lightly sautéed with garlic, coriander and brown mustard seeds). 'I was going to suggest a walk while the sun's still out. We can have the strudel when we get back. Let me clear up, Lara. You've already done enough today. Lunch was exceptional, as always.'

'Yes, thank you, darling. It was lovely,' Sylvia adds for the ninetieth time.

'Lovely,' Martin echoes and we all sigh with relief that despite my lack of job, life or anything interesting to talk about, we can always revert to my prowess in the kitchen.

'Boys, give us a hand taking this over to the dishwasher,' Ben says but they've already dispersed and despite my dogged attempts to carry the tower of dishes I've already constructed over to the sink, Sylvia bats my hands away and insists I go and put my feet up which I'd happily do if it weren't for Martin tickling Zac on the sofa while Oscar looks on from the armchair waiting for any opportunity to join in.

I smile graciously and slip unnoticed upstairs, closing the delighted squeals and other equally irritating voices behind the kitchen door. Jacob is already plugged into his console, feet up on his desk, by the time I peer into his bedroom but I ignore the fact he obviously wants to play and creep over to his bed.

'What are you up to?'

His back remains resolutely unmoved.

'… Jake, what are you doing?'

He makes a bit of a job of looking up as if he's only then noticing me, lifting one headphone from his ear with barely concealed impatience but I ignore that too and sink down onto his duvet.

'Forza Horizon.'

'That's the car one, right?'

'Yeah.' He sits upright now discerning my desire to avoid going downstairs outweighs my usual disinterest in hearing about every supercar he's earned or race he's won.

Oh, God. The headphones are down around his neck. He's going to tell me about them.

'Do you want to play?'

'Can I just sit here and watch you?'

'It's easy.' He hands me his spare controller. 'Look, this makes you move forward, this one's for speed. The one in the middle sticking out controls directions. Left for left. Right for right.'

I can't bear his enthusiasm. It almost makes me want to join in but not quite. 'I'm alright, honestly. We're going out in a minute. There's not really time for a whole game.'

'It's not a game.'

'Round. Lap. Whatever it is. You keep playing and I'll watch you until we have to head out.'

'Do I have to come?'

'Yes.'

He groans with well-practiced lethargy and his shoulders sink.

'Oh, come on. You used to love racing through the woods and feeding the ducks.'

'Yeah. When I was eight!'

'Oh, well. You can walk with me if you're too mature to run around and climb trees anymore. Tell me about all the girls you like. Or boys.'

He doesn't even grace me with a comeback. I count myself lucky he bothered to roll his eyes.

'Come on. You can't stay up here all day. Nanny and Grandpa have come all this way to spend time with you.'

'No they haven't. They're only interested in Zac.'

'Oh, come on, love. That's not true.' *That is absolutely true.* 'They're more focused on him at the moment, that's all. You can understand that, can't you?'

'Sure, whatever. Do I still have to come though?'

'Lara!' Sylvia trills up the stairs. 'We're about ready to set off down here.'

Jake looks at me pleadingly and I surrender.

'Just this one time,' I say and for a moment the unbridled joy on his face makes him look like my little boy again. 'I mean it. And don't sit here playing Forza all afternoon. Do your homework. Read something.' Which will be the bloody day. He's yet to bend the spine of a single book on his shelf (always handy during the odd last-minute hunt for a birthday present although it does make me hugely unpopular with his friends).

'Yesss.' Jake wrestles his headphones back over his ears and turns all his attention to the screen.

'You're welcome.'

'Thank you.'

'And don't forget to do your homework.' *Who am I kidding?*

Beasley looks even more glum than Jacob and it takes a few encouraging yanks to get him out of the house, but Zac speeds up the process with the sole of his boot and a motivational roar.

'Steady on, Zaccy,' Ben scolds with a forgiving grin designed to render any reprimand he makes utterly pointless.

'He's getting a bit slow in his old age after all. Like Nanny and Grandpa.'

'Ohh, don't roar at us whatever you do.'

No, don't. That's –

'Rooooooaaaaarrrrrrr.'

Jes-us.

Zac leaps on to Martin's back – well, lower back, waist, buttocks, then thighs as he tries to drag him down to the pavement and everyone laughs the way we used to when he was young and sweet and we hadn't realised his unruliness was a permanent state. Maybe I should have stayed behind and let Jacob teach me how to drive into a wall.

'Roooooaaaarrrrr.'

Fricking hell. This is what you get for encouraging him.

I stride out of the driveway purposefully, silently willing Beasley to tug on the lead, dragging me forwards to put some distance between us, but his heart isn't in it and nor are his joints. Instead he toddles behind me assessing the scent soaked into every tree we pass before disguising it with his own.

'Oh, come on, Beasley. Really? Do we have to stop at every one?'

The kids have run ahead into the woods and even Ben and Martin overtake us, heads jutting forwards, arms hanging loosely across their backs, each footstep a mirror image of each other's. Father and son. Before and after. Only Sylvia lurks behind.

There's no need. Don't feel you have to talk to me. Why don't you catch up with the others?

'Any news from Down Under?' she asks in an Indian accent. It isn't intentional. She's just not very good at Australian.

'Nothing new, no. The girls are both fine. Nick's still working at home so he's been able to help Casey out a bit more with them both, so that's one good thing to come out of the lockdown at least.'

'Gosh, it's been a while though, hasn't it?'

'Eighteen months now.'

'And still no talk of them opening the borders. You must miss your mum terribly. I'll bet she misses you.'

I'm not sure that she does. She certainly doesn't miss being here. Nick marrying an Aussie was the best thing that ever happened to her, especially when he followed Casey over there, had twins, invited Mum over to meet them (babysit) and reintroduced her to his wife's recently single dad.

That was three years ago and I've only seen her once in all that time and that was at the wedding – her wedding. To Harry. Which makes Harry our stepdad as well as Nick's father-in-law, a double whammy for him if ever there was one and also meant that when Australia announced there wouldn't be any more flights going back to the UK, my mum howled with relief that she was stuck on that side of the hemisphere, even if it does mean not seeing us 'until this whole ghastly business is over with'.

In her defence, no one could have imagined we'd still be in the grip of this whole ghastly business nearly twenty months later with no end in sight. But at least she has an outdoor pool

58

and a leathery tan to help her through the worst of it. We have a duck pond and the residing hope that Zac doesn't fall in it. Again. He's racing around in the style of a whirling dervish on a speeding trajectory out of a recently fired cannon. I wouldn't care but I haven't brought any spare clothes.

'She must feel awful about not being here for you.'

Again, probably not as much as you'd think. She was very fond of Elena. Less so of her offspring. Or The Destroyer as she calls him. No, I don't think she's too gutted about missing out here. Besides, there's Facetime and Whatsapp and loads of other ways to keep in touch now, all with video screens so we can see exactly what they're up to in the sunshine in their massive houses with huge backyards, barbeques and each other.

Good for them. If there was ever a life to escape, it's this one. I can't blame either of them for trading it in. For starting again. I could do it in a heartbeat. Walk away from everything we've built here. The woods, the park, the people, the ducks. The ducks.

"Zac. Stop that,' I yell. Uselessly. I'm still too far away to do more than frighten the jackdaws. 'Ben?'

He's got his head bent, staring intently at the ground as though whatever Martin's waffling on about might somehow materialise on it. Zac's flapping his hands and roaring again to the undisguised disgust of the blue-rinse brigade and Oscar's not helping matters by hollering at him to stop. I hand Sylvia Beasley's lead and pick up the pace.

'Muuuuummmm,' Oscar wails. 'He keeps chasing the ducks away.'

'Zaaac. Leave them alone please.'

'I'm helping them fly.'

'Muuummmm. Make him stop. He's scaring them away.'

The others finally seem to notice what's happening and Martin's answer is to sweep a bench clear of dried bird droppings and settle down for a well-deserved break.

'They're fine, Ozzie. They're used to it. I'd be more worried about what will happen to your cousin if he doesn't burn off some of that energy. You should take a leaf out of his book and run around while you've got the chance.'

'But he's chasing the ducks away, Grandpa.'

'Go and join in then before he sees them all off. Show us what you're made of. Go on. You can't let a six-year-old outrun you. Gotta man up, as they say.'

Oscar's cheeks are mottled, his lips are trembling and indignation catches in his throat like a shard of chicken bone. He runs like a new-born gazelle, as well Martin knows but even so, it's not the running that's the issue.

For goodness sake, Ben. Say something if no one else will.

'Come on, sunshine.' Ben eases himself up from the bench he was hoping to get more acquainted with. 'Let's go and find that tree you like to climb first. You can feed the ducks once Dr Dolittle's got bored.'

'If there're still any left by then,' Oscar mutters loping off in his dad's wake.

'Not one for joining in with the lads, is he, that one?'

'No, thank God, Martin,' I say. 'I don't think I could handle any more testosterone around here.' *Or tantrums, kickboxing, disruptions or brats.*

'Boys will be boys, as they say,' he crows and I want to smash the smirk clean off of his face. But I don't. I just tell him we usually prefer to play Frisbee or throw a ball about when we come here.

Rather than attack the local wildlife.

'Of course, you're not supposed to feed ducks bread these days, are you?' Sylvia has finally caught up and eases herself down on the bench with the air of a woman who has recently signed up for news alerts. In addition, she has yet to understand how algorithms work or realise that from now on she will be receiving a soul-destroying barrage of doom directly into her inbox.

'It's okay, I brought bird pellets especially.'

'Oh, that's nice. We never gave it a second thought in our day. That's what you did. Half a loaf of mouldy Mother's Pride and that would keep Ben and Elena busy for hours.'

Hours? It must have been a hell of a loaf.

'And then suddenly we find out we were killing them all that time. I don't believe it myself. They looked healthy enough to me.'

'It's to do with the lack of nutrients or something,' I say because for some reason I'm still listening.

'But then you read all these stories about how now the swans and what-have-you are dying in droves because no one's feeding them anymore.'

'It's tragic.'

Yes, Martin. It's tragic. Never mind your grandson kicking a few though.

'What are you supposed to think? You try and do your best...' Sylvia trails off and we sit in a companionable silence for five seconds before another thought strikes her. 'It's like recycling, isn't it? You spend half your day dividing everything up into paper, tins and glass, washing it up, putting it into the right boxes and then it turns out they're just shipping it halfway across the world so they can burn it all over there. Have you seen the pictures of all the plastic water bottles in their rivers? That's our plastic water bottles.'

'It's criminal,' Martin sighs.

'It is criminal. It makes you wonder if it's more responsible not to recycle at all. Just stick it all in our landfills with all the rest of our rubbish. At least we've still got room for it here. I mean if they're not going to do anything with it anyway. It's still pollution. It still makes it's way back over here.'

Martin nods his head sagely. 'She's got a point when you think about it.'

'It's hard to know what's for the best.'

It's not hard to know what's for the best. You recycle. You turn off the lights. You save the planet. You don't throw your

62

hands up in the air and give up because the system needs changing. You fix the system. God, Brexiters.

To be fair, she does have a point, but there's something about the way she prattles on mindlessly that always turns me into a petulant teenager.

'Maybe you should try petitioning your local MP, Sylvia, rather than stop recycling altogether. Put pressure on the government to enforce more control over the companies it's contracting these sorts of services out to. If you really feel strongly about it...'

'Oh, I know, dear, I should. I wouldn't know where to start though. It all seems so hopeless. I look around some days and wonder how long we've got left. You've got climate change, global pandemics and now look what's happening in Afghanistan again. Those poor people. What on Earth was the point of the last twenty years? We've just made it all worse. And every time we fix one hole, another one springs up in its place and it's this generation who are going to pay the price.' She flutters her hands towards the kids. Ben's finally got them both feeding a gaggle of geese and he's striding back towards us jauntily. Poor fool.

'I can't bear to think about the things they're going to see. It almost makes me relieved that... you know.' She takes my hand and shakes her head, her eyes filling again, that stupid look on her face, expecting me to agree.

My jaw clenches. I can't do this anymore.

'Mum,' Ben butts in at the tail end of her drivel.

63

'I'm just saying, darling. When I read the news sometimes I think what happened might have been for the best. Maybe we'd all be better off dead. At least we wouldn't have to watch this world die slowly. At least we wouldn't have to feel this pain everyday. Look at that little poppet.'

She means Zac. Zac's the poppet.

'What sort of life is he going to have without Elena here to protect him? Even if it is all too late, that's what mothers are supposed to do. Protect our children.' Her voice is shaking again and then her mouth twists and she spins around to me. 'Oh, sorry, love, I didn't mean –'

'I've got to go to Sainsbury's.'

'Lara –'

'Sorry. I just remembered. We're out of milk. The kids are going to need it for their cereal tomorrow.'

'I can get it,' Ben interjects, hopping from one foot to the other, swooping his arms in either panic or the brink of an impromptu musical number. 'Or we could all head back that way now... Mum, Dad. You're ready to go, aren't you?'

But I'm not ready to let them go.

'It's all right. You carry on to the playground. The boys will be disappointed if you don't. Besides, your dad's right. They could do with blowing off a bit more steam. I'll just pick up a few bits and head home. Make a start on the strudel.'

I'm up on my feet, pulling water and snacks out of my bag to get the kids through the next hour despite the fact they've just eaten. The shiny resolve on my face is like steel, unbending, unwavering and already half a dozen metres away from my parents-in-law. Ben bounds up behind me.

'I'm sorry,' he hisses. 'She doesn't mean it. It's just her way of dealing with everything.'

'I know.' My voice is light.

'She needs to focus on something other than the accident.'

'I know.' Still light.

Ben is galloping to keep up besides me. 'It's getting out of hand actually. The worrying. She's getting obsessive. I don't know what to do.'

'Spend some time with her maybe, for a start. Honestly, I'm fine. I'm just getting milk. Don't turn it into something it's not.'

'We all know how hard this is for you. And what you're doing for Zac. Everyone appreciates it.'

Even if they do think he'd be better off dead than stuck with me for a makeshift mother. At least giving up any chance of happiness or self-fulfilment for at least the next ten years won't all be in vain. 'I know. Look it's fine. I'll see you at home.'

'She wasn't talking about –' he calls behind me and I can feel him staring miserably after me as I take three strides to his every one but I don't care what she was talking about. She's always talking. She never stops bloody talking. She never comes up for air.

Better off dead than living with me. What I'd give to be able to close my eyes forever instead of pairing his socks, fixing his toys, washing his tiny pants, doing the school run twice a day. Every day.

'Hey, I thought it was you, Lara.'

My neck snaps with a jolt of recognition and the air catches in my throat like a cat with a foot on its tail.

'Sorry. Didn't mean to make you jump.'

'Lenny!'

Lenny looks confused. He also looks like he's made a horrible error of judgement but he can't put his finger on what.

'Sorry. *Mr Matthews*. I was miles away.'

'That's alright. I almost didn't recognise you without your dog.'

His step falls in line with mine, which is unfortunate because my legs are nowhere near as long as his and it's causing him no end of trouble, yet I'm the one with a sudden flush on their cheeks, a touch of breathlessness I put down to the rush I wasn't aware I was in. I slow down to let him pass but that only makes it worse. He double side-steps and then adopts a sort of funeral march before we finally settle into an almost comfortable wide-gaited shuffle.

How far is he going? Please, dear Lord, don't let him be on his way to the shops. I'm wearing an age thirteen boy's coat – which is short on the sleeves – complete with the muddy shoes Jacob outgrew three winters ago encased in four winters' of mud. And I'm not sure I even brushed my hair this morning.

'I was just thinking about you.'

'Me?' *Zac surely. Me? Really? Me?*

'Yes, well, Beasley actually.'

Could be worse. 'Oh, yes?'

'Well, you've inspired me.'

Moi?

'To finally get a dog. A beagle actually.'

Huh.

'And I wanted to pick your brain a bit, since you're the expert.'

Oh God. What made him think I had a brain?

'I wouldn't say expert,' I snort. I actually snort. I have to look away to compose myself and by compose, I mean wipe the end of my nose with my sleeve.

'Well, you know more than me, that's for sure.'

Hold it together. Good grief. How long can it possibly take to get to the high street? What have they done with it? 'Feel free to try me, but I'm more of a cat person really.' Then feeling guilty. 'With the exception of Beasley, of course, but he's not really mine.'

'But he's good with your cat though, right? I heard beagles got on well with other animals.'

'I suppose so. I think that was one of the reasons Elena got him. She had this manky old tabby she thought might take to him at the time. He was very keen on her, she was less impressed, as I recall.'

I can picture poor Beasley now, ever the optimist, wagging his whole tiny body in glee whenever they crossed paths only to whimper away moments later in a stinging retreat. It was a lesson he failed time and time again making him either incredibly thick-skinned or dim-witted. A touch of both is probably fair but either way no amount of indignant rage could prevent him from trying to befriend that cantankerous creature. In the end, at a loss of what else to do she resorted to dying – I suspect, out of spite.

'Oh.'

'Have you got a cat then?'

'No, no. Not that I know of anyway.' Lenny waggles his eyebrows and flashes a grin I have no idea how to interpret. Assuming he's never shagged a cat.

'Sorry, that sounded funnier in my head.'

'No judgement from me. What you do in your own time…'

'Oh, Christ,' he blunders furiously backtracking, shoulders hunched, arms swirling in denial. The orange Sainsbury's sign is finally in sight and I can't tell if I'm relieved or slightly disappointed. Either way it would be rude to rush off.

'I don't have any secret love kittens, just to clarify.'

'That you know of…'

'That I know of.'

'And you're getting a puppy –'

'Well, a puppy or better still, one of the post-lockdown rejects I keep reading about. I'm thinking it might be cheaper.'

'And in desperate need of a home, of course.'

'Of course.' He throws his hair back and laughs.

I'd forgotten about that little gap in his teeth. It's still there. I wonder what it feels like? To him, I mean. To him.

'Well, good luck with that, I guess… I don't know much about puppies.'

I do know Elena stopped researching after she read 'good with cats' and it wasn't until after she brought her beagle home that she realised the next paragraph was all about how mischievous, un-trainable and stubborn they are.

Nine times out of ten she'd arrive back from a walk with just the dog's lead, anything left within jumping distance was immediately demolished and he once ate an entire IKEA sofa in a single afternoon. He needed walking for at least two hours a day, couldn't be left alone without alerting the neighbours, would wolf down an unclaimed poo faster than a Mars bar and his bottom burps could clear a room.

It was lucky for him he was good looking and lucky for us that he'd grown out of most of these endearing qualities long before we got him. Not that a Tic Tac would go amiss and I'd have to be passed out in a crumpled heap before I ever let him lick my face (side note: If I ever am found inexplicably in a pool of my own blood at the bottom of the stairs it will be because Sharon has finally succeeded in tripping me down them. Either Sharon or Zac anyway).

Even so, as far as advice is concerned, I'd say steer clear of dogs and get a cat. Even a cantankerous one.

But I don't say that. I say, 'If you need any tips in about ten years time, I might be able to help you out. Talk you through the different stages of incontinence and dementia. Beasley's, not mine.'

'Oh,' Lenny throws his head back again. He's so easy to please.

'I'm heading this way.' I point towards the plum-shaded uniform of the mask inspector manning the sliding doorway to the store and we stumble to an ungainly halt on the pavement. 'But, you know. I am happy to help, if you do have any questions. If I can. I'm better with cats though' I raise a hand to the side of my mouth and whisper 'Always use protection, that's one failsafe.'

'I'm never going to live that down, am I?'

'I shouldn't think so.'

He shakes his head and hides his face behind the palm of his hand. Then he touches the top of my arm and my pupils dilate. Ever the poker face. *What is wrong with me?*

'Thanks for making my weekend, Lara,' he says and it's not until I get home that I realise I've forgotten the milk.

Five

The mince is bubbling away on the hob, permeating the kitchen with a hint of late summer in Sorrento. Without the heat. I stir the ragu one more time and pour a packet of spaghetti, upright and unyielding into a pan of boiling water. The sauce is thickening and spirals of steam rise and straggle away leaving behind a trace of garlic and oregano that tingles my nostrils when I inhale. I salt the water freely, coercing the pasta to soften and bend against its will.

Everything is on track. Even Sharon has abandoned her usual post on the island and is perched on the schoolbag Zac dumped as soon as we squelched into the house, shoes squeaking, coats dripping and staining the floor. She's in absolute heaven. Not only is she painfully balanced on the sharp edges of the pencil case poking through the bag, but it's also uncomfortably wet. And to add a sweet cherry to her cake, Beasley seems to have picked up a cold. *Sorry, Beasley.*

A current of cool air sweeps into the room as the door clicks behind me but for once the hairs on my neck don't stand on end.

'Be about 15 minutes.'

'Great,' Ben says, leaning towards me for a kiss.

He's only been working upstairs. I don't know why he always acts like he's been on a trip on the Voyager every time he comes down. He's wincing and though I'd like to take credit, I've been pulling the same face for the last half an hour every time Oscar hits a high note. Or doesn't hit a high note, I should say. He's stretched out in the sitting room, headphones on, getting our money's worth out of his Sonos playlist under the misguided belief that if he can't hear us, then we can't hear him. Which will be the day.

Ben waves at him from a distance and slides in next to Zac at the breakfast bar where I've confined him until he finishes the dregs of his hot chocolate. So far I seem to have emptied out most of it myself, one layer of congealed skin at a time.

'How was school today, buddy?'

'Good.'

It was always 'good'. That was all I got for eight years. Now I get 'Boring. We got given three homeworks.' It's something at least.

'What was so good about it?' Ben perseveres, resting his elbows on the surface before whipping them away just as quickly with confused disgust.

'Nothing.'

'Interesting. Did you drag Aunty Lara to the playground afterwards?'

'She dragged me. I didn't wanna go. It was raining.'

'It was not. There was a slight drizzle. Honestly, who complains about going to a playground?'

I pull a fresh bottle of Pinot Grigio out of the fridge. Don't point out the empty one in the recycling box or the Nutella tumbler I slipped into the dishwasher earlier. I just get out two fresh wine glasses. The ones with stems that are harder to pass off as anything else.

'I didn't have anyone to play with. They all went home.'

'Yes, well, I'd rather have you climbing the walls in the playground than here.'

I pass Ben a glass and he taps it with his own, his eyes burning into mine as if there's a faint chance of us ever having sex again, let alone bad sex for the next seven years.

'The only person there was Mr Matthews and he's a teacher.'

Ben looks at me uneasily. 'That's a bit odd, isn't it?'

'He wasn't at the playground. He was just leaving the school. It's not like he's a weirdo or anything.' There's a tone in my voice I need to soften.

'Oh, well that's nice. Did he see you?'

'Aunty Lara made me go and talk to him even though school had finished and he said you're brave staying out here in the rain and I said I just want to go home and then it got really dark and we said we had to go and then it did rain and I got soaked right through to my socks and I had to get into my pyjamas even though it's not bedtime.'

'Oh, dear. That doesn't sound good.'

'You didn't do too badly out of it, Zac. You got a hot choc after all.' Then under my breath 'Even if it is more of a frappé now.'

Jacob's old Spiderman mug is cemented to the breakfast bar, surrounded by sticky congealing craters. Ben stares nostalgically beyond the sloppy stains at it, tiny now and impossible to imagine in clumsy teenage hands. He makes as if to pick it up, but even the handle is filthy. His eyes flicker away quickly and he leaves it to me.

Smoothly done, darling.

'With marshmallows,' Zac boasts as though they were in recognition for some achievement, not simply a glib attempt on my part to cushion the invariable onset of pneumonia.

'Can I have a hot chocolate?' Oscar pipes up from the next room.

'No! Cos you didn't get freezing and wetted!' Zac jumps down from his bar stool, careers across the wooden floorboards and lands with a thud in, what I take to be, Oscar's lap.

'Oww. Muuummm.'

'How many marshmallows, did you give him?' Ben says but he's smirking and for once I don't feel like wiping it off his face. 'Talking of which, I was going to say, what do you think about us having less meat?'

I lower my wine glass and stare at him. 'I don't think about it. Not since I last tried to get any of you to eat anything without a pulse and what's that got to do with marshmallows?'

'Just that they're not vegetarian.'

'Neither's Zac.'

'No, but Elena was vegan, so he did use to eat a lot more plant-based food. I just think... it's something she'd want. You know, if it's not too much trouble.'

'You want me to start cooking separate meals for him?'

'No, I mean, we could all probably benefit from eating less meat and fish, you know – with the planet and all.'

'Is this your mother again?'

His face tells me everything I need to know about that. His eyes dart away and he goes for the mug. Desperate measures and all.

'She mentioned it, yes. But she's right. You were right, I mean, when you wanted us to try it before.'

'I only wanted to cut down a bit and all any of you did was complain. You more than anyone as I recall.'

'I know, but I just feel like it's something we should be doing. For Elena.'

'I've already made spaghetti Bolognese. What do you expect me to do with it?'

'Nothing! We'll eat it of course. I don't mean every day. Just maybe two or three nights a week...'

'The boys will have something to say about that.'

'I don't mind,' Oscar cries out, his buttocks grinding into Zac's vertebrae like barren gums gnawing on a corncob. 'We watched a documentary in Ms Howell's class about the ice caps and the rainforests and how the world's going to end if we keep killing animals.'

'There's a bit more to it than that, Oscar,' I growl.

'He's right though. We should all be playing our part and Zac's fine with it. He was more used to vegan food than meat before he came here.'

'Sorry for feeding him.'

'You know what I mean. Oh look, forget it. It was just a thought. I didn't mean to start an argument.'

I'm not arguing. I just – Christ, it's hard enough trying to keep everyone happy without adding all this to it. And I love the way they're acting like I've never made a vegetarian meal before when they're the ones who continually turn their noses up at anything that isn't made – primarily – from flesh. I'd given up trying and now listen to them.

'Fine. I don't mind. I like vegetables. I'm happy to eat more, but seriously, if I hear one complaint about it – you especially Oscar –'

'Muuuummmm. tell Zac to get off the sofa. I'm trying to relax.'

'Thank you.' Ben eases himself off the stool, edges behind me and slides his arms around my waist. His chin is resting on my shoulder, his breath on my neck.

'I need to go and help, Oscar,' I mutter and push him away.

'My teacher's vegan,' Zac pipes up hours later when I'm putting him to bed which is proof in itself that he does hear everything, despite me having to ask him eight times to put his pyjamas on. It's also typical of him to bring up something like that right as I'm trying to sneak out of the door. I could just ignore him and turn off the light but I probably shouldn't be too dismissive, not when he's opening up to me like this.

'Really? Mr Matthews? How do you know that?'

'I told him Mummy's vegan.'

'Did you?' I lower my hand from the switch above his bed and sweep the hair out of his eyes. Ben's eyes. Elena's eyes. Beasley's eyes actually, when he thinks I don't know he's trying to get one over on me.

'Were you telling him about Mummy?'

'Mm-ha.'

'What were you saying?'

'That she's pretty.'

'She was pretty. She was beautiful.' I say reaching out to run the back of my finger down his nose before a sudden aversion makes me turn the movement into a swipe, brushing his cuddly toys across the bed instead. 'She looked just like you.'

'I'm not a girl.'

One side of my mouth curls into a half-smile but my chest catches. I have to breathe in and exhale before I reply. 'You still remind me of her though.' My voice is strained and each word scratches my throat like fingers grating down a chalkboard.

'I drew a picture of her.' He pulls back the bedclothes and raises himself onto his elbows.

'No, no.' I whisper, pushing him gently down. 'You can show me tomorrow.'

He sinks back into his pillow.

'What else did you tell Mr Matthews?'

'I don't know.' His eyelashes are beginning to quiver and droop with the effort of staying awake. He's losing the fight.

'But he said he was vegan?'

'Mmm.'

His eyes roll back once more and his breathing begins to deepen and slow. His lips part, slack with exhaustion and sapped of the strength it takes to survive, the exertion that drains him and in a fleeting moment I see my own face in his. We are the same, he and I. We're both bystanders caught in the crossfire and scarred by shrapnel. Reliant on sleep to numb us for a few short hours before the sun casts a light on our new unsought world. Forcing us up, forcing us out, forcing us to start each day again, to carry on.

I lean down and inhale the scent of his dewy skin, the shampoo and innocence, the soft cheek, the blameless vulnerability and as I kiss him, I feel for the first time some growing sense of hope. An almost tangible dream that we've passed a hurdle. That things will start to get better now.

But so much for dreams. It's less than twenty-four hours before I get a call from the school office telling me there's been an incident and by incident I mean *Zachary appears to have bitten another child.* And by appears to have, I mean he did. He doesn't even deny it. He has no qualms at all about attempting to gnaw a two-inch chunk out of an *unnamed pupil's arm* (Nico, it was Nico. Zac was less concerned about the importance of anonymity than the school and besides which 'it was all his fault.' Apparently).

Funny thing though – I'd spent years squirming with guilt any time I'd forgotten to pack the boys' swimming kits or sign a form before the deadline but the one time I get summoned in to discuss an act of violence worthy of notifying social services, I feel quite chuffed about it. Can't put a finger on why, but predictably, *Mr Matthews* is all charm and perfectly understanding. Cautiously unbiased and diplomatic, some might say. I'd go so far as to add *unacceptably lenient* were it my child with a fresh jaw-shaped scab on his arm but, of course, it isn't so I'm more than happy to let Lenny make excuses for Zac's frankly outrageous reaction to Nico using his purple felt tip. He has been through a lot, we have to agree.

'Talking of biting children, Zac tells me you're vegan.'

'Ha. That's quite a segue.'

'I thought of it more as the opposite extreme. Not that he's ever actually eaten another child.'

'Well, that's good to hear.'

'Unless it was barn-raised.'

Lenny looks as though he can't tell if I'm joking and his mouth is suspended on the brink of a smile he's not confident enough to stand by. He twitches his head and shakes it away, veering instead towards an attempt at professionalism. *Very sweet.*

'I hope it's alright that I told him. I'm not even sure how it came up. He was talking about his mum.'

'No, it's great. It's good for him to talk about her.'

'Good, I'm glad you think so and yes, anyway. I am vegan. I usually give people a minute's grace to get as many jokes out of their systems as possible. Feel free to kick off anytime you like.'

'No jokes.' I wave my hands, all animated cheekbones and denial. 'I was after a few tips, that's all. Everyone in my household has suddenly decided we need to eat a more plant-based diet after years of moaning if I put so much as a pea on their plate, so now I have to come up with even more ingenious recipes they'll actually eat.'

'Oh, don't worry about that. There are loads on the Internet. Just Google whatever ingredients you've got and pages of ideas will come up. Plus with all the supplements around these days, you can pretty much make whatever you'd normally have, but substitute the meat.'

What could possibly go wrong? 'Well, that's the other thing,' I exclaim, a little too keenly on reflection. 'How am I supposed to get enough protein in their diets? It's hard enough to fill them up at the moment. The little bastards won't stop growing.'

Probably shouldn't say 'bastards' in a PG-rated environment, but Lenny pretends not to notice. I'm sure he's said worse. He's got a class of thirty of them to deal with. Even so. Better show some restraint.

'Easy. It's a myth that carnivores are healthier than vegetarians. On the contrary, the protein in plants is far easier to access than the protein in meat.' He looks like he's about to say something else, but he pulls himself up on it. 'I'm sorry. I'm not trying to ram my opinions down your throat. I just find the science behind it quite interesting.'

'Please. Don't apologise. I need all the help I can get. Ram away.' Eww. Bit strong. He has the good grace to ignore it.

'Well, the latest research suggests that plant-based diets are a far more efficient means of improving everything from speed and agility to bulking up. Even healing injuries. Loads of top athletes swear by it these days. Arnold Schwarzenegger's basically vegan, Patrik Baboumian…' He raises his eyebrows triumphantly.

'Is that supposed to mean something to me?'

He lifts his palms with assurance. 'Strongest man in the world. Also a vegan.'

I mouth 'Wow' with exaggerated awe and Lenny grins.

'I did warn you…'

'No, no. This is great. Please. Go ahead.'

He shrugs and smiles again. 'You just need to pack in the lentils and pulses. Chickpeas are great, sweet potatoes. Honestly, it's not hard and it tastes amazing. There are so many incredible flavours out there that you never really think about until you cut meat out of your diet. You'll enjoy it, I promise. Your family will never look back.'

'Alright, alright.' I laugh (giggle like absolute pillock). 'You've convinced me. I only really wanted a few recipes, not the sales pitch.'

'Well, I do a pretty mean harissa, red lentil, and squash tagine, but you'd have to look it up. I can't remember what's in it.'

'Okey dokey. I will. And if it stunts the boys' growth, I will be writing to your manager.'

'They'll be pulling trucks with their teeth within the month, you'll see.'

'Good grief. I hope not.' *What a thought.* Still, it certainly doesn't seem to have done him any harm, not that Arnie would have anything to worry about in an arm wrestling contest. Lenny's more lean than buff, although who knows what he looks like without any clothes on? *Where did that come from?*

'Anyway, I've been ranting on for long enough. I should probably go and rescue Mrs Haverstock.' (The harassed TA who will no doubt be mentally formulating her letter of resignation if she's left on her own for very much longer.) 'Thank you for coming in and sorry it was under these circumstances. As I said, we'll look at bringing in an additional classroom assistant who'll be able to intervene more quickly whenever Zachary's behaviour begins to escalate so we can hopefully avoid these sorts of ...'

'Incidents.'

He nods. 'Exactly.'

I stand, more easily this time because somebody's had the forethought to bring in another human-sized chair and I can't help but feel it has my name on it.

'Well, thank you for your time,' I smile.

He says 'It's been a pleasure' and I must say, I agree.

Six

I wish there was a way I could get Zac to school everyday without seeing anyone else. Apart from Lenny obviously. Lenny's fine. Don't mind that. It's just the other parents that get on my nerves. Or rather their insane enthusiasm for cake sales and talking to me.

'Why do they feel the need to talk to me, Beasley? It's perfectly obvious I'm at least ten years older than all of them. I've already been through the school system twice. I could teach the curriculum myself, if they didn't keep changing it.'

I'm not sure he shares my confidence.

'And how come they all seem to have expensive new coats and their own shoes? It's like they still have a disposable income even though they've all got snot-smeared toddlers in tow. Toddlers they think *I* should be interested in hearing about. As if I care whether they're obsessed with Peppa Pig or Bing Bunny. I've been there. Done that. Didn't buy the T-shirt. Don't like it. It's bad enough that I have to do this bit all over again. It's frankly unreasonable to expect me to give a shit about their babies as well, especially the ones that look like potatoes.'

Bad choice of words. Beasley likes potatoes. He perks up expectantly but I'm otherwise occupied with a butternut squash and even he thinks better of investigating further. He knows when to leave me alone.

Kay, on the other hand, is determined to draw me into the fold whether I like it or not. She's forever inviting me to join her and the other mums, when all I want is to wither away in the background, cursing quietly under my breath and judging people. Avoiding all those inevitable questions. *How many kids have you got? What do you do?* Watching them take inventory of my answers, assessing how old I am. Forcing me to listen to them comparing their fabulous careers, gifted children and the stunning Airbnb they rented down in Dorset over the summer ('*Cornwall's so overcrowded these days*').

'I wouldn't mind but they all seem so confident. It's like they can do anything.'

Beasley groans.

'It's true. I think I made a mistake giving up work when I had the boys, now I look back on it. I just didn't want anyone else raising my kids when I could be looking after them myself, especially not when I would have spent almost as much as I earned on childcare costs.

'But what you don't think about is how hard it is to get a job that fits around your new life five or ten years later. I'm competing for the same part-time positions as six million other mums and were I to try to go full time, I'd be up against kids straight out of university with no commitments and no financial restrictions. I bet most of them still live with their mum and dad. I'll certainly bet they don't have to do the school run at 3.20.'

That's not a bet Beasley's willing to make. Sharon stretches out across the chopping board and glares at me. She's sick of hearing this too.

'I know. Shut up and do something about it. Funny thing is, I wouldn't mind spending all of my wages on childcare now, if it got me out of the house. But I think I've missed the boat.'

She flicks her tail in the tagine. She's very passive-aggressive these days.

'Talking to the cat again, are we?' Jacob appears out of nowhere and hisses in my ear, taking a year off my life and an unintentional inch off the squash. At least on balance, it wasn't my finger. Or a tail.

'No. I'm talking to the dog. Sharon hasn't spoken to me for months. She's still miffed about Beasley.'

Jacob loops around the island and wrenches the fridge door open letting the cold air stream out like he's cooling himself down on a hot summer's day but it's October and the electricity bill still needs to be paid. He slams it shut with an audible sigh, slumps his shoulders and drags himself past me towards the cupboards.

When we first moved here we had a tiny galley kitchen only one person could fit in at a time. If I was cooking I used to have to stand out there on my own while everyone else hung out together elsewhere so when we renovated, I was careful to fully embrace the joy of open-plan living. It took months but when it was finally finished it was wonderful to be able to make meals in the same room as my family. For about a week. Now I'd lop my legs off at the knees not to have them all under my feet.

'What can I eat?'

My jaw clamps down for the fiftieth time since school finished. I'm going to have to start wearing my mouth guard during the day at this rate. 'For goodness sake, Jake. Can't you wait? It'll be time for dinner soon.'

'But I'm starving. I haven't eaten since lunchtime.'

It's all I can do not to crack a molar. 'You had a bowl of cereal when you got in.'

'That was ages ago. Is there anything I can have now?'

'Good grief. Look in the fruit bowl. There's plums, bananas, oranges. I think there might be some grapes in the fridge.'

'Why don't you ever make any of that nice stuff any more? All those things on sticks and spicy Scotch eggs. They were good. Especially those king prawns in that funny bread.'

'You make them sound so appealing. I didn't know they'd made such an impression on you.'

He's rifling through the cupboards with complete distain. 'Can you make them again?'

Of course, darling. I'll whip a batch up for you now. Help yourself to the caviar while you wait. 'Not really. They're a bit fiddly. I was just experimenting with different canapés when I was thinking about setting up that catering thing.'

He draws out a box of cereal, examines the cheap, off-brand packaging and discards it on the counter with a sneer. 'Aren't you still doing that? Why did you stop?'

'What do you mean why did I stop? When would I have the time to start a new career with everything that's going on?'

He shrugs. He doesn't put anything back in the cupboards either, but that's okay. I'm at a loose end. It'll give me something to do.

'Why can't you cook it when we're at school all day?'

'Do you have any idea how long it takes to make that sort of food? Not to mention all the other hundreds of things you have to do when you start a new business.'

'I'll give you a hand. I'll be in charge of the marketing.'

He strides back to the sofa, shoves a banana in his mouth and stretches out like a cat, feet hanging over the armrests while he simultaneously scrolls though my phone. No doubt he has sticky fingers but at least he's getting better at multitasking.

'You can start by sorting out your social media profile. You haven't posted anything on Instagram for months.'

'What do you mean? I've never posted anything on Instagram. You used to do all that for me. I wouldn't know where to start.'

'God, old people. Look, it's easy.' He drags himself back up and shambles across to me again with the poise of a plumber explaining a query on a bill.

'Do we have to do it now? I'm right in the middle of something.'

'You're always in the middle of something. Look, all you have to do, is arrange some of that in a bowl, stick a few green leaves on the top, what's it called? Cilantro –'

'Coriander. We're not American.'

'Whatever. It's only a demo. Just take the photo so I can show you how to upload it.'

I snatch my phone in mock exasperation and point it at the bowl of vegetable peelings, curling and greying on the side. The picture's blurry and the subject tricky to discern with my finger blocking the top right-hand corner and the flash reflecting off the bowl.

'Well, that's awful.' He plucks the phone off me and aims the camera at the tagine simmering on the stove. 'Now we just need to edit it a bit, try a different filter, make it brighter. There.'

He shoves the photo in front of my face triumphantly but without my glasses there's no difference between whatever he's taken and the compost waste in mine.

'Very nice.'

'Now. You just click on the send icon here.'

I squint at the screen. It's no good.

'Choose Instagram –'

'Do I need a password?'

'No, well, yes, but it's all set up on here. Just listen, woman.'

I can feel my anxiety going through the roof at the mere thought of having to do this myself.

'Press that button. There you go, look. That's your latest post and you can see all the other ones from before here.'

I brush my hands down on a tea towel and exclaim, 'Ahh. Simple as that. Now I just have to cook a small banquet and upload it.'

'Visualise your goals, Mother. Stop procrastinating. Isn't that what you're always telling me?'

'It does look pretty.'

I scroll through the photos Jacob posted during lockdown when I first started messing around with the idea that I could turn my hand to something more interesting than the frustrated housewife cliché that had crept up, unnoticed upon me. The kids were finally old enough not to need me at all hours and little by little, I was beginning to shed the dull, dreary skin that had been obscuring the person I used to be.

I was itching to get my teeth into something new, face fresh challenges, do something for myself and the eye of a global pandemic felt like the right time to do it. It wasn't as if we could go out anyway. There was nothing to do but hone my skills in the kitchen and even after cooking ten thousand meals week in and week out, year after year, the prospect of putting my hard-earned talent to use was exciting.

I allowed myself to fantasize that I could make something of it. Be that successful businesswoman catering for everything from weddings and dinner parties to glittering star-studded events with maybe a line of frozen food available in individual boutique outlets or even some of the posher supermarkets (you know who you are). I'd even gotten as far as registering the company name – which sucked some of the joy out of the

89

process – but then the world came crashing down. All of a sudden, I was in a worse position than I'd ever been before but that was changing now. Life was beginning to open up again.

'You just have to do it, Mum. Stop making excuses and get on with it. Isn't that what you'd tell me?'

I laugh but for the first time in ages a small spark of hope fires up in me. A world of possibilities within arms' reach.

'What are up to?' Ben says, creeping up behind me and I drop the phone back on to the worktop. 'Was that your food thing? Are you thinking about starting up again?'

'No. Yes, maybe.'

'You should,' he exclaims. 'You'd be brilliant at it.'

He's trying to be nice but my heart sinks and reality takes over. 'There's no point thinking about it. I don't have the time. How am I supposed to get anything done with Zac around? Even if I could deal with the prep work during the day, I'd still have to put the final touches together in the middle of his tea and bedtime. Not to mention, delivering it all and serving it –' *For God's sake. It's a daydream, that's all. Don't you ever need an escape from reality? Don't ruin this for me.*

Sharon arches her back and vaults off the island, horrified at the rate of escalation in my voice.

Oh, stop exaggerating. I'm perfectly within my rights to get hysterical.

'I could help out with Zac. I only have to go into the office once in a while now. I'm sure we could make it work.' Ben scans the room looking for back up, his eyebrows high, forehead bunched.

'I've already said I'll handle the marketing.' Jacob raises his eyebrows too only his are darker and harder to ignore.

Oh, for goodness sake. 'It's just not practical,' I sigh, reining my tone in.

'Come on, Lara. It would be really good for you. For us as a family.' Ben looks down again sharply. 'I could help you build a website or design some flyers or something. What was it called again?'

Of course, he doesn't remember the name. I only used to talk about it all the time. 'Contemporary Cooking.'

'Oh yeah.' He looks like he's considering something, but he bites his tongue.

'What?'

'Nothing.'

'What?'

He pauses and then speaks too quickly. 'It's just, it's not very catchy, that's all. It sounds a bit formal.'

'How is that formal?'

'I don't know. *Contemporary Cooking.* It's just a bit...'

"Oh forget it. It's not going to happen anyway.'

'Co-co!' Zac whirls in from the hall with a pair of imaginary maracas. At least that's what I take them to be. They could be nunchucks, now I think about it.

'Contempry Co-co. Get your cocos here. Nice fresh coconuts.'

91

'Heeyyy! Coco. I like it.' *Oh, Ben.*

If only all my problems could be solved so easily.

'Coco. It's like a play on words too. Coco - Cocoa'

'I know what it is, thanks.'

I could pick up the frying pan and end this conversation with one well-aimed blow but that sort of reaction isn't even acceptable in children's cartoons these days. And now Jacob's slipping away just as I was sharing a moment with him.

'I could mock up some logos if you like. Want to give me a hand, Zac, since you're the one with all the good ideas?'

"For goodness sake, Ben. Can you just stop going on about it?'

His mouth twists and his hands fly up as if he's about to be hit by a runaway truck.

'Sorry, sorry. Just trying to help.'

He backs off and we fall into an uncomfortable silence. Uncomfortable for him at any rate. I was quite enjoying it but he turns to Zac and asks him if he wants to play Uno, which of course he does because dinner's nearly ready and I'll have to be the bad guy again when I need them to pack up so I can lay the table.

Perfect.

Zac bowls in from the sitting room clutching the cards and Sharon springs back onto the island out of his way. She narrowly misses the salt, but in my haste to grab it I knock over the pepper grinder, cracking the lid against the granite worktop and scattering small hard black balls all over the floor.

Christ.

Ben doesn't react. In fact, he's avoiding looking at me at all.

Good. Less inane conversation to put up with.

Zac launches himself across the room again and my first instinct is to snap at him to stay away but instead of stamping the peppercorns into the ground, he kneels down and picks them up one by one, balancing them in his tiny hands.

'Thanks, Zac. That's very nice of you.'

He's too busy concentrating to respond but Ben finally looks up and as our eyes lock, we smile. Then Zac gingerly raises himself to his feet, grins at me with untainted delight and flings his arms open like a flamboyant guest at a wedding.

'Yayyyyy!'

'Zac!' *For Christ's sake.* 'Get the dustpan and brush now.'

The sudden downpour has aroused an interest Beasley's not shown for years and Ben leaps up to prevent him from scooping up the confetti with his tongue. Zac dives between them, crushing the pepper into fragments under the heel of his foot and for once Ben actually reacts.

'That's enough, Zac! Get the dustpan and brush. Now. *Now.'*

Zac spins round, eyes glittering, mouth curled savagely, but instead of heading for the cupboard, he roars at Ben and barges past him into the hallway. I slam a pan down onto the hob and dig my fingernails into the couscous with a force that threatens to split the packet but if there was ever a time to do it, it might as well be now. Ben is massaging his temples, the look on his face beaten-down.

Welcome to my world. My arm shakes, rigid with fury as olive oil glugs into the saucepan and I fire up the gas a split second before I realise Sharon has curled up next to it and the air fills with the smell of – well, burnt cat, I suppose. I bat the flame out of her tail with a jerky flap of a tea towel and she stares at me with utter contempt.

It's just a bit singed, that's all, Sharon. You'll be okay.

I don't think she actually noticed I set her on fire but my heart's still hammering in my throat when Ben says, 'I saw that,' and I turn to him baring my teeth apologetically, my eyes contrite.

Sharon's gone back to sleep and as I stare at him aghast, we start to laugh, him first, then me. Short snatches of air erupting into cackles, blurring our eyes with tears that roll down our stretched cheeks. Beasley joins in with a sneezing fit and Sharon shoots us all a glare that sets us off again.

'That was classic.'

'You can't tell anyone I just did that.'

'It was her own fault. Daft cat. Couldn't you find anywhere more inconvenient to sit, Sharon?'

She's not in the mood for small talk and we crack up again as she leaps down from the island and stalks past Beasley startling the poor creature with an unprovoked slap that sends him back to his bed.

'We live in a madhouse,' Ben cries and I say, 'It's the only place that'll have me' and he smiles and lightly brushes my arm.

My eyes drop automatically, tearing away from his and he pauses and then pulls away.

'I'll clear this up,' he stammers.

'I'm…' I meet his gaze for the first time in probably months. 'I'm sorry about earlier. I know you're trying to help. I just feel a bit overwhelmed right now.'

'I know. I know you do and I'm sorry there isn't more I can do to help.'

'You do enough.' Ben squeezes my hand sadly, lingering too long, drawing out the moment until I shake it off, affably. For once not angry with him.

'Something smells nice,' he continues pressing past me to fetch the dustpan and brush. We both know without saying, it'll be easier to do it ourselves than drag Zac back in here. 'What are you making?'

'Harissa, red lentil and squash tagine.'

'Mmm.' I hold a spoonful up towards him and he slides it into his mouth, revealing the fraction of a smile the instant before his eyes widen in horror and his lips purse, panting out quick short plumes of steam.

'Sorry.'

'Oo-oo-oo. No, no, ooo – It's – ooo – mmm – delicious,' he garbles. 'Hot.'

'Sorry.'

'No, no. My fault. I should have blown on it first.' He stokes my arm. 'It's very good.'

'It's very vegan.'

'Thank you.'

I smile again, the knot in my stomach gently unfurling, the noise in my head quietening.

'I'm looking forward to it actually, this new diet of ours.' He's on his knees sweeping the floor, chasing the peppercorns as they ping and scatter out of his reach. 'Are you more into the idea too now?'

'I was always into it. You were the ones who insisted on eating meat.'

He pauses. 'Oh, okay. I didn't think you really wanted to –'

'Yes, of course I do. I'm always up for experimenting. I was just a bit worried about the boys having a balanced diet but loads of people you wouldn't expect are plant-based now. Arnold Schwarzenegger, Patrik Baboumian...'

'Who?'

'Patrik Baboumian. The strongest man in the world.' I can't help but say it like I don't know what planet he lives on half the time.

'Oh, old Paddy B. You should have said.' He grins, raising himself with the grace of an upturned tortoise. 'Well, you've certainly been doing your research. And I'm happy to be your guinea pig if everything's as tasty as this. Where did you get the recipe from?'

'Just the Internet.' *Sort of.*

My mind flicks back to the look on Lenny's face when I said Zac only ate barn-raised children. Ha. It was a picture. I'll have to tease him about it next time I see him. Thank him for the tip about the tagine too. I could take him in some for lunch tomorrow. See how it compares to his. Or would that be weird? I serve up a bowlful, arrange some garnish on the top and angle my phone to get the perfect photo.

'That for ya Insta, baby?'

'Yep.' It's bizarre. I'm still not irritated with Ben and to be clear, he is being irritating now. 'Might as well start putting some stuff up when I get the chance, just to fill the page or however it works. You never know, I might have more than three minutes to myself one day.'

'It's a good idea, love. I will even be the first happy customer to leave a review. The first of many.'

He smiles so kindly, so hopefully that for a moment I forget about everything else. But just for a moment.

Seven

Oh Sharon. Why do you only ever want to sit on me at night?

It's three thirty in the morning and she's kneading her claws into my chest, her face pressed into mine, purring like an engine revving. I read somewhere this behaviour stems from either her instinct to prepare her bed before she sleeps (not going to happen.), is reminiscent of how as a kitten she would paw at her mother's nipple to stimulate milk (also not going to happen.) or else it's to mark her territory with scent, warding off other animals as though a troop of foxes and hedgehogs are making their way up the stairs as we speak (not entirely impossible). Personally, I think it's payback for having to put up with Beasley.

She never used to be allowed in the bedrooms at night for precisely this reason, but it seems cruel to make her sleep downstairs with the dog so now she has free rein of the house, which would be fine if she didn't announce every visit. Every morning I swear I'm going to start locking her in the kitchen again but by the evening the guilt and alcohol have set in and I feel bad trapping the pair of them in together. Bad for Beasley mainly. Besides it's quite nice having some company in the dark.

I was awake before she got here today. Had been for ages. I'm halfway through my nightly three-hour sleep cycle – or non-sleep cycle – I should say. Three on, three off and then two and a bit if I'm lucky. Really, really lucky. Usually one.

Zac tends to get up at six and while I'd be happy to direct him to his tablet, it only drives him to appear even earlier the next day. So I get up and boil the kettle, feed the animals, make a coffee, get out the cereal, tell Zac we're not having pancakes for breakfast, make the sandwiches, tell Zac we're not having Haribo for breakfast, pack the lunches, tell Zac that's the only cereal we've got, unload the dishwasher, tell Zac to hurry up before his cereal gets soggy, re-heat my coffee in the microwave, tell Zac to hurry up before his cereal gets soggy, forget where I put my coffee, tell Zac to eat his cereal even though it's gone soggy, make another coffee, throw Zac's cereal away because it's soggy, tell Zac to get dressed, wipe down the breakfast bar, tell Zac to get dressed, have a shower, tell Zac to get dressed, brush my teeth and hair, tell Zac to get dressed, finish my coffee, scream at Zac to get dressed, get Zac dressed, tell Zac to brush his teeth and hair, make another coffee, tell Zac to brush his teeth and hair, brush Zac's teeth and hair, tell Zac to put his shoes and coat on, put my shoes and coat on, tell Zac to put his shoes and coat on, put Beasley's lead on, tell Zac to put his shoes and coat on, kiss Jacob and Oscar goodbye as they head out the door, scream at Zac to put his shoes and coat on, put Zac's shoes and coat on and practise his spellings on the way to school.

Is it any wonder I drink? I should be necking back cans of White Lightening by drop off. Makes my medicinal glass or two of white wine in the evening practically homeopathic. They are large glasses, I have to admit, and occasionally there's more than two of them and I don't always wait until the evening but even so. I like to reason that as long as I only drink when I'm cooking dinner, it's perfectly acceptable. Of course, dinnertime has been creeping forwards lately. I think I had them sat at the table by four o'clock every day last week, which meant I started cooking at about three thirty.

Look at that, Sharon. Only twelve hours to go before I can justify unscrewing the Sauvignon Blanc.

I used to drink red but black teeth are a dead giveaway and when Ben finally appears at six o'clock after the chaos has cleared, I can always feel him surveying the scene – not that he'd ever say a word about it, of course.

Oh, Christ, Ben. He sounds like a cruise liner sailing into port. I give his arm a short shove and his jaw snaps shut but he doesn't roll over. That means he'll start up again in a second. There he goes.

Honestly, between you and him. Oh, you're off now are you? That's it, is it? I need a wee anyway.

I throw the duvet back and waddle slowly out to the landing clutching at the bed frame and feeling my way down the walls.

Ow. That was my toe. The door must be somewhere near here. The hall glows in the soft light cast by the street lamp outside and I sneak into the bathroom avoiding the floorboard that creaks. My bladder is on the brink of bursting and if I had been asleep, I'd have no doubt been dreaming that I was in a queue for the toilet. Those dreams have been getting increasingly frequent. It's only a matter of time before I don't make it.

Oh, for goodness sake. There's barely a tinkle. *What was the point of getting me out of bed for that?*

Sharon is pleased to see me up, however and happily winds around my legs meowing.

Shhh. You'll wake up Damien.

I edge back around the bed and slide under the covers to spend another hour and a half contemplating bugger all again. Ben likes to tell me he always sleeps badly too in which case, I wish he'd stop braying like a donkey all night. It's a touch unsociable, especially if he is – as he usually claims, wide-awake.

I used to nudge him gently when his snoring reached the point where astronauts would have been within their rights to send letters of complaint and every time he would bolt up in bed shouting 'What, what?!?' as if the house were engulfed in flames. And then the next day he'd grumble that he couldn't get back to sleep for hours (again, the foghorn suggested otherwise) so we agreed the only time I would ever wake him was if his snoring was getting out of hand. Now if he gets a short shove in his ribs, he simply rolls over onto his side without the hysterics. It's cut some of the drama out of process and the only downside for him would be in the event of an actual fire (but every plan has its flaws).

Sharon jumps back onto the bed and settles down on my feet.

Couldn't you snuggle up next to them rather than balancing on top? It's not very comfortable. For me, I mean. I know you like it that way.

She buries her nose into her paws, instantly comatose and my thoughts return to this so-called catering idea I can't quite shake. It seemed like a good solution to my jobless frustration this time last year, but so much has changed since then. The name for a start apparently. *Coco.* Bloody ridiculous. How would anyone know what it was supposed to be? Where's the brand identity or whatever they call it these days?

Oh, yes. Well done, Zaccy. Aren't you the gift that keeps on giving?

It's of no consequence anyway. I was getting ahead of myself. What do I know about starting my own business? Or cooking, really for that matter? Yes, I enjoy it, yes, I'm better at it than some people but am I better than a trained chef with qualifications and years of experience behind them? Probably not, no. Not to mention the fact I don't know anything about the accounting side, the tax, the health and safety. I don't even know what I don't know.

But it would be so nice to do something different. Something for me. And I can cook, usually better food than they serve at pubs and restaurants. That's what started this whole delusion off in the first place. The endless disappointing overpriced meals that put me off eating out even when we barely went out at all. Paying those sorts of prices when I'd have preferred to have made it myself. It took any pleasure out of having the night off and ignited a flame – a preposterous, misguided belief buoyed on by my overinflated ego – the pretentious notion that I could compete with professionals.

And yet I can see it all so clearly in my mind, as real to me as anything else in my life. I spent so many months fantasising this career change into existence, it's a shock to realise it didn't actually happen. Those images in my head aren't memories. They're the fragments of a pipedream so vivid I can no longer distinguish between them and reality. It's only the fact I'm still here doing nothing and life is passing me by that proves beyond any doubt that it was all an absurd fantasy. A pointless lunacy even to imagine a lucrative trade that would fit around my schedule, earning me a small fortune and a mantelpiece full of accolades.

Oh, Sharon. Why can't I live inside my head? It's so much nicer there.

She doesn't stir but no matter. I know what she'd say.

Because you need to feed me.

Eight

'Oh, we're having tagine again.'

Ben leans over my shoulder, inhaling the fragrant steam rising from the saucepan bubbling away on the hob.

'Is that a complaint?'

'No.' He pulls away like I've slapped his wrist, twisting towards me, the sincerity etched onto his face. Too much sincerity to be truly convincing.

'Hmm.' I raise an eyebrow, not keen to let him off the hook yet. 'I'm adding chickpeas to give it more consistency and flavour. More protein too.'

'Good idea. It smells delicious.'

'You did say you wanted to eat less meat.'

'I know. I said it smells delicious.'

I let the implication that he's being ungrateful hang in the air but I don't really mean it. I haven't felt quite as annoyed with him as usual. Not since I started thinking about the business again, trying out recipes, new ingredients. It's silly, but even the thought of having a proper stab at it has given me the boost I didn't realise I needed.

I was picking Lenny's brain the other day for more ideas. I'd been called in again to talk about Zac, but I've got to say in his defence, it could have all been an accident or at least bad luck this time. He'd somehow Velcro-ed the strap of his shoe to Lottie's ponytail and it had caused all sorts of alarm when he stood up. Understandably, of course. It must have hurt having her hair ripped out like that but then it is very long and where's he supposed to put his feet when they make them all squeeze onto that horrible mat together?

Not that I'm downplaying what happened but the poor girl seemed to think it was deliberate when sorry, but if you're going to wear your hair like that you have to take some responsibility for what might happen. Maybe a bun, or a bob even, would be more practical for school. Or any kind of confined place. It's common sense, that's all. Anyway, suffice to say, Lottie is no longer enamoured with Zac.

Still, it got me out of the house and once we'd dealt with all that, Lenny mentioned Buddha Bowls, which I'm ashamed to admit, I'd never heard of. He filled me in, much to my embarrassment and since then I've been going mad for them at lunchtime and Ben has been trying to get in on the act. They're basically plant-based bowls full of healthy goodness (I've been practicing my spiel) usually on a bed of whole-grains like quinoa or bulgur wheat with maybe some lentils mixed in. Super healthy and topped with roasted root veg, sautéed greens, avocado, pumpkin seeds or anything you can think of with a drizzle of dressing to pull it together. Tahini with maple syrup perhaps, garlic and chilli-spiced tomato, carrot and ginger, freshly squeezed lemon. The options are endless.

Oh, God. Listen to me. I sound like Lenny.

He couldn't stop going on about them either. It was making my mouth water just talking about it and I must remember to tell him I'm pimping up the tagine recipe he pointed me towards a few weeks ago. In all honesty, I'm enjoying this experiment so far. Apart from the tofu. I haven't learnt to like that yet, but I'm working on it. Lenny says it's fine to use the meat-free substitutes if I prefer, only not to overdo it because they're pretty high in salt. The kids like them though so that's the main thing, as long as I cook everything else from scratch. I'll make a gradual move towards unprocessed alternatives once we've acclimatised. It's certainly been useful having a real-life vegan to help me through it. Not sure what I'd have done without him.

'You've started early,' Ben says materialising behind me and at first I think he means on the wine but he was referring to dinner.

I push back a wave of affronted indignation and take a sip of my lemon tea knowing perfectly well that the need, the urgency to down a cheap liquid sedative won't hit me until about three twenty-two. Earlier on weekends. It's very strange. I'm completely fine without a drink in the day. Wouldn't think about it, but for some reason pickup triggers a raw desperation to take the edge off everything. Blur the lines. Blot out the noise. I can't think why.

'The sun's out. I'm not going to get away with dragging Zac straight home after school. Be lucky if we make it back before five. Can't wait until they put the clocks back. At least everyone deserts the playground by quarter past four.' I turn the hob off and leave the tagine to thicken of its own accord. 'Are you off for a bike ride?'

'No, I popped down to see you.'

'You must be bored.'

'Can't a man spend a few minutes with his one true love without having to explain why?' he says heading towards the fruit bowl, his arm stretched towards a banana.

'No need to explain. You were hungry and I happen to be in the kitchen.'

'You're a cynic, Mrs Harrison.'

I'm a realist and besides which, your one true love is in the garage with a deflated wheel you still need to pump up. I let the creases in my forehead do the talking and concentrate on uploading a photo of the tagine on my phone.

'Anyway, I'd better sort the old dear out while I'm down here. Her chain needs more oil and I have to pump that wheel up.'

'Mm-huh.'

He swings the bin out from under the sink and drops the banana skin in with a flick of his wrist, magicing the remnants off his fingers in small circular motions (that lead directly to the floor).

Aren't you going to wash your hands? Her standards must be slipping, I don't say but he turns as though reading my mind and rinses them under the tap.

Can't have her thinking you haven't made an effort, hey? Not with all those other Lycra-clad dad bods out there competing for her attention.

He kisses my cheek again and his breath smells sweet. There are worse things and I make a perfunctory attempt at returning it, knowing that as soon as he's finished out there, he'll have to take her out for a quick spin in the park to check she's in perfect working order. And, why not? I would try to avoid being here when the kids get back too if I didn't have to look after them, one after the other in an endless relay, handing out food and helping with homework. It's not half bad this 'working from home'.

'Have a nice time,' I say even though he has yet to admit his intentions for the next few hours, even to himself. He saunters out with a baffled shrug and I glance at the clock on the wall. Time has gotten away from me as usual but Beasley knows exactly what's going on. He's been playing dead all afternoon but I can tell by the way he's subtly stiffened that he's realised it's pickup.

'Sorry, love. I would leave you here but you'll only disgrace yourself later. Besides, we might see your biggest fan. That would be nice, wouldn't it?'

He rouses himself laboriously as I click the lead on. He used to wear a harness but it's been so long since he tried to run off, there's no danger of garrotting him with the collar.

'One less thing to worry about, hey, boy?'

109

He doesn't answer. He just potters along until we get to the school gates and then braces himself for the inevitable rush of adulation and air as Zac zooms past the doting crowds of infants into the playground.

'Hi there. Bye there.'

Beasley and I both shudder and shuffle back across the road.

Here we go again.

It's cold but bright outside. The few remaining brown leaves cling to near-barren trees while others scatter in the breeze, their fragile webbed bronchioles spreading across the field where they collect in windswept piles - crunching underfoot, decaying on the sparse muddy grass, their purpose over.

'I hate this time of year.'

Beasley whimpers and keeps his nose firmly to the ground avoiding eye contact.

'I used to love it. The colours, the smells but I don't know. It's so depressing now. It's such a long wait until spring and don't get me started on winter. It'll be here again before we know it. You wait. As soon as Halloween is out the way, all the shelves will be full of Christmas crap again. Spend spend spend.'

'Hello.' Kay bounces up besides me, her crooked teeth quietly conspicuous behind a faltering smile. She cranes her head quizzically, edging the final few inches, her finger pointing to an imagined AirPod in my ear. 'Ah, sorry. Are you...?'

'No. I'm talking to Beasley.'

Her eyebrows knit together, unsure whether to interrupt.

'It's fine. We've finished.'

'Ahh.'

'Take it you're going to the playground.'

Her eyes narrow comically and she shakes her head even though she means yes. 'It's too freezing. I said, "Theodore. Let's go. You've got homework" but he said "No, Mummy. I want to play with my friends".'

Oh God, what do you mean they've got homework? I almost say but then I realise she's one of those first-time-mums who's actually invested in their kids and makes them study when they get home instead of sticking them on their tablets so they don't feel compelled to talk to each other.

'I know. It's miserable. We should petition the council and get them to close the park down as soon as –'

'Wo-hoo, you two.'

Oh Jesus wept. I've inadvertently wandered over to the Gold Class Mums™. My eyes swing on pendulums seeking Zac out among all the other blonde boys but he's at the top of the slide, kicking one of the juniors who's trying to climb up it. *For heaven's sake.*

'How are we both?' one of them asks.

I really should learn their names. I manage the stretch my mouth across my face even though my lips crack which I put down to the cold, rather than lack of use.

'We are good,' I reply, then indicate down to Beasley in case the 'we' comes off as patronising, which was the idea but it sounds harsh now it's out there.

'Ahhh, hello little sweetie. Are dogs allowed in this bit?'

'No.'

'Oh.'

'We were just discussing Stella's fortieth party.' A short dark-haired woman who seems to think I know Stella leans forward and says 'fortieth' in a revered tone better suited to announcing she's due a telegraph from the Queen.

'Really?' I say, feigning interest while broadly not giving a shit. The tall, heavy-set woman from the other week – *Oh God, it's Lottie's mum* – waves a dismissive hand in front of her Slavic cheekbones (possibly not Slavic given that this is presumably Stella which doesn't sound at all Eastern European, but they are large and pronounced either way).

'It's hardly a party. More of a get-together. Can't really call it a celebration, can I? Although it's better than the alternative.'

Cue bumbled shuffling and downward stares. *Boring.* I know from experience I'm the only one who can smooth this social impasse over but I'm tempted not to. I fancy spinning it out for a few moments longer, revelling in their mortification but even I break in the end.

'How lovely.'

'Well, I don't know about that. It's all rather stressful. It's been a while since I've organised anything as big as this and this lot here are such youngsters, I'll be setting the benchmark for all fortieths to come.' She looks me up and down, appearing to size me up. 'You must have been to a few. Any tips will be gratefully received.'

Ohh, like that is it? I'm starting to enjoy this. 'When is it?'

'Oh, a few weeks' time. Two and a half, is it? I can't keep track. I should probably be freaking out.'

I am clearly not on the party list. A less arrogant woman might have been embarrassed but then I remind myself that I'm not friends with this arrogant woman, I don't want to go to this awful party and my nephew may well have intentionally probably ~~tried to~~ scalpe(d) her daughter. Fair play. Bring on the alternative. I'll take that instead.

'Oh, Stella,' the short dark-haired woman dives in. 'What else is there to organise? You've sorted out the venue. You've decided on the food and the booze –'

You're certainly eager to please.

'And the theme!' a tall, redhead with a beaky nose and no chin breaks in. She tilts her neck towards me and giggles expectantly.

Oh, the theme. I know. I love a good theme.

'What food did you choose eventually?' Kay ventures. She's so tiny compared to everyone else she has to stand back a little so as not to strain her neck looking up at them all. Or is it that they're looking down on her?

'I'm still a little torn actually. I'd been set on Arno's – you know the one near Waitrose? I know a few people who've used them before for events, but we went in at the weekend and the tasting menu was very disappointing. New chef apparently. Just my luck so now I'm screwed.'

I never rated Arno's when the old chef was there. How crappy must it be now?

I participate in the round of sympathetic murmuring but stop short at the back rub. Still, my heart goes out to her, poor love. What a thing to have to go through. Eager-To-Please suggests ordering takeaway from a curry house to which Stella lifts her chin and snorts so derisorily Eager has to join in as though she was being facetious all along. The birthday girl turns to me again.

'Who did you use for your fortieth? Fiftieth?'

I smile sweetly but we all know what's going on. 'I did my own actually.'

'Oh really? Was it very low-key?'

'Not at all. I'm a caterer. Weddings, functions, you name it. It's what I do.'

'Really?'

No. 'Yes. Contemporary Cooking. Feel free to look me up.' *Please don't look me up.*

'Is that right? What sort of food do you do?'

'Anything really.' *Why am I still talking?*

'For parties…'

'Well, canapés are always very popular.' *Who am I trying to impress? Beasley do something. Zac. Anyone?* 'Duck satay with peanut sauce, dolcelatte-stuffed figs, prawn and chorizo skewers…'

She's still waiting blankly. I rack my brain for the recipes I messed around with back in lockdown.

'Um, caramelised mushroom tarts... Arancini?'

I'm losing my nerve. *Oh good God. Surely you get the idea.*

'Mmm. To be honest, I don't know if I want to bother with all those bits. They always get cold so quickly, don't they? Whenever I get that sort of thing in at Christmas, it's always such a disappointment.' This woman has clearly dealt with a lot of disappointment in her life. 'I mean I'm sure yours are better, but you know what I mean? It's hard to picture it all. Have you got a website?'

No, no. Stop it. Please ignore me. I'm talking out of my arse. 'Not yet, sorry.' *But she's so freakishly intimidating.* 'I'm on Instagram though.'

'Right.' Her phone's in her hand.' Let me look you up then. Contemporary, what was it? Is that the one? Contemporary Cooking? Oh no, it's not that. Imagine. How corporate. Sounds like something from the eighties.'

'Coco. It's Coco,' I blurt like a fucking imbecile. 'It does stand for Contemporary Cooking but that's kind of a joke. Like a retro, sort of, nod at... You know. We don't want to take ourselves too seriously.' *Wahhhhh.*

'Oh, right. Well, Coco's good. I like Coco. Oh. You've only got twelve followers. Is that right?'

'It's a glitch. We're in the middle of rebranding, that's all. My son's got to bring all the old, um, people across.'

'Okay, well make sure he sorts the name out. It still says Contemporary Cooking, here.'

'I'll let him know. He's very good at the technical, um –'

'Let's have a gander anyway. Oh, wow. Very nice.'

Well, she's a bigger woman than me, I'll give her that. Beasley gives me a look. *I didn't mean it like that.*

'This could actually be quite scrummy. What is it?' The other mums crowd around the screen, straining to examine the pictures I hadn't really intended anyone to see.

'Oh, that. That's last night's tea. I was just checking the, you know, uploading.'

'What is it though? Middle Eastern. Mmm.'

I guess… No, sorry. Can we circle back to the 'big' thing? I genuinely didn't mean it like that. Don't get me wrong. I don't like this woman but that's not cool. Alright. I'll stop going on about it if you stop looking at me like that, Elena. Beasley.

'You know, that's more the sort of thing I was thinking. Just a few huge bowls of tagine and couscous and then whatever goes with it on the side. Baba ganoush and some of that bulgur wheat thingamebob. You know what I mean? Rather than fussing around with all those little bits and bobs that nobody really likes anyway.'

'I'm sorry. Are you asking me to...?'

'Well, why not? I've always been one to let bygones be bygones. What say you? Think you could put something together for about fifty of my closest friends and family in less than three weeks' time? Ha ha ha.'

'Of course, of course, that's fine.' If this woman wanted me to serve her the kid's tea, I could do that. I could do that with my

116

eyes closed. 'I can do one beef, date and honey tagine with almonds and one chicken and apricot?'

'Better do one for the vegetarians too. They're bloody everywhere these days.'

'Well, I can recommend the harissa, red lentil and squash tagine. That's the one you were looking at just now'

'Perfect. You certainly know your stuff.'

I'm pretty certain she doesn't think I know my stuff.

'Why don't you put together a quote and get it to me over the weekend and then perhaps you'll indulge me in a little tasting session. Just to be sure, of course.' She guffaws and touches my arm, bending her head towards me. Her breath is warm and tinged with Chardonnay but there's something in her eyes that I can't read.

'Great,' I say and then Zac pulls up behind me demanding something to eat so I bribe him with a slab of chocolate cake if he agrees to come home immediately. Stella makes a sort of 'message me' sign in the air as I'm wrestling him into his jacket and I attribute the white sweat beading on my forehead to the effort it takes getting him to the gate. Not sure anyone else is convinced but they wave enthusiastically, seeing me in what I take to be a whole new light.

Oh, Lenny. Where are you? I could really do with a chat right now.

Nine

'You did what?' My mum's voice is shrill and just slightly over-exuberant given the circumstances. The glare from the sun shining over her shoulder surrounds her with an ethereal glow, but I can read the delight in the arch of her eyebrows despite the shade the contrast is casting on her face.

'I know,' I sigh, propping the iPad up against a cereal box while I rustle together a bunch of snacks ready to feed Zac and Oscar immediately after breakfast, on route to football practice, at halftime, all the way back home and just before lunch.

'Well, you'll just have to tell her you can't do it.'

Every so often the light makes the side of her head look like it's been caved in. It's very distracting.

'I can't do that. I have to see these people everyday. It'll be humiliating if I say I can't do it.'

'It'll be more humiliating if it's an absolute disaster. You can always say you don't have time at the moment.'

'But I do have time and I don't know, maybe I'd like to do it.'

'Lara! This isn't some family barbeque. You're talking about catering for a huge event.'

Bob is pottering about in the background in a pair of Bermuda shorts that bunch tightly around the crotch.

Oh dear, Bob. Put some clothes on. 'It's not going to be that huge. Besides, I've been experimenting with new techniques and recipes since you've been away. I'm sort of quite good now. I think I can pull it off as long as I get a few dry runs in first.'

My mother manages to roll her entire head in lieu of her eyes and once again I am eight years old and clearly very stupid.

'Look, we all know you can cook, Lara. You get it from me.' I do not get it from her. 'But this is too much. Surely. Given the situation. I mean, maybe in a year or two but right now... With everything that's happened.'

'It's exactly because of everything that's happened that I need the distraction.'

'But The Main Distraction, if you get my drift, will still be there.' She leans towards the camera and hisses 'Surfing the kitchen surfaces no doubt.'

She means Zac. I haven't told her Sharon's the problem on that front.

'— and it's not like I'm in a position to help you out by taking him off your hands for a few hours while you get on top of it all. Hours. Ha! Days, it'll be.'

'You're never going to be in a position to help me out, Mum. You live nine thousand miles away.' *As if you ever would anyway.*

'Oh I just mean with this blasted lockdown. Bob and I will come over and stay for a few months as soon as we're allowed.'

Oh, fabulous. That's just what I need.

'Won't we, Bob?' She calls over her shoulder and her mouth disappears in a ball of sunlight.

Her husband sidles over toasting me with a beer bottle in one hand while signalling thumbs up with the other. Seems a little early at eight in the morning but then I'm reminded by the glorious daylight streaming in behind them that they're ten hours ahead.

'Hi, Bob.'

'Lara.'

He's a man of few words. Mum takes his Foster's and waves him away.

'You drinking lager now, Mum?' I don't think I've ever seen her with a beer in her hand in my life. She's always been a wine snob. Won't even drink Prosecco. It has to be Champagne. *'There's a difference, you know!'*

'When in Rome.'

Good grief. Rome's one thing. At least they do a decent Chianti there. Even I avoid Foster's if I can help it and I've got a six-year-old sociopath living under my roof. I watch fascinated as she draws a long swig from the bottle, her fingers grasped delicately around the neck.

'I take it you're all settled in nicely there now.'

'Well, it's not the Adriatic but you know me and sunshine.'

Must be lovely for some. I shove a thermos of hot coffee into my rucksack, swing the kitchen door open and shout, 'Leaving in fifteen' up the stairs.

'Sorry,' I say returning and adjusting the screen so I can quickly fold the washing at the same time. 'Football.'

'Urghh,' she shivers. 'I thought they were giving that up.'

'Zac loves it and it's the only exercise Oscar does so I'm forcing him to keep going even though he hates it. I've said he doesn't have to enjoy it but it's one of those things boys need to know about and that might sound sexist but it's true. I don't care if he never plays again when he's older but at least if someone starts a game in the park or whatever, he'll be able to join in if he wants to. He doesn't have to be good, but I can't have him being left out for the rest of his life just because I gave in to him when he was twelve.'

'I can't see Oscar giving two hoots about being left out of anything but the Tony Awards.'

'I know. I still have to give him the tools to make choices though.'

'My sweet darling.' Not me. 'How is little Ozzie anyway?'

He's always been her favourite. I don't know why. She doesn't usually like to share the limelight.

'Not so little now. He's almost as tall as me. Another few centimetres…'

'Oh, no. I feel like I'm missing out on so much.'

You are.

'And how's the demon?' she whispers into the microphone.

'The demon's fine, Margaret, thank you,' Ben chirps, breezing into the kitchen in a pair of skin-tight cycling shorts and a neon T-shirt I can see his nipples poking through.

I press my hand against my chest to slow my heartbeat and re-angle the tablet away. My pulse isn't racing because of the T-shirt, I should clarify. It's only the one thing I didn't do when designing this room was anticipate my husband popping up in it at all hours of the day and certainly not in that sort of attire.

'It's Maggie now, don't forget.' I say, taking the opportunity to mock her while she's too flustered to talk.

'Of course it is.' Ben continues. 'Much more laid back, hey? More fitting with the new lifestyle. And can I discern the hint of a twang in your accent now?'

'I –'

'I've got to say, I'm always surprised at how much you like it out there.' *Being an uptight cow,* he doesn't say, although I know it's what he's thinking, but he always gets that wrong. It isn't that she's uptight, she simply doesn't like him very much. Wasn't best pleased when he steered my focus away from her and encouraged me not to give in to her demands for attention. He was right, of course, and he certainly got what he wanted. There's plenty of space between us now.

'Hello, Ben. You're looking very yellow,' she says, her voice clipped.

'Thank you, Maggie. You too.'

He grabs one of the muesli bars I've laid out for the boys, kisses me on the cheek and trots off without so much as a goodbye. They're as bad as each other. They're both so used to people falling for their charms, they can only assume any absence of adoration is down to some personality defect in the other. Ben, for his part, has also latched onto the fact she hasn't made more of an effort since our world's been in turmoil.

'She didn't even send flowers, Lara,' he'd cried, vindicated for once and not thinking for a moment how hard his righteous indignation makes it for me to even Facetime her with him skulking around in the background ready to maul our conversations apart the moment I hang up. And even before.

'Still in the throes of a mid-life crisis, is he?' My mum purrs now that Ben's safely out of earshot. The kitchen door clicks before I can decide how I want to answer that and Oscar shambles in.

'Come and talk to your gran while I finish getting ready. Where's Zac?'

'Still in bed.'

'Oh, for crying out loud.'

'Hi Gran.'

'Ozzie Lozzie, my handsome boy. Have you been practising?'

Oscar's taking part in a singing competition at school and has most definitely been practising. At the top of his lungs at all hours of the day and occasionally night.

'Let's hear it then.'

I leave them to it and peg it up the stairs two at a time. Well, I peg two stairs up, two at a time and then think better of it. Zac's door is ajar but he's still wrapped up in his duvet.

'Up. Now. We're supposed to be leaving in ten minutes.'

'I'm tired.'

'Nope. I'm not falling for that again. Up and get ready please or you'll be bouncing off the walls for the rest of the day, driving me mad and breaking things.'

He groans and flings back the bedclothes, shuffles towards the ladder and eases himself down as though entering the Atlantic from the side of a boat in a storm. He could probably do with a lie-in but if I don't get him up now, he'll leap out of bed in an hour's time and spend the rest of the morning leaping over everything else until I'm so wound up I end up screaming like I'm the crazy one.

'Quick as you can please.' Taylor Swift's *Look What You Made Me Do* is reverberating through the floorboards and it's not Taylor Swift singing it. The neighbours must love us. 'You'll be fine when you get there.'

Twenty-five long painful minutes later, I'm standing at the sidelines with Beasley wondering why I bothered.

'Come on. Let's stretch our legs,' I suggest and he reacts with no more enthusiasm than either of the kids. 'What is it with you lot today? Come on. Over here. It'll make the time pass quicker and oh, look, there's another beagle. Look. Over there. Well, you could pretend to be interested. Ahhh, it's a baby. There was a time when you used to be as cute as that. Oh.'

125

'Hi Lara. I was hoping I'd bump into you.'

'Lenny!'

Lenny looks confused. 'Oh, because of the –' He swirls his hand around his face and smiles goofily.

'Sorry. I mean *Mr Matthews*.'

'Oh, Lenny's fine. I'll take it as a compliment. Not sure he would.'

There's nothing I can say to that without sounding even more idiotic than I already do so I turn my attention to the main event.

'You did it, then? Beasley, look. You've got a new friend to sniff.' I bend down to the short chubby puppy thrashing its tail around in excitement at my feet. Beasley couldn't care less. 'Girl. Boy?'

'Girl. Didn't think I could cope with having to mark every lamppost.'

'Well, that's what the dog's for.'

There's a pause and then a crimson flush creeps up Lenny's neck, his laughter light and contagious.

'I keep walking into it, don't I?'

'You certainly make it easy for me.' I crouch down to rub the puppy's fresh, gleaming coat, her muddy paws pressing against my thighs, her tongue rasping against my cheek. Beasley's too old for this sort of nonsense and stands to the side staring out into the middle distance as though his train's been delayed.

'Don't mind him. He's a grump. Come here, you gorgeous little thing. What's your name?'

'Coco.'

I look up, but there's no mirth in Lenny's eyes, only infatuation and much as I'd like to suggest otherwise, it's not directed at me. I think.

'No way. My catering business is called Coco. Contemporary Cooking, actually, but Coco for short.' Oh, God. I'm off again. What is wrong with me?

'Really? I didn't know you had a company.'

'It's new. But we don't want to talk about that.' *We certainly don't.* 'We want to talk about you, don't we, Coco?'

Coco leaps up onto my lap and out again.

Thank God. My knees are starting to go. I take the opportunity to stand before I seize up and have to roll myself onto all fours to get some leverage.

'How's it going? When did you get her? How old is she?' The questions tumble out before Lenny has a chance to answer and we both laugh, drawing closer to one another as Coco spins around me twisting her lead into mine.

'Exhausting, yesterday and twelve weeks in that order. This is the first time we've been out. We haven't got very far.'

'Ahh, it's all new. You've got to explore everything, haven't you, darling? It's probably Beasley you can smell. He's a stinker. Yes, he's a stinker.'

Beasley is not impressed by either my animated baby voice or the fact I've thrown him under the bus.

Well, that's what you get for rolling in fox poo. I can't be nice all the time.

'Are you here on your own?' Lenny asks.

'I wish. No.' I nod my head towards the crowded field. 'Football practice. That's my youngest propping up the goalpost over there. I only make him keep coming for the exercise and then he spends the whole time standing around in goal.'

That's not entirely true. The main reason I make him come (apart from so he can bond with men in social situations when he's older) is because I paid for it a year and a half ago before the bloody lockdown and I'm determined to recoup my losses.

'He looks like he's having a great time.'

'Oh, he is. Look at him. He's your typical alpha male, is Oscar. Huge football fan.'

Lenny laughs with the empathy of a man who's never seen the point of kicking a ball about either.

'No, Zac's the only one who's ever been really into it. If you can imagine that.'

Although he's making a poor effort today, it has to be said. He's hardly tackled anyone to the ground and his kit still looks relatively clean. Most tellingly, the ref isn't following him around like a sheepdog with a rabid lamb.

'You've got your hands full with two boys to deal with.'

'I've got another one at home in bed.'

'Ill?'

'Teenage.'

'Oh dear. How's that going?'

'Not too bad, actually. We've just had a lot of grunting so far. And selective hearing.'

'No dramatic exits and doors slamming then?'

'Only by Zac. Jake gets a bit stroppy from time to time, but that's about it. I feel like I hardly see him anymore, he's always out with his friends or up in his room gaming but that's normal, isn't it? I try to make the most of it. The less I have to deal with the better.'

'I'll bet. Sounds like you're getting off lightly. I was a nightmare when I was a teenager.'

As if you could ever be a nightmare. Look at you. 'Oh, don't get me wrong. I'm in danger of forgetting what colour his eyes are, he rolls them into the back of his head so often but yes, so far so good. And Oscar's fine. I never need to worry about him. It's just Zac, to be honest. I know how horrible that makes me sound but he is a lot. Well, you of all people probably know what I mean.' *Why am I telling you this?*

'It must be hard.'

'Hard? The other two were hard. A good day with Zac is like the worst day I ever had with either of them at the same time and then double that.'

Lenny bites down on his lip, his eyes warm and understanding. I shake my head.

'Sorry. That sounds awful. I'm awful, I know it.'

'I don't think you're awful. Not at all. I understand. It's…it's a… God, it would be hard even if you weren't juggling two other kids. And look, you can talk to me. If you…'

I can't talk to you. I can't talk to anyone. I shouldn't be saying this. But I say it anyway. 'It's just that life was finally getting back to normal and then this happened and it's so terrible and tragic but it's also so consuming and that makes me sound like such a selfish dick and I'm not. I promise you.'

'I can tell.'

'He's such hard work though. He's such hard work. Aside from the circumstances, which are horrific in themselves, aside from the impact it would have on anyone, the stuff we're all having to deal with, emotionally ourselves, aside from all of that, he's still a little nutcase.' *Stop talking. Stop talking.* 'Sorry.'

Lenny forehead is furrowed with concern but his expression falters when I say *nutcase* and he wavers.

'Sorry. I don't mean to...' he sniggers and then both our faces crumple into foolish, sheepish grins as we bite back laughter. High-pitched hysterical laughter in my case. More restrained, I suspect, in his. 'It sounds awful.'

'It is awful. It is unimaginably awful and I'm a selfish bitch for even thinking it. You're the first person I've ever said all that out loud to. I'm just... There's this catering thing that's come up. An opportunity and it's everything I've been dreaming of for the last few years and I keep swinging between thinking I should go for it and realising I don't have the time or experience.'

'What is it then?'

I glance around the field as though somebody might be listening, but everyone's miles away, occupied with their own lives. Only Coco is paying us any attention at all, but I suspect she can be relied on to keep her mouth shut and as for Beasley? He's too busy fantasizing about chasing off the flock of seagulls ahead, who conversely, have no fear of him chasing them off at all.

'It's just one of the women at school – Lottie's mum. It's her fortieth and I may have slightly exaggerated my credentials to her and all the other mums. As in, when I say I have a catering business, I mean I've registered a business, I've thought about it. I've got great ambitions to do something with it in the future when I've got time but I've never actually cooked for anyone apart from my family but now I've sort of landed myself in a situation I can't really handle. I've made out I'm this big hotshot caterer and really, I'm not. I'm just a sad old housewife.'

'Oh, come on. I'll bet you're a sad old housewife who's made thousand of meals. Who cares if you've never charged anyone before...?' His voice has a playful teasing tone that makes my stomach flutter more than it should.

'Or catered for fifty people...'

"You're feeding three growing boys. They probably eat more than fifty grown adults between meals.'

'But what if anyone finds out I lied?'

Coco has twisted her leash around my ankles so many times, I'm in danger of falling and being dragged across the playing field on my back. She is adorable but she's making it very difficult to have a meaningful conversation. Lenny holds my arm to steady me as I step out of the noose, bending down to loosen it, his head disconcertingly close to my legs. I tense my thighs and buttocks even though it's of no consequence. That much consequence anyway.

131

'Everyone lies. It's the first rule of business. You've gotta fake it till you make it, isn't that what they say?'

'If I make it.'

'Look. Every single person out there has blagged a job interview. We're all making it up. Look at social media. It's just one big lie, or at the very least it's only a sliver of reality. We present the side of ourselves we want other people to see. No one's posting Instagram shots of themselves waking up with their hair sticking up and a crusty old trail of drool on the pillow. It's all about perception and the spin you put on things.'

'I'm really out of my depth though, this time. It's all Jacob's fault, my eldest. He got me going. Made me think I could do it. I mean, if this is what my life has come to – taking careers advice from a teenager – it's no wonder I'm in trouble.'

'Sounds like he's got a good head on his shoulders. Like his mum,' he says and I'm not sure how that makes me feel.

Beasley's had enough of Coco sniffing his bottom and desperately rolling on her back to entice him towards her. A low rumble that could pass for a growl if she flings herself under him one more time brings me to my senses and I pull on the lead.

'I should get back to the boys. It's nearly time for the final whistle, thank goodness.'

'Sure.'

'Thanks for the advice though. You're right. I need to stop taking myself so seriously. Get out of my head.'

'It'll be fine. You can do this.'

132

I can't do this. 'We're here every week,' I call turning away from him before he reads anything into the smile I can't shake.

'I'll keep that in mind,' he replies.

Oh God. Sort yourself out, you silly woman.

By the time I get back across to the kids, the walls of spectators lining the pitch are breaking up and meandering in fragmented groups towards the exits.

'Zac. Time to go. Oscar, come on.' He's by my side. It's the quickest he's moved all morning.

'Have we got anything to eat?'

'Yes. Start walking. I'll get you something in a second. Zac.'

Zac is standing around staring at the cones he normally races around collecting at the end of the match.

'Take your vest off! Leave it there! Come on.' I rummage around the bottom of the rucksack as I walk, finally landing on a squashed brioche I shove at Oscar's midriff, much to his disgust. 'That's it until lunch, ok? There's not a hope in hell you burnt off enough calories to justify having four breakfasts. You hardly moved at all in that game.'

'I was in goal. I'm not allowed to go anywhere.'

'The whole point of you coming here is to get fit. It's the only exercise you ever do.'

'I do loads of exercise.' Which he fails to demonstrate by bursting into a breathless sweat trying to keep up with me. 'I ride my bike to school most days. I walk the dog.'

'Occasionally standing in the garden with Beasley does not constitute a walk.'

'I'll start taking him for walks then. Please. Can I just stop coming here? I hate it.'

I turn and look at him. 'What other interests do you have though? If you drop football, you won't have any hobbies at all. Come on, Zac! Catch up.'

'I do. Singing. I should be practicing for the MODHO awards right now, instead of standing around getting cold and damaging my voice.'

'You should be running around. That's why you're cold. Damaging your voice...'

'Mummmm, please.'

'Oh God. Alright. We're all paid up until the end of half term but you can drop it then okay? On the condition that you actually make an effort for the last few weeks. Zac!'

'Yes!' Oscar punches the air with his fist. 'Did I tell you what I'm doing for the competition?'

'No, but I heard you singing to Gran.'

Zac is dawdling so far behind us, I have to hold out my arm in front of Oscar to get him to stop.

'Wait here for a sec so he can catch up.'

Oscar, realising he has a captive audience, turns and starts belting out his audition song a shade too loudly for my liking but he's confident, I'll give him that. And only slightly off-key. Beasley looks mildly horrified and seeks shelter behind my legs either for protection or out of sheer embarrassment.

I could really do with a cup of tea. My toes are freezing. I just want to get home now and you know what? Lenny's right.

I'm going to go for it. I'm going to palm the kids off on Ben as soon as he's back from his bike ride and make a start on that quote. Bearing in mind I'm the only person who knows where food and socks are kept in the house so I'll be interrupted at least thirty-two times, of course, but I can't let that put me off.

I have to stop procrastinating and using Zac as an excuse not to get on with my life. They're back at school on Monday so I'll have plenty of time to put together a tasting menu for Tuesday or Wednesday. Knock it out of the park, get the gig and still have a week to organise everything else. Research the menus. Put in the orders. What was I worried about? There's no reason in the world why I shouldn't do this.

'Zac! Can. You. Come. On!'

Zac finally shuffles up looking shivery and pale and very sorry for himself.

'What's wrong with you? Can you hurry up please? I've got loads of things I need to get on with back at the house.'

'Okay,' he says in a pitiful voice And then he coughs.

Ten

'Covid? For fuck's sake. Covid. Why now? Why does he have to go and get it this week of all weeks?' I stare down incredulously at the NHS text that's just pinged through on my phone even though I knew what it was going to say before I opened it.

'It's going around the schools apparently,' Ben states knowledgeably. 'Loads of kids are off with it.'

'I know. I told you that, but for fuck's sake. Why him? Why now? Just as something finally starts to go my way, he's going to be off for ten days. Why does this keep happening? It's like Groundhog Day. Every time I think I've got a minute to myself, they all turn up again. If it's not lockdown, it's half term or Easter or Christmas. Or this! It's unbelievable. How the hell is anyone supposed to function? It's no bloody wonder I can never achieve anything.'

I yank the fridge door open and reach for the bottle of wine on the top shelf. It's emptier than I expected. *Damn it. I'm going to have to switch to red in a minute. Have we got any red?*

'I can help out. In the evenings.'

Oh great. The evenings. I'll just do everything as usual then. Look after an ill child all day, homeschool him, run around making meals for everyone, cleaning and doing the housework

137

and then quickly whip together a banquet for fifty random strangers when you're done prioritising your life.

We pay the mortgage when I prioritise my life he doesn't say because of course, I don't say what I'm thinking either. I say 'There's no point. It's never going to work. I am literally cursed. I don't know who did it, I don't know why, but my life is screwed and it's never going to get any better.'

'Lara. You are a strong, capable woman and you can do this. Stop catastrophizing. I said I can help.'

God, you can be a patronising prick when you want to be, Ben. I take a long cold swig of white wine and slam the glass down, sinking my head back and staring at the ceiling. 'Arghhhhhh.'

'It's okay,' he says, tentatively taking me into his arms. 'You can do this, I know you can. I'll let them know I might have to do some flexitime, free you up as much as I can. The party's not for a few weeks –'

'Less than two weeks now.'

'He'll be out of isolation and back in school by then.'

'None of that matters if I don't even get the job. I'm supposed to present Stella with some samples by Wednesday and I haven't even finished the quote yet. I don't have any of the ingredients –'

'Right. Go. Go and sort it out. I'll look after the boys today, keep them out of your way and then tomorrow, I'll need to work in the morning to get on top of things, but I should be able to swing a few hours to help out with Zac in the afternoon. Just

138

stick him in front of the telly anyway. He's ill. It's not like you have to do anything with him.'

No. Stop it. I need to be mad at someone. Why are you always so nice when I want to bite somebody's head off?

'What are you waiting for? Go.'

My top lip trembles and all I can manage by way of thanks is a hard squeeze that goes on for a fraction too long.

I can do this. I know I can.

And I do. Despite Sharon's repeated attempts to sit on the laptop obscuring the screen and deleting three columns of calculations (twice) I get the quote done and emailed across. To be fair, I get through it more efficiently once I make the decision to fudge the whole thing and add a massive mark up to ensure Stella will balk at the figures and politely decline (I hope politely anyway) thus enabling me to walk away from the whole charade with my head held high. A cunning plan which fails to take into account the fact that around here my idea of an outrageously inflated invoice is someone else's crate of Bollinger and sushi rolls on a Friday night. Just because.

And so there's little I can do to justify turning down either the money or Stella when she agrees without the hint of a haggle and proposes bringing the tasting session forward to Monday (otherwise known as tomorrow) so that essentially, she still has time to throw a load of cash at something else if my cooking turns out to be crap. Which I'm beginning to suspect it may well be after all.

'Oh, come on, Mum,' Jacob sighs at the sight of me floundering around the kitchen, emptying the cupboards in a blind panic while simultaneously scribbling down an extensive list of ingredients which will later prove to be as outrageously overpriced as my quote implied. 'If I can race a BMW i8 against a Maserati MC20 with a six point advantage and win, you can make dinner for some rich old lady. All you need to do is serve tiny portions on massive plates and go on about all the weird stuff you put in it – the way you always do.'

'She's only forty.'

'That's what I said.'

'Hmm. Right. Out of my way. I'm off to the shops. They shut early on Sundays. Unless you want to come with me…?'

'I'd rather die.' Everything stops for a second and we stare at each other.

'Sorry,' he blurts and I take a step towards him, my breathing shallow, cautiously restrained behind a stiff smile that doesn't reach my eyes and I run a thumb down his cheek. And then I leave without a word because there are none.

But time keeps moving forward and having spent the entire weekend in bed, which was categorical proof were it needed that Zac actually was ill, he is naturally up and raring to go at six o'clock Monday and while I'm not entirely pleased at the rate of his recovery, all is not lost because Ben, my darling husband who is actually deserving of applause and not the mean things I usually think about him, has promised he will come down and take over as soon as possible.

I am so relieved I don't even mind spending the morning helping Zac make an armoury of knives and guns out of A4 paper, all the cereal boxes we're still using and sticky plastic that keeps splitting into useless shards of gum that take the varnish off the table top. I don't even lose it after an hour of colouring them in when he says we also have to make an RPG, which turns out to be an even bigger weapon than anything we've made before and a lot more fiddly. I am fine. He is perkier than yesterday but still not a hundred per cent, which is an almost perfect state for him. If only he could always be a little bit under the weather.

I'm confident there's no chance in hell I'll feel obliged to make him fill in four pages of maths or complete the missing words in his English workbook on today of all days so I ignore his schoolbag and give us both a break.

Not that break means I get to relax while Zac potters around entertaining himself. Not at all, but I'm happy to go along with whatever he wants to do to keep him quiet. I'm just counting down the minutes until Ben comes downstairs and relieves me. Frees me up so I can kick everyone out of the kitchen and let me do what I do best. Not that I've set much of a bar there, but still, it'll be fun and I'm only feeling very occasionally overcome by hysteria now instead of all of the time.

'Let's play Monopoly,' Zac cries, his animated face still smeared with the evidence of Saturday morning's football, his hair matted into greasy clumps.

That might be pushing it. I'm only human after all. 'Ohh, Zac. I don't mind playing a board game but not Monopoly. It goes on for too long.'

'But I'm off all week, you said.'

'I know, but we can't spend the entire time playing Monopoly. I do have other things I need to get on with, you know.' And then I remember that Ben will be down any minute and he loves this sort of thing. 'Actually, tell you what. Set it up and I'll play with you until Uncle Ben comes down and he can finish it off.' (Over the course of the next sixteen hours.) *Ha!* It only gets really boring when someone buys Mayfair and Park Lane and nearly bankrupts you anyway.

Time does drag during this game and in Zac's company so I don't realise for a good while that despite all his promises Ben has yet to appear by two o'clock and when I manage to break away for long enough to bang on the study door, he looks up, flustered and preoccupied. I stand in the doorway, my hand on the handle, my head straining into the room with unbearable restraint.

'Erm...'

'Right, sorry,' he garbles accusingly. 'I know I said I'd help out but we've got three people on the team down with Covid and we're supposed to be presenting the final package to Xtra-Line on Wednesday. We're nowhere near bloody ready and now I'm going to have to take over the whole project as well as fixing the mess they made of the Croft account. We were barely breaking even as it was and now we're going to be working at a loss. The whole thing's an effing disaster.'

Of course it is, of course it is. And you couldn't have told me that this morning when I was faffing around making RPGs?

'Aunty Lara,' Zac yells up the stairs. 'Hurry up. It's your turn.'

'Can you stick him in front of the box or something?' He turns back to the laptop, the issue of my dilemma clearly resolved.

'Can I...? Do you know how many times I've tried to get him to watch TV today so I can have five minutes to myself?'

'Well, it's good that he hasn't been stuck in front of a screen all day, I suppose.'

My nostrils stop him in his tracks.

'Look, I'm really sorry. I'd take over if I could.'

Of course you would. My jaw tightens and the words I want to say get caught in my throat. I need a drink but the odds of winning this contract are even slimmer than they were a few minutes ago. I can't risk dropping any more balls (though I could happily twist both of Ben's off right now).

'Aunty Lara!'

My teeth clench at my husband's carefully constructed remorse, the helpless regret settling into his eyes. The hopeless shrug of his weary overloaded shoulders.

Wanker!!!!!

143

All I can do is slam the door shut and launch a chilling attack on the banister, my fingernails digging into my palms, my mouth stretched in a silent scream.

'It's your turn, Aunty Lar–'

'Jesus Christ. Enough!' The thump and wallop of the stairs shuts even Zac up as I thunder towards him, the set of my eyes murderous and blazing with the impatience I've held in all day. 'It's time to go on your tablet.'

'But we're in the middle of a game.'

'Just leave it all out. We can carry on tomorrow. I'm behind on everything I needed to do today.'

'But I'm winning.'

'You'll still be winning tomorrow.'

'But I want to play now.'

'For the love of God, Zac. Just go and watch your tablet. Put the telly on. Do something, anything that doesn't involve me.'

'But –'

'I'm not asking. I have a thousand things to get on with and all I've done all day is play with you. You're supposed to be ill, for Christ's sake. Can't you just take a break? Why did have to pick today to suddenly want to spend time with me?'

'But –' He stands over the Monopoly board, the little metal dog drooping in his hand.

'Leave me alone, Zac!'

And just like that he bares his teeth and swings his hand across the table sending hours of hard-earned houses and hotels skidding across the floor, his piles of money the tail end of a tornado, swirling and scattering all over the room.

'Well, that was stupid.'

His eyes contract, glittering dangerously, his mouth still contorted in rage as he screams in fury, demolishing the wrecked remains of the game, his arms thrashing, lashing out at anything within reach; his latest artwork bending gently on the sideboard, the scented candle, the wall of photo frames –

'No!' I grab his wrist, my rage a match for his own, my knuckles white, his skin beneath them bruising with the force it takes to hold him back and we stand, rigid and unyielding, locked in front of Elena's serene face until the anger ebbs away from us both and he throws himself limply against me, huge harrowing sobs racking his chest. Sharp, shallow sobs in mine.

'It's okay,' I say knowing it will never be okay again and we stand for a moment rocking in a silence punctuated only by our laboured breathing, both of us brittle and broken and bathed in his mother's gaze.

In the end I swallow and withdraw first, my hands still resting on his shoulders all the while my feet are already edging away.

'Look, Sharon's come to see if you're alright.'

The cat's winding herself around Zac's legs in concern the way she does whenever anybody cries. It's either maternal instinct or she's a dreadful busybody but whatever it is, she's strangely comforting in a crisis and as Zac bends down to stroke her small plump body, I step away.

'We'd better pick this lot up before Beasley does it for us.'

He's up too and searching for any scraps of bacon or strings of sausages that might have been flung onto the floor during the height of the drama. He moves faster than you'd expect.

'Quick, quick. He's eating the boot. Oh no, Beasley…'

That gets Zac laughing at least. It's gone and no, before anyone asks, I will not be rooting through his every bowel movement until I find it. I would rather buy a whole new board and throw every other piece away. No one likes the boot anyway. Now if it had been the hat…

'Listen, this is what we'll do. You set up a new game while I make a start on the food and then you can throw the dice for me and move my bits around. That's the best I can do until Oscar gets back and he can take over, okay? But I do really need to get cooking, Zac. I need you to be as good as you can for me now. It's really important.'

'Okay.'

'And you're sure you don't want to go and watch telly or something now? You have been at it all day.'

'No.'

No. 'Okay. Set it up then.'

And so that's how we play. Me standing at the island prepping the veg, marinating the meat, draining chickpeas and measuring spices into ramekins ready to be fried up later while Zac sits at the table moving the pieces around the board and prising money out from under Sharon who has curled up on the bank.

146

It's not where my head needs to be but it's the best I can do and it's almost manageable, even when Oscar does finally appear and then immediately disappear upstairs to go to the toilet, which takes far longer than usual and leaves me questioning the benefits of a vegan diet. Only the fact he's massacring Arianna Grande at the top of his lungs and no doubt disturbing Ben brings me any joy at all until he saunters back half an hour later and my heart leaps with relief.

'Good grief. Where've you been? I told you I need to you play with Zac for an hour or so. Please,' I say, apparently under my breath because he makes no sign of having heard me.

'Next time you go to town, can you please get some more red nail varnish?'

'What? Why?'

'Because the one upstairs has run out.'

'You mean *my* one upstairs has run out.' I don't really care. Most of my make-up dates back to university. I'm amazed it hasn't all dried up. Besides I have more pressing concerns like braising the aubergine. 'I thought you were going to the loo.'

'I was.'

'How have you managed to do your nails then?' I haven't done my nails in fourteen years. I don't even file them unless they break off and start catching on my cardigans. Oscar thinks better of answering and transfers any guilt he feels into admiring his hands.

'Let's see,' Zac cries and Oscar flashes his fingernails so quickly he'd need special powers to see them.

147

'Show him properly Oscar,' I snap.

He sighs and stretches them out on the table.

'They're ladybirds,' he explains as if they need explaining. He's obsessed with *Miraculous: Tales of Ladybug and Cat Noir*. He's watched all four seasons twice and it's not a cartoon by the way. It's a highly sophisticated animation for teenagers dealing with secret crushes and hidden personas. What's not to like?

'Can you do me some?' Zac squeals, splaying his own fingers across the now abandoned Old Kent Road.

'No. They take ages.'

'Oh, go on, Oscar. It would really help me out if you could spend some time with him. I did ask you to earlier.'

'There's no red left.'

'Use the yellow one then, like some flashy European ladybird. Or a bee. I'll get you some more tomorrow.' *If I can ever leave the house.*

'Yayy.' Zac zooms upstairs like a homing missile and misses the face of doom Oscar's composed for the occasion.

'One red and an orange,' he bargains.

'One red and an orange but be nice and don't let him touch anything until it's dry.'

Oscar slopes off despondently but I know he's secretly delighted.

'Love you.' *Fanbloodytastic*. It'll take at least fifteen minutes to apply and then another ten, sitting stock still while it sets. This is genius. I'll pick up one of every colour in the rainbow if it gets me through the next week.

The dodgy floorboard creaks in the study and I hear Ben exclaim as Zac bowls past.

Don't you dare bring him back down here. I freeze, my ears pricked, my eyes wide at the thump of footsteps coming down the stairs and it's only when Ben bursts into the room that I realise I've been holding my breath. He's alone. *Thank Christ.*

'Good to see Ozzie and Zaccy getting along so well.'

Good to see them at all since you've been upstairs all day instead of helping out like you said you would. 'You know they sound like a couple of hamsters when you use those stupid pet names.'

'I'd never really thought of that.'

'No. I wish you wouldn't, that's all. It's very twee.'

'Sorry. I'll never refer to the children again.'

If you ever did more than just refer to them it probably wouldn't grate so badly.

I fling a cupboard door open pointedly spilling packets of pine nuts and raisins onto the counter and rifling through jars of couscous and bulgur wheat. My hands are skittish with adrenaline. My mind's whirring with nerves.

'I was going to take Zac off your hands but I just persuaded Oscar to keep him busy for a bit so what can I do instead? Put me to work.'

Oh, you *persuaded him. What would I do without you?* 'What about all your disasters? I thought you were 'putting out fires' all afternoon.'

'They'll have to wait for a bit. I told them my highflying wife needs help with her fancy catering business. Besides I sent them everything they needed earlier. There's nothing I can do until they get back to me.'

How much earlier? How long have you been sitting up there playing with your hose as the smoke was clearing?

'Okay, well, thank you.' *I suppose.* 'All I really need is a bit of space so I can get it done. Give me a couple of hours and I should be able to take it all across to Stella by eight o'clock.' Under the pretext that it's better to wait until the kids are in bed so we can properly concentrate on the task in hand. Nothing to do with the fact I am highflying by the seat of my pants.

'Will you be able to manage it all? Are you going to drive?'

'It's fine. It's only around the corner.'

'It's not that near. The food'll get cold.'

'Oh, it's fine. There's never anywhere to park around there and if there is, you have to pay for it.'

'Not after 6.30.'

'Ben. I said it's fine. I'd rather walk.'

'Just trying to help.'

Well, you're not.

'I can take you if you like. Drop you off.'

Jacob will be home by then. He could babysit and it would be easier... but then my reasons for not driving don't stand up. 'Seriously, I've been cooped up in the house all day. I need some fresh air and some headspace.'

'Well, do you want me to chop anything at least?'

Which would actually help but I'm far too controlling for that. It's a bad habit of mine I know, but I cannot abide being presented with uneven chunks of vegetables that cook at complete odds to one another, half a piece chargrilled to a smouldering ember while another is still raw to the bite. *No, thank you.*

'Honestly. If I can have the kitchen to myself and you can ward off Zac later when Oscar gets bored, I'll be fine.'

'Happy to taste test anytime you like…'

'Yes, alright.' *Go.*

And then an extraordinary sense of calm envelops me as I claim the space as my own. As I spread spices and tins and jars over my work top, a jumble of clutter to some but organised chaos to me. The start of a new beginning. The start of life as it was always meant to be. Apparently not the end of everything else but I can do both. I have to. It's that or nothing at all.

Eleven

Oh, Sharon. Settle down. I'm so hot. This has got to be the menopause. The peri-menopause. Or is it the cat sitting on my chest? I'm burning up. What did I drink last night? I don't think I went over half a bottle but I've thought that before and then realised there's only a drizzle left. I'm drinking too much, I know I am. It's not like I'm hiding vodka in the washing machine or anything but I can't think of a time when I last went an evening without a glass of wine or two and I never used to be like this. Now I wake up most nights dripping in sweat, hot to the touch. Spinning like a roast chicken in a rotisserie. When Sharon's not pining me down. I must be peri-menopausal. It can't be the wine. I should cut down though, before it gets to be a habit. More of a habit. Before it's not just Zac that drives me to it.

Thank Christ he's back at school now, that's all I can say. What a few weeks that was. Was it two? Ten days? Felt like ten weeks.

I can't go through that again. Not with him anyway, Sharon.

I mean it's bloody ridiculous. This new variant is bloody everywhere. If you haven't been vaccinated then more fool you. Except for the unfortunate few who really can't be for medical

153

reasons or whatever but how many people like that are there really? We've all had enough now. Let everyone look after themselves. I'm done. Ten days locked inside with a bored six-year-old bouncing off the walls did me more harm than Covid ever could. Ten days and I couldn't even take him out for a medicinal hour of exercise a day. The furthest we got was the driveway and even then one of the Gold Class Mums™ immediately appeared and made a more poignant than jokey comment about him staying two metres away from the pavement and not facing downwind.

Ha ha. Don't worry. I've told him not to breathe until we get back inside.

Did she really think there was a hope in hell I could keep him cooped up in his room the whole time, passing him food through a flap in the door and hosing him down every morning? Believe me, I'd have done it if that were an option.

You were great though, Sharon, thank you. You're always very good with sick people. Sick, irritable little people who think they shouldn't have to do schoolwork at home even when they've been more ill coming off a rollercoaster than they ever were while they were contaminated. More manageable too.

And bless Lenny, when I did eventually get to palm Zac off on him again. He must have been gutted, especially after nearly two weeks of peace and quiet. He probably felt like he had a whole new class. New job too.

The TA was less professional, I must say though. I'm sure she swore under her breath when she saw us waiting outside the classroom for the doors to open, not just on time but ten minutes early, almost as though I was trying to get rid of him.

Ha! If I could have left him there at six in the morning, believe me I would have. She did a good job of pulling it together by the time he bolted in though, I'll give her that.

Of course the downside of getting there early was having to wait outside with all the other keen parents who I suspect were, by contrast, more organised than desperate to dump their kids for a few hours. Old Chinless Beaky Nose did say Stella had been very complimentary about the tasting session though so that was nice to hear, especially as a few of the others were within earshot. Might as well enjoy a little notoriety for the right reasons for once.

The sample testing had all gone pretty much as predicted. To pot in my opinion. The beef tagine needed at least another few hours stewing in the slow cooker rather than ramped up high on the hob, the squash was overdone and the chicken was fine but lacking in the depth a little more time and less stress would have lent it. Even so, Stella does like Arnos so overcooked and bland was seemingly 'not a disappointment'. She may well have been starving too since I didn't actually get there until quarter to nine in the end and she said she'd been 'saving herself'. She hadn't been saving herself for a drink though so I could have served up a platter of Pringles at that point and she'd have said they were 'surprisingly tasty' (I'm not going to dwell on the 'surprisingly').

And it was so sweet of Lenny to remember. As I was leaving (leaping euphorically out of the doorway) he tapped my arm and mouthed, 'How did it go?'. Naturally, I did a thumbs up and pulled a stupid manic grin that made me look like an imbecile but he just winked and said, 'Knew you could do it'.

Which is where I should have left it but I tried to wink back and honestly, I'm not sure what I did, but I think I must have shut both eyes but not quite at the same time. With any luck, he just thought I'd walked through a cloud of dust. I need to work on my technique before I try it again. Or not. I should probably stop trying to wink at all. The fact Lenny always manages to pull it off is no guarantee I'll ever be able to accomplish more than a wonky blink. And really, winking? I don't know why I suddenly find it so appealing.

Oh, flashback, Sharon. I've just had a flashback. God, it's been awful. It really has been a bag full of shite. Well, you know. You were there.

I can still picture myself crumpled on the floor, head leaning back against the sitting room wall, biting back tears as my eco-friendly disposable serving dish research lay abandoned by my side. Zac using the furniture as an obstacle course with me as the finishing line, my thighs starting blocks, my feet hurdles. Balancing on the arm rests, jumping off the back of the sofa, splattering himself across the blankets. The windowsill a plank he could vault off onto a pile of well-placed cushions, invariably kicking me on his way down no matter where I positioned myself. And every time I snuck away he'd just follow me with his Nerf gun spewing bullets all over the house, roaring incessantly, refusing to do any work unless I bribed him and even then he got through it all so quickly he'd be back and under my feet again before I'd even emptied the dishwasher.

And don't get me started on the other two. They were no help at all. Jacob refused to come out of his room the minute he got home from school under the guise of 'stopping the spread' and Oscar spent the entire week locked in the bathroom practicing for the MODHOs (which he won by the way but that hasn't stopped him singing. If anything he's even worse now, buoyed on by fame and adulation).

And of course, of course Ben had to go and get Covid too, didn't he? He didn't mind taking time off then. Letting the rest of his team down. He should have been hospitalised he suffered so horribly, the poor man. I mean, he seemed alright to me but then I am 'unbelievably unsympathetic' and I 'need to brush up on my bedside manner.'

The only good thing to come out of him taking himself off to self-isolate on the sofa bed in his office with a box full of snacks and Netflix on the laptop while I continued to look after his nephew on my own, was having the bedroom to myself for ten nights (I insisted even when he felt better 'just in case').

Ten nights of not being pinged out of the bed every time he rolls over as though he's making the most of his last minute on a bouncy castle. Ten nights of not imagining trains pulling into a station every time he inhales. Ten nights of not flinching away in response to his elbows grazing past me, his breath on my neck.

No jostling, no snorting, no noise at all, apart from the cat who despite having the whole bed to stretch out on continued to prop herself on top of me.

And did I sleep any better? Did I heck. Not that I told Ben that. I just didn't feel as irritated as usual when my brain clicked into action and I lay awake for three hours every night. Every single bloody night. Tossing and turning, sighing, drained with nerves sometimes. My heart hammering like a debt collector at a door, banging furiously. The untameable surge of my pulse straining against the veins in my neck, filling me with anxiety, dousing me with doubt. I can feel it coming on again at the thought of it. That hot fear, the prickling sweat drenching me.

Oh, Sharon. I need to take the duvet off. What do you mean why am I telling you? Because you're on it.

Oh, Christ. What have I done?

What have I done, Sharon?

So what if I fooled some half-cut idiot with low standards into thinking I was any good at cooking. I only had to put together three small dishes for her and that nearly broke me. How the hell am I going to feed fifty people in a few hours' time? I can't cater for a massive event. The most I've ever done is family birthdays and barbeques where nobody minded if the sausages were overdone or the chicken was an hour late coming out the oven. This is totally different. Nothing can go wrong, I can't just wing it. Not when I'm charging people.

Dammit to hell.

What on earth inspired me to exaggerate like that? It'll be a disaster and then I'm going to have to see them all every day for the next five years. Why, why, why did I say I could do it? I was just showing off. Trying to pretend there was more to me than some boring stay-at-home mum. Trying to pretend I was interesting like them. That I hadn't just wasted the last fourteen years of my life. It's going to be awful. Thank God it's the half term break straight afterwards and I won't have to see them all for a week. Maybe they'll have forgotten by then.

Oh, Sharon. I'm so screwed.

What would Lenny say? Lenny would tell me to 'fake it till I make it'. Which is all very well but it's hard to fake a good tagine. It's either nice or it's not.

What time it is? Five o'clock. Sod it. I'm not going to get back to sleep at this rate. I might as well get up and make a start on it all now.

Come on, Sharon. I know it's still dark out but there's no point lying here worrying I don't have time to get everything done when I can get it done now. Just don't wake Beasley up or he'll be in a bad mood all day. Oh, now, Sharon. That's not nice.

Actually, you stay here. I'm banning you from the kitchen. Don't look at me like that. It's just for today. You can keep Ben company and kneed his chest to shreds instead. You might as well. He's going to say you kept him awake half the night anyway. It's okay. No one believes anything he says.

Now, wish me luck. I'm going to need it.

159

Twelve

The kitchen smells like heaven and looks like hell. Frying pans are looming over the sink defying gravity in unstable towers and assorted saucepans rest sticky and steaming on the hob. Oily pools of marinade have collected around discarded bowls, smeared and dripping with aromatic spices that will stain the worktop. Nuts are strewn across every surface and grains of uncooked rice crunch unswept underfoot. But it is done.

'Oh, Lara. You really have excelled yourself this time,' Sylvia gasps salivating pointedly at a plateful of leftovers and when I say leftovers, I mean dinner for the next three weeks. I was so anxious not to fall short when it came to portions that I ended up making enough to feed an army of rich, middle-aged drunks, over-enthusiastic husbands, starving teenagers and my in-laws, which is fortunate as they have invited themselves to stay overnight, allegedly to help Ben keep the boys out of my way, but in reality to regale me with fascinating tales about people I've never met and yet must seemingly hear all about. All while trying to concentrate on the most complex meal I have ever made and *no, thank you. I do not need a hand.*

Except with loading the dishwasher but apparently 'everyone has their own unique way of filling those things so it's best to stay out of it' (which is true but I'd have made an exception today).

'Thank you, Sylvia.'

'No, I mean it,' she says, implying that she doesn't usually. 'I absolutely love this one with the aubergines and I'm not normally a fan, as you know.'

I didn't know actually. I know someone-Ben-went-to-school-with's-mother had gall stones last year and their neighbour Jan had to cancel her trip to Borneo in the end, but I never knew Sylvia didn't like aubergines, which is borderline interesting after twenty years of cooking them for her.

'Not sure about the one with raisins though. I prefer it without.' A gravelly voice breaks through my musings with a note of pretentious authority.

'Oh, Martin –'

That's alright. Any complaints from you are confirmation that I'm doing something right.

'– I love the one with raisins,' Sylvia exclaims in the same tone she uses to admire the children's art projects. She leans forward and sniffs tentatively at the plate, her glasses clouding with half-moons of warm fragrant air. 'What's in it?'

'Couscous obviously,' Quick smile to soften the *obviously.* 'Golden raisins, toasted pine nuts and fresh coriander.' *Fried onions, cumin and vegetable stock but let's not get lost in the details.*

162

'Ohh. And this one?'

'That's kisir. It's bulgur wheat with walnuts, pomegranate seeds, parsley, chilli, just a bunch of stuff really.'

'Nope. I don't like that one.'

Thank you, Martin.

'You can do the rice again though. Rice and pasta. Very strange but it works. Are you writing this down, Sylvia?'

Sylvia rolls her eyes, her head bobbing to and fro, a deep sigh on the way. 'Don't mind him, Lara. It's all very good. Delicious. I'm sure this Stella woman will be delighted. What's this one?'

'Butter beans.' *Gently infused with olive oil, garlic, lemon juice, Dijon mustard and parsley with a light seasoning of pink Himalayan salt and black pepper. Now shut up. I've got to go.*

Ben swings around the doorway, his cheeks flushed from the night air and the effort of loading the car (after wrapping the boot in tarpaulin as though he's about to commit murder inside of it, not spill a little tagine if he takes a corner too sharply). He's tipping his head and jangling the keys at me like I'm a dog and I normally hate it when he does that, but tonight nothing can upset my mood.

I have, short of dropping all fourteen large recyclable foil containers en route to the Boat Club, pulled it off. Of course, it's not entirely beyond me to do that so I won't get too smug until I'm in and out of the doors and the food is Stella's responsibility. But it all looks and tastes pretty spectacular, if I do say so myself and Martin's disapproval only confirms that.

Not that I ever want to see another tagine again (the boys can finish it. I'll be on cereal for the rest of the month). Being absolutely sick of cooking wasn't a drawback I'd considered when I invented this career. In fact, I'm fairly certain if I had been doing it for as long as I've pretended, I'd be ready to knock the whole thing on the head by now. Burn my wooden spoons, smash my saucepans to smithereens and dump the whole lot in a landfill site along with the sodding parsley.

Did I mention it's good for bad breath, Martin? You should try it.

'Shall we?' Ben asks and I take a last inventory. All fourteen food trays packed in the car. *Check*. Extra fresh herbs ready to sprinkle on top in a small pot on the passenger seat. *Check*. Kitchen a health and safety nightmare I won't be posting photos of on Instagram. *Check*. Incompetent but legally acceptable child-minders stuffing their faces with eight different dishes at least one of them would prefer was a steak and ale pie. *Check*. Children nowhere to be seen. *Check*.

'Yup.'

'Let's do it then.'

'Ohhh,' Sylvia makes a task of swallowing her mouthful without breaking eye contact or letting me leave until finally she gulps, dabs her mouth, half-rises from the chair and cries 'Good luck with it all. You're going to knock their socks off.'

'Thanks, Sylvia. We'll be back in about half an hour. Don't worry about the boys if they're happy on their screens. They've already eaten. And help yourself to seconds. And thirds.'

164

'We will. Don't you worry about us. We'll –'

'Thanks, Mum. Come on, Lara. There's fifty people out there waiting to sample some Contemporary Cooking.'

'That's Coco to you.'

Ben grins down at me, holding the door open as I slip through. 'Coco it is.'

We drive in silence for the most part, but for once the atmosphere isn't charged with simmering resentment. Even so, my chest feels tight and I have to stuff my fingers under my thighs to stop them trembling. Ben lets go of the gearstick and gently rubs my leg, then instead of withdrawing he rests there for so long I eventually reach up to take his hand in mine. The warm orange glow of the streetlights illuminates his face as we pass beneath them. He turns his head and my heart reaches out towards him in a way I never thought it would again. His eyes are kind, his expression hopeful.

'Thanks for driving and doing the heavy lifting. I couldn't have managed it all by myself,' I say and there's no need to fake the gratitude in my voice.

'No probs.' He presses my thigh again, squeezing it before he takes his hand off to change gear. 'Are we here? Can you see anywhere to park?'

'We'll be lucky. We might have to double up in front of the entrance and I'll –'

'Here's one.'

'Oh.'

He reverses smoothly into a space I'd have barely dared ride my bike through and in the moment that follows, my stomach twists like a bagful of puppies weighed down by stones. Ben turns to me.

'Are you ready, Chef Harrison?'

'As ready as I'll ever be, I guess.'

'You guess? This is it. You've done it. You're a caterer now,' he beams and I mirror the curve of his lips, nerves settling, anxiety morphing into excitement. A spark of elation at the cusp of my throat.

'I'm really proud of you. You've worked so hard to get here and I genuinely hope it makes you happy.'

My smile wavers but I hold his gaze.

'Happier, I should say.' And then he squeezes my hand once again and we stare at one another as though there's no one else in the world.

'Jesus!' Ben rears back, his eyes wide and startled.

'Hi-ee, Lara.' Kay's face peering through the window rips a hole in the mood. 'Are you coming in?'

I wave my pot of coriander erratically and try to unfasten the seat belt, jolted from my composure.

'That's one of the mums. You don't know her,' I say – unnecessarily. Ben doesn't know any of them. 'Listen, before we go in, I wanted to say... I haven't told them about the accident. Not in detail. There hasn't been a right time and well, you know...'

Kay bangs on the glass and peeps in again. 'Shall we wait?'

I try to tell her I don't give a shit either way but there's no real middle ground when it comes to gesticulating and besides, we do need to go. The food's getting cold.

'I just mean, I'd rather not –'

'Understood.' Ben says. 'We're not stopping anyway, are we?' He swings the door open and steps into the crisp breeze drifting up from the river. I shuffle back around and clamour to catch up with him, but he's already unloading the trays by the time I manage to extract myself.

'Thanks, mate,' he says to the tall, dark-haired man he's loading them onto. 'Think we can manage the rest.'

Well, this isn't what I expected.

'My husband, Paul,' Kay says.

'My husband, Ben,' I reply and we all rinse our foreheads for what they're worth since a handshake is out of the question, let alone a pre-Covid hug or a kiss. Shame. He's unexpectedly good-looking, though I don't know why I'm surprised. Kay is a doll after all and she looks even more stunning tonight in an eighties style rah-rah skirt, pink fluorescent tights, fishnet gloves and a short denim jacket. Assuming that's the theme. Otherwise, she looks awful and a little bit nuts.

FYI he's a banker, not an English teacher, it turns out. As is she. I should probably already know that. Note to self: I must try to show more interest, particularly since I've already wasted valuable time getting to know them both better.

It's a dark, uneven walk from the pavement and the entrance to the Boat Club is distinctly unimpressive. Only the sound of

Wham pumping through the first floor windows indicates anything more exciting than an AA meeting has been scheduled for the night.

Unimposing though the stairwell may be, however, Stella has gone to town with the function room, decorating it with silver streamers and shiny self-indulgent helium balloons. I can't tell whether the shimmering disco ball spinning on the ceiling is a recent Amazon purchase or it came with the hall but it takes me back to an age of school discos and alcopops. Dressing up in oversized T-shirts, dyed Levis and DM boots. Too red lipstick inexpertly applied, streaks of bronze blusher topped with cheap mascara clumping at my eyes.

Maybe it's the thrill of knowing I'm there in an official capacity or the unanticipated yearning not to be, but I'm wired. Alive and awakened and not even irritated one bit when I'm temporarily blinded by the strobe lights. Quite the opposite in fact and before I know it, the rhythm vibrating through the lino is working it's way up my body and I find my head jerking, hips swaying, feet tapping to the beat. I'm barely moving but it's the most I've danced in years.

'Careful with the chicken,' Ben bellows over the music.

'You're here!' Stella cries, dashing over with an armful of bangles and a cleavage that makes focusing on anything she says a challenge. 'I smelt you arrive before I saw you.'

'I'm always telling her that.' Ben guffaws and leans in eagerly towards her bosom, no doubt just to be heard. 'Shall we pop it all over here? Starboard, as it were.'

168

Why not? Batten down the hatches. I don't say although I could and no one would notice but for once I don't feel like starting an imaginary fight.

'Thank you so much, everyone.' Stella jangles her arm generously at the four of us, sweeping the table free of birthday cards as she does so, either by accident or to make room for the food, it's hard to tell. She's propped up somewhat unsteadily against Ben's forearm, which makes me nervous on behalf of the tagine, but he seems happy enough.

I swear to God, if you drop that thing…

Kay steps in and takes it from him, but the look we share suggests we'd both quite like to see what would happen if Stella fell into it. I gently lift the last of the lids off and add the final touches of coriander with a well-earned flourish.

'Well, that's it then,' I shout like I'm caught in a wind tunnel. 'We'll be off. I hope it lives up to your expectations.'

'What? You're not staying?' the birthday girl slurs through a smudge of pink frosted lipstick.

'I didn't think we were invited.'

'Of course you're invited. You're already here, aren't you?'

'I –'

'Stay.'

'I'm not dressed.' I am dressed. In fact I even put on a hint of make-up in anticipation of everyone here looking even more glamorous than usual. Of course I should have opted for blue eye shadow but at least most of my wardrobe is several decades old.

'I did wonder. Still, you look fine.'

Ben and I turn to each other. Stella is pawing his arm now and he shrugs hopefully. "I can always text Mum. Ask her to put Zac to bed. They won't mind.'

'Text Oscar. She'll never see it otherwise.'

'Is that a plan then?' he says, reaching for his phone hesitantly. 'Stay for a bit?'

'I guess. If you're sure, Stella?'

'Course I'm sure,' she enunciates far too emphatically for anyone still able to speak straight. 'I thought you were staying anyway. Come with me, Lara's man. I'll get you a drink. No point eating on an empty stomach.'

'I'll have a gin and tonic too,' I call in their wake, though I'm fairly certain by the time I get to *tonic* I'm well out of earshot. Maybe I'll get lucky and Ben will bring me a pint of gin instead.

'This looks amazing, Lara,' Kay yells.

'Kay said you were a chef,' Paul bows down to my ear and for a moment I'm so distracted by his breath tickling my neck that I don't fully savour the fact that I am. I'm an actual chef. I'm a caterer. I'm not making it up. Everyone can see this, not just me when I close my eyes and fantasize about it. Not just Sharon when she sits on my recipe book or Beasley when I bore him with all the ambitious plans I've cultivated overnight. I've done it and as long as no one's hospitalised as a result, this will be who I am now. How these people see me. Not just a housewife or a mother but a talented businesswoman. I have proof. Fifty of Stella's closest friends and family have descended on the table and are eating my food.

'That's right.' I can barely contain a giggle (but that's as much as to do with having a gorgeous stranger's lips brushing past my ear as anything else. It's such a shame about the halitosis).

'You made it!' Beaky-nose cries throwing her arms around me, global pandemic or no.

I really must try to find out her name. All their names. They're all here now, the Gold Class Mums™ surrounding me with their backcombed hair and pushing drinks in my hand. Insisting I need to catch up. *Tell me about it!* That the food smells sublime. *Thanks!* Asking me how I'm enjoying my freedom now Zac's back at school. *I haven't had time to notice. I've been up to my ears in chickpeas!* If I escaped Covid this time around. *I did, but my husband likes to think he got my share too!* Men! *I know!* How I got into catering. *By chance, really.* How I come up with fresh ideas. *Guesswork, half the time.* What I've catered for before. *Birthdays, mainly. Family gatherings, anniversaries, everything really.* If I want to dance. *Dance?*

'Yes, come on,' Lucy or Lois squeals. Wait. No, it's Rachel. Or something like that. 'I love this song.'

And so does everybody else and the next thing I know, I'm up on the dance floor, chugging back plastic tumblers of Prosecco, waving my hands in the air and swinging my hips. Throwing my head back and straining my voice along with the chorus. Twisting and twirling. Weaving to and fro, mimicking their jubilant expressions until I'm no longer imitating them, I can feel it. I feel what they're feeling. The sense of abandon, the ecstasy. And it's not just the alcohol. It's the flushed faces beaming all around me. The music. The untameable fire inside me. The muscle memory kicking in as I lose myself in dance. If you can call it dancing. The boys would die if they could see me now.

It's been so long since I've let myself go like this. Since I got drunk with a group of friends and had fun. We used to do it all the time when we first moved here, back when there was a group of us in Jacob's class with younger children and we'd hang out after drop off enjoying the sun as the kids played. Life was one bit round of coffee mornings and girls' nights out. Camping trips every summer with all six families, the sixteen of us gathered round the campfire toasting marshmallows, turning to eighteen as the years went by and the last of the babies arrived. The Kingston Crew we called ourselves, delighted to have found each other and more importantly that our husbands and children all got along too.

It was idyllic but then the littlies went to school and the last of the play-dates after drop off fizzled out and by the time they all graduated to secondary school we were down to a night out every six months. If it hadn't been for Covid, we might have kept the camping trips going too but life had moved on. The dynamic had changed but that was okay. People grow apart. They fall out of touch. I didn't need them. Not like Elena. Elena was my best friend. She was my person. She was the one I had to speak to every few days even if it was just to tell her about something ridiculous that had just happened or a thought that had popped into my head. She was the one who made me laugh until tears rolled down my cheeks, who understood me in a way no one else ever could or would. Who finished my sentences, matched me drink for drink, always had my back and danced like we were still at university, drunk out of our minds on Snakebite and Blacks. Knowing that this thing we had between us would never change.

I push the thought of her out of my mind, the spike of anger deep down inside me and throw my arms in the air, screaming the lyrics to whatever's playing at the top of my voice. I scream something anyway. The noise is buzzing in my head. My forehead's clammy with a thin sheen of sweat and my cheeks hurt from smiling. I grab hold of Kay's arm.

'I need the loo,' I mouth.

'WHAT?'

'The loo,' I yell as she squints, angling towards me, her crooked teeth suspended with the strain of listening. 'THE TOILET. Don't worry. It doesn't matter.' I grin and shake my head, wobbling away over-confidently, every stride determined, my chin held high as though no one will realise I'm not entirely sober. Not that they'd give a hoot. Nor is anyone. I stagger past Ben and surprise myself by being mildly relieved to see he's managed to disentangle himself from Stella's breasts and she's staggering decisively back towards the others, her drink swilling on her hand as she turns an ankle and swiftly corrects herself.

Ben is deep in conversation with Paul, no doubt about something footbally. *Holy Moley*. They look serious. Still, you never know. Maybe they're analysing the latest season of Love Island. I gesture to him but he barely lifts his eyes. God, Brighton must be doing badly by the looks of things.

You see, Oscar. This is why I've made you stick with it all these years. What would your father talk about if he didn't have the Premier League?

It's one of those wees that goes on for ages and then keeps going even when you think *crikey, this is lasting a while* at least three times and I'm starting to feel self-conscious about the queue I can hear forming outside. It's a relief when it's over but when I look up at the mirror as I'm washing my hands, the hot sweaty face looking back at me reminds me of someone I used to know. There's a spark back behind my eyes and I can't help but grin at myself. At the memory of this evening even as it's still happening. At the thought of moving on. Of making friends again. Turning a corner. At the realisation that things could start to get better now. I stifle a titter and give myself a congratulatory wink (not sure if I pulled it off. I couldn't see with both eyes closed).

By the time I step back under the scattered glint of the disco ball there is, as always within an hour of these things, an almost perfect segregation of men on one side of the room and women folk on the other. Ben nods to me as I swagger back past him, lifting his drink, his smile forced and twitching as though I've interrupted tragic news about next week's line up.

Oh, get over it. It's only a game.

But then my heart skips a beat and my head starts to spin. Nobody's dancing anymore. They're huddled in a group around Stella, their faces ashen, glancing towards me and away again just as quickly and I know instinctively that they know. That they'll never ever look at me the same way. That I'll never be not just a housewife and a mother but a talented successful businesswoman.

I will always be defined by the accident and the crushing blow we were dealt. By the trauma of watching it play out over and over again in my head, invading every minute of every day since.

Kay starts to walk towards me, but I back away. I keep treading, feet tripping and tumbling over each other until I crash. Crash into Ben and he takes me in his arms, spins me on my heels with that pitiful look in his eyes. That sorrow. That harrowing pain unmasked by alcohol and confession.

'No.'

'I'm sorry.'

'I asked you not to.' My voice is hard, my throat strangled.

'What could I do? She asked me what happened.' Stella's clawing her neck and clinging onto someone's elbow, the anguish on her face an empathetic endeavour meant for me. And the rest of her audience.

'It wasn't your place to say.'

'Whose place is it if it isn't mine? You're not the only one –'

But I've already grappled myself out of his grip and pulled away. I'm already heading for the exit, stumbling down the stairs, my slippery palms franticly seeking out the walls, the bannister, the cold prickle of the metal bar on the fire door. The sobering bite of winter as it hits me in the face. The sting of tears finally spilling from my eyes like barbed wire scratching down my cheeks. And a sound I don't even recognise as human erupting from the very depths of me.

The door smashes back against the wall again and in an instant Ben's behind me, wrapping my coat around my shoulders, pulling me into his arms again but I can hardly breathe.

'You didn't have the right.'

'It just came out. I'm sorry. I'm not like you. I can't hold it all inside. I can't pretend it never happened.'

I can't speak. I can't even look at him.

'You're always so angry,' he says softening his tone, pleading with me to prove him wrong but he's not.

'Yes, I'm angry. I'm angry all the time. I don't understand how you're not.'

'Of course I'm angry. But more than that I'm sad. Really, really fucking sad and you're not anywhere anymore. It's like I lost you too.'

'Fuck you.'

Ben's head snaps back as if I slapped him.

'This is not about us. You do not get to do this.'

'Jesus Christ. When are you going to forgive me for not being there? When do I get to grieve?'

I stare up at him, my lip curled, my nostrils flared and he lowers his voice, taking me into his arms. 'When are you going to come back to me?'

I swallow to hold back the fury rising up from my stomach. Beat my hands against his chest and wrench myself free.

'When I can sleep at night and not see it happening time and time again.' The front half of the car crushed like a Coke can underfoot. Elena's neck bent at an impossible angle, her eyes glazed and staring through me. 'When I stop reliving it every day.'

'Lara. I love you and I'm sorry, but it's not our fault. It was the other driver's.' *And Elena's. And Zac's. And mine.* 'But he's dead. It's over. You have to stop punishing yourself like this. You have to stop punishing me. I can't do anything about what happened. I wish I could but I can't take it away.'

'I know you can't. All I asked you to do was not to tell everyone so I can deal with it in my own way.'

'They're your friends.'

'They're not my friends. I don't even know them. I'm just going to be stuck with them for the next five years. Me, not you. You don't have to see them every day and worry they're going to bring it up in the park or after drop off. Know that when they ask you if you're okay, they really want to know exactly why you're not.

177

You're up in your office all day, tucked away from it all. You can tell whoever you like. You'll never have to stand outside the classroom avoiding eye contact in case someone gives you that pitying look. It's all I can do to hold it together at the best of times…' I don't have any more words for him. I don't have the strength to explain. To burrow away at that furrowed confusion, the lack of comprehension scored into his forehead. 'Oh, forget it. You're never going to understand. Just leave me alone.' I snatch my coat out of his grasp, reeling around and stumbling backwards.

'Wait. Let me drive you home at least. We're miles away. Please stop.'

But I don't. I keep on walking until I can't hear him shouting after me anymore. I keep walking through the blurred veil of the tears streaming down my face. I keep walking away from my husband and I don't know if I'm ever going to stop.

Thirteen

The sun is beginning to break out from behind the clouds lending an aura of wonder to the crisp frost glazing the stiff grass. The sheen of ice that seems to stretch across the football pitch, peppering puddles and patches of mud. Even the frozen dog turd Beasley's sniffing is tinged with majesty as it glistens in the misty morning light but even so, I yank him away.

'Leave it.'

A high pitched yelp of disappointment cuts through the air and he strains at the lead, his nose buzzing, senses tingling with desire.

'That's a bit mean, isn't it?'

Footsteps crunch up behind me but I don't turn around.

'It looks like a good one.'

'I was saving it for Coco.'

I bend down to ruffle her head, stroke the length of her body as she squirms, delighted by the attention and providing a diversion in which to compose myself. Wipe away any traces of emotion. Bury them deep, deep inside where they belong.

'Thanks but she had a big breakfast.'

I look up at last, wondering when I finally do why I stalled for so long. I'm instantly calmed by Lenny's presence, the warmth in his eyes. That gap in the heart of his smile.

'You okay?'

'Yes. Sorry. Miles away.'

'How did it go?' he asks as though he's been holding it in and even without any context, I know exactly what he's referring to. The shorthand is growing between us.

'Good. Your tagine was a firm favourite with everyone.'

'Really?'

No, the chicken went first, then the beef, then the sauce the chicken came in but everyone who tried the butternut squash did say it was better than they expected. I smile. 'Hands down.'

'What do you know?' He tilts his head contentedly. 'Maybe there's hope for the world after all.'

'I should have saved you some. God knows, I made enough.'

'Next time. Assuming there's going to be a next time…?'

Coco is tugging at the lead, frisky and desperate to explore the pungent musk diffused across the playing field, so I pull Beasley to his feet and start walking, eyes cast to the ground once again.

'Apparently so. Three more times off the back of Stella's thing alone.' *Three pity pledges probably. Three more opportunities for the rubber-neckers to have a good stare at the wreck.* 'Canapés this time for a Halloween party on Sunday.' *Zac's not invited.* 'At least, I hope it's for the party, not the trick or treaters who come to the door. Imagine their disappointment

180

at having to choose between a salmon and sepia crow's nest and an eyeball blushed with beetroot purée?'

'An actual eyeball?'

'Quail's egg.'

'Nice.'

'I mean, that's just begging to get tricked.'

'It's even providing ammunition...'

'That's true. Plus at forty quid a tray, it's excessive, even for Kingston.'

'Well, as long as you're getting paid.'

'Hmm.'

'And the others? You said there were three.'

'Two more provisional. One's a Christmas work-do but there's plenty of time for things to go wrong before then and the other's a wedding anniversary in November. Plenty to go wrong there too.'

The keen glow behind Lenny's eyes is beginning to fade. He stares down at Coco but his ear is cocked towards me, his tone overly casual when he finally speaks. 'You okay? I thought you'd be more excited. Isn't this what you wanted?'

'Yeah. I'm, yeah. No, it's great.'

'What's up? You don't seem yourself.' He stops abruptly and turns to me, his eyes narrowing in concern, seeking an answer I can't begin to contemplate. I look away, bite down on my back teeth before I break down. Shake away the urge to confide.

'Oh, you know. It's just half term, that's all. I'm looking forward to having the house back to myself. We're all on top of each other. Gets a bit much trying to keep them entertained.' *Keep them entertained without spending a fortune, that is. Without spending anything if I can help it.*

Money's been tight for a while but lately prices seem to be to going up quicker than I can get to the check out. It's good to finally be able to contribute to the finances after all these years but a few hundred quid here and there barely touches the sides of the debt we've accrued within the last six months alone.

'I'll bet.'

'It's all adding up and, you know...' *It's not just having an extra mouth to feed, it's all the other outgoings that come with having another child in the house as well. The clubs, the clothes, the shoes, the additional cinema tickets, the extra university fund. The new toys to ward off the tantrums, the new games to numb the pain. On and on like drips slowly spreading across a ceiling and we cover it all like mildew but the mould keeps coming back.*

'There's only so many times you can take them to feed the ducks, I suppose.' Lenny smiles, but it's no smiling matter.

'The ducks? I should be so lucky. We've already done that twice this year. You should have heard the fuss when I suggested going back again.'

He laughs with the complete lack of understanding that can only belong to someone used to children doing everything they ask. As soon as they ask.

182

'Honestly. Don't have kids. It's exhausting trying to come up with new stuff to do all the time that doesn't break the bank. Even a trip to the supermarket ends in tears or a trolley full of Oreos, whether they're on offer or not. It would be cheaper to take them to Chessington World of Adventures the amount it costs me trying to keep them from having a melt down before we get to the drinks aisle.'

He laughs again. 'And I thought dogs were expensive.'

'Oh, they are. Of course we've got one of those now too, but at least Beasley's got a shorter shelf life than a six-year-old.'

Six years old! And the few savings he has are all tied up in trust until he reaches eighteen. His mum's flat was rented. There's not even a lousy absent father in the background to turn the screws on for some basic maintenance. It was typical of Elena not to make any plans and just expect us to clean up the mess, particularly when that mess is an ever increasing, thankless financial pressure weighing down on us. And that's without Brexit or Covid or the economy going to shit anyway.

'Must be tough.'

'It is a bit.'

Ben's parents have offered to help out wherever they can, but he's too proud to take it. He'd rather see us all out on the street before he accepts a penny from them. At least then maybe he'll let them throw some loose change into a little hat under whatever bridge we end up at. It's not like it's charity. Zac is their grandson, after all.

'How's your husband coping with the change?' Lenny asks evenly, but my stomach twists and I don't know if it's at the thought of Ben or the sound of those words on Lenny's lips.

'The same way he copes with everything. Nothing ever seems to faze him.'

Except for me. He's been tiptoeing around since the party, trying to lighten the mood with impromptu cups of tea and offers to take the boys out so I can prepare for Halloween. Showering me with over-enthusiastic appreciation for the spooky hors d'oeuvres lining the worktops. Drumming on about what a success the business is becoming, what it could be and how it's all thanks to my hard work. He's nothing but flattering, gushing and completely insincere. Terrified even.

'Does he help out with the kids at all?'

Coco has stopped to sniff the entirety of a tree and I glance across the field to check that football practice isn't winding down early but it's all a blur from this distance. A flurry of reds and blues, gradually turning to brown. Either way, it hardly matters. It's not like Zac ever leaves on time.

'When he can, to be fair.' *I have to give him that, but when he can isn't enough. It doesn't even touch the surface.* 'He's busy with work this week, of course.' *It was too much to hope he could take even one of the kids off my hands. Especially when the age gap makes it twice as hard to do anything together and even if he wasn't prone to hissy fits, the youngest child in a family always determines what the rest can do.* 'It's been a bit full on to be fair. I haven't been able to organise any play dates, what with most of the country going down with this new Omicron variant. Not to mention, Zac not having any friends to speak of.' *Certainly none with parents that will let him redecorate their houses or redecorate their kids if they leave them with us.* 'The most exciting thing I've done is take Zac and Oscar to see Peter Rabbit 2 at the Odeon.' *The 10 o'clock showing because it only cost £2.50 a ticket and I could smuggle in shop-bought popcorn.*

'Your eldest didn't fancy it then?'

'He had to revise for his exams. If I'm to believe he even got out of bed before midday.' *Besides which, he's apparently too old for kids' films now but could we bring him back 'some sweet chicken chilli with sticky rice from the pop up Korean shack in the market?*

I'd always imagined he'd be hanging out on street corners by this age, eating McDonald's or KFC and no doubt dropping the wrappers but all he and his friends want to do is take eight-mile bike rides around Richmond Park and eat fancy stir-fry (with chopsticks). I teased him for being so perfectly middle class but I was only half-joking. That was why we moved out of central London after all, to give them a future like this. A clean lifestyle, only now it was me 'treating' them to cheap fast food because a Gregg's steak bake was £1.55 while a small pot of so-called street food cost six quid.

As soon as we got back he asked why I hadn't bought more when I knew he hadn't had anything to eat all day (despite the empty box of Honey Nut Cornflakes languishing near – but not in – the recycling bin). He then promptly ate the pasty in two bites and shot out the door until it got dark.

'Of course, he managed to find time to hang out with his friends most afternoons though.'

'Must be hard to let go when they become more independent.'

I smirk and a noise not unlike the one Beasley makes when he sneezes punctures the atmosphere. 'Yeah. It's weird. You spend years counting down to a time when they won't need to rely on you for everything and then all of a sudden they're making their own decisions and you have no idea what's going on in their lives.'

But it was okay. There's something sad and wonderful about watching him grow up. Turn into a man. A balanced, thoughtful, considerate human being who maybe one day will be able to occasionally empty the dishwasher without being asked and put things away after he's used them. Or not.

'I'm just very fortunate because now he's a teenager, he knows absolutely everything. He literally has an answer for anything and thank God, because I'm usually wrong.'

'That must be a tremendous relief.'

'As you can imagine.' *I'm only kidding. He's a good boy really. Reminds me of you. Or what I hope is you.*

And he's in with a nice crowd, thank goodness. It had been the right decision to send him to Deer Hill Secondary. There were two comprehensives to choose from and most of his Park View gang had gone to Kingston Court, which was also good but we were closer to the one in Richmond. The one with huge playing fields and open spaces, a mix of modern and traditional facilities, the all important excellent Ofsed report and a catchment area wide enough to include us but only just.

He's still in touch with some of his friends from primary school but they'd mostly drifted apart and the new kids he hung out with, both in the flesh and virtually, live on the other side of the river. All very nice, all very polite, all cheeky enough to be fun, but I wouldn't recognise a single one of them if they walked past me on the street. Not like the tiny scrimps we used to spend our weekends with and have around for play-dates after school, now towering over me. Them I'd recognise anywhere even as they duck their heads to avoid making eye contact with me.

'Talking of which, I should go. If I don't get him out of bed now, he'll insist on staying up until God knows what time tonight and then he'll be foul all day tomorrow because he's tired.'

Lenny slows down but neither of us makes a move to leave, shuffling on the spot instead as Beasley drops to his hind legs, head aloft in anticipation of a lingering goodbye. Coco is instantly upon him and as if by his command, a shrill whistle pierces the air and the football players begin to melt away from the pitch.

'I really do need to go.'

Lenny reaches out and his touch sends a jolt through my arm that burns long after he takes his hand away. 'I'm usually here at

187

around six most evenings, if you ever want to talk. And walk the dogs, I mean.'

My smile flickers but I hold it together 'That's good to know. I'll keep it in mind.' And then I have to break away because I don't know what I'll do if I stand there looking at him for much longer. 'Come on, boy.' I tug at Beasley's lead. 'Let's find Zac before he gets himself into trouble.' Before he's not the only one.

If my nephew has one function in life, it's to clear up playing fields with his football kit. There can't be any mud left on the ruddy thing. It's plastered to his shirt, smeared on his shorts, caked onto his shoes. Even the trainers he wasn't even wearing during the match look like cow pats.

'Good grief, Zac. Take them off before we get in the house, please.'

'All of it?'

'Yes. Leave your boots outside and everything else in the utility room. Just keep your pants on unless they're filthy too. Go on.'

I turn the lock in the back door and usher him in but clear instructions were never my forte and he goes bowling on straight through into the kitchen, trailing grass clumps and, if I'm not wrong, a worm.

'Oi. Get back here.'

Oh, Christ. Oscar's up and is making the most of his new found freedom on a Saturday morning by giving Mariah Carey a run for her money.

'Pipe down, Oscar please. You don't have to sing so loudly. You're going to shatter the windows one of these days. Zac. Off the sofa. Now.'

'That's not very nice,' Oscar pouts, one hand on his hip, the other nursing the strawberry milkshake he's helped himself to. 'You'll wish you hadn't always been so rude to me when I'm a world-famous pop star.'

'When you're a world-famous pop star you'll be able to buy your own house and sound-proof it. Until then try to keep it down to ninety decibels or below. Zac. Shoes. Now.'

Oscar's off again. He's got a lovely, powerful voice, but my God, he doesn't let up for a minute. And when he's not crooning his head off he's on about getting singing lessons. I told him to check out YouTube. It's the best I can do on a budget. Fame might have to wait until the head chef at Waitrose reaches out to me.

'Oscar! Tone it down! Zac! Get. Out!'

I'm standing in the middle of the kitchen, my face puce, legs fixed, one arm rigidly pointed to the garden when Ben creeps in through the back gate on his bike looking contrite and wary. He lifts his eyebrows in place of his usual condescending greeting and for a split second I think the trepidation in his eyes is due to me shouting, but it's actually in anticipation of my reaction to

189

Zac flinging his shoes across the floor and ripping his filthy shirt over his head.

'Put it in the utility room. Don't you dare –' But he does. At any rate he must have because the shirt smacks onto my head, hovers there as if deciding what to do and then slides very slowly down my face. Ben is staring through the bi-folds, half gaping in horror, half in glee, weighing up the stance he's about to take.

'Zac!'

He goes for horror and then disapproval, laying his bike down and gingerly stepping into the house. Even Oscar's stopped singing and is wearing that glazed hopeful expression the kids always adopt at the slightest hint of one of the others getting in trouble.

'Sorry!' Zac giggles as remorsefully as he can while skipping out of his shorts and slinging them up in the air, this time entangling them on the lampshade. For a moment, Sharon looks like she might get off the hob, but she clearly thinks better of it and settles down again.

'That's enough, sunshine,' Ben says pulling the shorts down and pressing them against Zac's chest. 'Put your stuff next to the washing machine and go up and get changed. I've booked us a lane at the bowling alley. You too, Oscar.'

'What? When? I haven't had lunch yet.'

'We can get something when we're out.'

'McDonald's?' Oscar's voice arches hopefully.

'Sure. Whatever you want. Just be ready to leave by the time I am.'

And with that both the boys go scarpering up the stairs like they're being chased with feather dusters.

'That okay?' he says turning to me and I shrug.

'Do what you like.'

'It's not what I like. I'm just trying to get them out from under your feet, that's all. Give you a bit of space.'

'Sure.'

He sighs, unclips his helmet and lowers it onto the worktop. His hair looks ridiculous.

'Unless you want to come too…?'

'To a bowling alley followed by McDonald's?'

'We don't have to –'

'We sort of do. You've promised them now.'

'Well, do you want to come? We can amend the booking when we get there.'

'No, I've got too much to do.' I draw a long breath, steeling myself against the counter and staring pointedly at the food containers on the side. 'Besides I thought we were trying to save money.'

'It's not that much. They've been good all week.'

Really? How would you know? 'Fine.' I wheel around slowly, away from him, willing him to leave. His peripheral outline is blurred but I can feel him staring at me imploringly. Pathetically.

'Is it?'

'Yes, great. It's brilliant.' *I'll be the one that scrimps and saves and makes them eat damp sandwiches in Richmond Park every day and you be the fun one. That seems fair.*

Ben nods his head slowly and looks away. 'I'll jump in the shower then.'

'You do that.'

The door closes a little too loudly on his way out.

Unbelievable. Like he's got anything to be upset about.

Beasley pads over to his bed and Sharon and I both glare at the mess he's made around his water bowl.

'For God's sake. Can't any of you clear up after yourselves? Just once.' I slam Oscar's empty glass into the sink.

'You alright, Mother?' Jacob's hair is slick and sticking up in a way that could have taken him ages to get right or simply be a by-product of spending most of the morning in bed. He stretches both arms wide, his T-shirt riding up above his waistband, his fingers curling into balls as he yawns.

'Goodness. Didn't expect to see you for another few hours,' I say, trying not to react to the sight of the new hair rising up his stomach. He smells like bin day.

'You've got your idiot son to thank for that. He sounds like he's murdering bagpipes up there.'

My tongue clicks on the top of my mouth and I flick the kettle switch, averting my eyes. 'Alright. There's no need to sneer like that.'

'There's no need to sing like that.'

'Alright,' I repeat warningly. I swing open a cupboard and pull out a teabag in one practiced move. I wave it at Jake but he shakes his head and I drop it into the cup I was using this morning. 'He's not that bad. In fact, he's very good. He's just overly loud, that's all.'

'And overly inconsiderate.'

He pulls the milk out of the fridge and at first I think he's passing it to me, but of course he's just getting a glass for himself. I wrench it away from him as he's putting it back. For the first time ever.

'Well, you should be up anyway. It's eleven o'clock. Aren't you going to get ready? Your dad's reversed the no spending policy he's been ramming down my throat all week. If you're quick, he might pick you up a Ferrari.'

'I'd rather have a McLaren,' he grins through a semi-skimmed moustache.

'You might have to make do with McDonald's. You'll need to hurry if you want to go with them though.'

'Nahh. I'm alright, thanks. I'll just have some of these.' He picks up the largest of the food containers on the side, opens the lid and pulls out one the sepia tinted vol-au-vents I made at six o'clock this morning.

'Put them back. They're not for you.'

He takes one anyway.

'Have you even tasted them? They could be disgusting. I'm doing you a favour.' He lifts the pastry and gnashes his teeth playfully waiting for me to roll my eyes and say *go on then*.

193

'For goodness sake, Jake. You've breathed all over it now. Have that one and then get yourself a bowl of cereal.'

It's gone in one bite.

'Mmm. I'm not sure. It was too small to draw any conclusions. I'd better check one more.'

I tut but it's a losing battle. There's no fighting Jacob when it comes to food. He's at least a head taller than me now and even without brute force, he has me wrapped around his little finger. It's lucky I made twice as many as I needed. Or maybe I saw this coming.

'Have the wonky ones at least.'

He shoves two in his mouth. Flakes of pastry fall from his chin and onto the floor, Beasley lifts his head hopefully, but at that distance the crows' nests probably look like deer turds. There was a time he'd have wolfed them up on that basis alone. He really must be getting old.

'Can you get a plate, please?'

My tea is the perfect shade of beige and I stir it one more time before squeezing the bag with a spoon. It drips into my palm as I whisk it over to the sink to let it drain and I lick it, surprised at how quickly it cools against my skin. The few seconds of distraction is all Jacob needs to flip open another container and form a pyramid of green arancini, which he will demolish in less than a minute.

The boiler suddenly stops humming gently in the utility room and upstairs the crash of the shower doors smashing together breaks through Oscar's high note. I blink involuntarily, pushing away the image of Ben stepping onto the warm heated tiles, pulling his towel off the radiator, furiously rubbing away his chest. That horrible moss-like hair creeping over his shoulders. I shudder. My top lip is taut. Jacob tosses one of the small balls into his mouth levelling his eyes at me.

'Why are you angry at Dad?'

I come to. 'I'm not.'

'Yes, you are.'

The cup feels awkward in my hands and I slam it down too quickly. Liquid, searingly hot this time, spills onto my fingers and over the side.

'Damn.' I wipe down the worktop with a few quick, purposeful motions but Jacob stands there, waiting expectantly for an answer as I rinse the dishcloth out under the running tap, shake it out and hang it irritably over the tap. 'He told some people something after I asked him not to.'

'About the accident?'

I don't reply.

'She was his sister, Mum.' He takes another mouthful but continues to speak before he swallows, spraying flecks of fried rice into the air. 'He's got a right to be upset.'

'I know she was his sister. She was my best friend. I was closer to her than he was, but it's not a competition. The point is that I asked him not to tell anyone about it and he did anyway.'

'But why shouldn't he –'

'Because, because Jacob. It's our private business and I don't want to have to explain it all to everyone I meet. I don't need their curiosity or their sympathy. I need to be able to walk into a room full of people and know that no one will ask me how I am in *that voice*. That bloody voice. I need some anonymity.'

'But maybe Dad needs to talk about it.'

'Then your father can talk about it to me or his friends. His actual friends, not these strangers we've just met that I'm going to have to spend the next five years bumping into each day. Not him. Me.'

'That seems a bit...'

'What? Unfair?' I spin around. 'You're right, it is unfair. Life's unfair. I thought you knew that by now.'

My neck angles up towards him, the set of my chin non-negotiable, but he stares me down, no longer intimidated. No longer the child I can shut down with a look and an edge of cut glass in my voice.

'Maybe you should give him a break.'

'And maybe you don't know as much as you think you do, Jacob,' I snap, ripping the empty plate out of his hands. My lips are drawn back over my teeth, stretched into a snarl that begins in my eyes and Jacob looks down at me, slowly raising his hands in mock surrender, backing away. He nods his head, his mouth dragged downwards, unimpressed and I reach out to him, my shoulders suddenly listless but it's too late. The hostile bitch in me is stronger than the sensitive man emerging in him and he shrinks away, recoiling with a twitch before disappearing off again.

'Sorry,' I whisper hoarsely to Sharon, awake now and ready to bolt. I falter, an explanation for my outburst caught my throat. Some sort of justification, vindication, an excuse, but she settles back down onto the gas ring with a look that could curdle milk.

'Sorry,' I say again but it's too late. There's nobody there.

Fourteen

The breakfast bar is a jamboree of cereal bowls, milk rings, upturned spoons and stray flakes of Weetabix rapidly hardening into mortar. The clash of china against metal as I clear up fails to drown out Oscar and my mother belting out the song that thrust him into stardom mere weeks ago. The fact she's on the iPad in the front room is of no consequence. I could turn it off and her tinny rendition of *Look What You Made Me Do* would still be audible nine thousand miles away.

God, to live vicariously through your grandchildren. Could anything be worse? Apart from not being able to live vicariously through me, I suppose. A flair for the arts and any musical talent definitely skipped a generation. Not Oscar though. He really does have something special, if a little raw. It would be a shame not to see how far he could take it, even if it never came to anything.

I'll speak to the school later, see if they can recommend a good (cheap) singing teacher in the area. I got a few more potential bookings out of the Halloween do yesterday and a definite one through word of mouth on Instagram this morning. I'm at the stage where I'm not even surprised to be asked for a quote anymore.

How crazy is that, Mother? And there was you hoping it would be a disaster so you could say I told you so. I collect up the last of the clutter and rub down the surfaces before the cereal fuses to them.

'Have you brushed your teeth yet, Zac?'

'Yes,' he lies blatantly as he does every morning.

'Go upstairs and do it now.'

'What?'

'It's pardon, not what and you heard me.' To be fair, he may not have. 'Oscar, say goodbye to Gran and go and put your uniform on. You're going to be late.'

But they're only on the second verse and my mum is clearly on her third or fourth bottle of Foster's. And yes, it's sunny again over there casting some sobering perspective on the mild spell we've been enjoying ourselves.

'Zac. Teeth. Now.'

Ben slides past him through the door, tapping the mop of blonde hair as Zac skulks up to the bathroom to run his toothbrush over his gums like he's wiping a banister. The cabaret hit the chorus and Oscar points accusingly in time to the music, hips swinging, knees bent, lips confidently petulant. Ben ignores them both. He even forgoes a snide comment about my mum or a display of sudden over-interest in how late Oscar's going to be for school.

Instead he walks straight up to me as I'm filling dishwasher (in my own unique way) and says, 'I've been thinking.' So there's a first. 'I'm going to ask Steve if he can make Sundays instead so I can take Zac to football.'

I shoot up, a sticky bowl still in hand. 'What?'

He takes a step back and braces himself against the worktop. 'I'm not going to be cycling on Saturday mornings anymore so you won't have to do the football run,' he says studying me.

I scan the room, almost expecting to be confronted by some sort of damning evidence spread out amongst the breakfast debris. A photo of me having fun. A recording of laughter. Beasley glowering traitorously at me from his bed.

'You said Steve couldn't make it any other day.'

'Think he prefers it, that's all.'

That's all? I don't remember my preference being taken into account when you first announced how I was going to be spending my weekends.

'Besides, if he can't change it, I'll go by myself.'

'Why?' I still have the bowl in my hand but it's beginning to droop and there's a good chance I'll drop it.

'So you don't have to do it.' His voice rises an octave and we both pretend it's only to be heard over Oscar. I shake my head.

'It's fine. Don't bother,' I say, taking charge of the dirty crockery once again. Bending down to the half-filled machine.

'I don't mind,' he protests, still unnaturally loudly.

'Neither do I. It's about the only time I spend with Zac when he's not furious at me for making him do something he hates.'

Ben pinches the bridge of his nose and then looks up sharply. 'Oscar, tone it down,' he chides sharply, takes a deep breath and continues, the new familiar edge to his pitch unmistakeable. 'Even so, it would still be nicer to have some time to yourself, wouldn't it? You could meet up with some friends. Go for a massage. Do something special. Something to cheer you up.'

Zac has hurtled down the stairs into the front room and is attempting to join in with the last verse.

'Stop it!' His reluctant band mate wrestles him away from the tablet and I can make out my mum's contemptuous composure from all the way over here. Even so, she hasn't paused for breath.

'You're ruining it.'

'Boys. Keep it down,' Ben yells over the squawking. 'We're trying to have a conversation in here.'

'Make him go away.' Zac is splayed across the adjoining doorway, his arms and legs akimbo, clinging on to the architrave and scratching at the paintwork with Oscar bulldozing into him from behind, his feet slipping on the floorboards. 'Muuuuumm.'

'Lara. Some help here.' My mother cries with lofty disapproval, clearly enjoying the drama and the fact there's bugger all she can be expected to do about it.

'Quiet!' Ben roars, storming towards them, slapping Zac's hand down from the doorframe and wrenching him up by the wrist, one finger jabbing the air between himself and Oscar. 'Go upstairs now and get ready for school. And you.' Bending down. 'Calm down. Put your shoes and coat on. I'm taking you to school today.'

The room is quiet now but the atmosphere is heavy and both boys do as they've been told with exaggerated aplomb, shocked and unified by Ben's completely unprovoked outburst as he stands in the sitting room pressing the heel of his hand into his forehead, his eyes crumpled, mouth twisted downwards.

'Goodness.' The microphone makes my mum's voice more grating than usual and Ben's back instantly stiffens, his eyelashes unseal, fingers curling until his nails dig into the flesh.

'What's got you all riled up?' she chirps and without turning around, Ben strides across to the utility room, grabs his coat and the base of Zac's neck and gently pushes him out of the back door, laces dangling on the ground both and Zac with only half a foot in his shoe.

'Well, I knew he had a temper but I've never seen him like that,' my mum persists, luxuriating in the opportunity of finding fault with her son-in-law.

'Just leave it, Mum, please.'

'Well, I'm only saying… I hope he doesn't batter you around like that.'

'He didn't batter anyone around. He just handled the situation.' Why am I defending him? He's a complete tool. If it weren't my mother picking holes in him, I'd be reliving every argument we've ever had. Every time he raised his voice. 'Plus it doesn't help with you two making that sort of racket in the mornings. It's stressful enough trying to get them off to school.'

'I'm just showing an interest in my grandson,' she frowns. 'Honestly, it's about time someone did.'

The doorbell rings and I know without even glancing up that it's Melissa, Oscar's BFF since they first sat at the same craft table stringing together beads and pipe cleaners at nursery. She's one of those small mousy girls who'll take off her glasses some day and everyone will suddenly realise she's turned into a beauty. Either that, or she'll dye her hair black and get a face full of piercings and tattoos.

Oscar comes pounding down the stairs to answer the door, tie askew and barely scraping the barrel of the uniform policy but almost decent and at least four minutes late.

'Bye, Gran. Love you.'

'Bye Ozzie,' she cries in return toasting his retreating back with a bottle that sparkles in the sunshine, reflecting iridescence across the screen. 'Love you more. Keep those pipes tuned. I want to hear more next week.' And then in a quieter, more indulgent tone. 'Beautiful boy.'

I bite back a retort. He is a beautiful boy. I'm just not keen on the way she plays favourites, even if Jacob's happy to be ignored. He's finally up and dressed too, racing around the house in a frenzy, dumping last half term's rubbish out of his bag and stuffing his packed lunch into it in its place. I wave him over.

'Say hello quickly,' I mouth but he shakes his head frantically, his eyes expanding in horror either at the thought of speaking to his crazy grandmother or being even later for school than he already is. *Fair enough.*

'Who are you talking to?' Mum probes, craning her neck as though she can bend the camera angle at will.

'No one. Beasley.'

'He's still going is he?' Even the dog isn't safe from her damnation.

'Listen, Mum. I have to go. I've got to pick up a few bits from the supermarket. We've run out of everything.'

'Are you going to drive?'

I inhale. Arrange my face. Try to sound neutral. 'No. I'm just going to take my old lady shopping trolley and a rucksack. I could do with the walk.'

'Thought you said you'd run out of everything.'

'Well…'

'Come on, Lara. You need to get back into a car and start driving again. The longer you put it off, the harder it's going to be.' It's like talking to Ben only shriller and more patronising.

'It's fine, Mum. I really need the exercise. I'm still trying to shift all the weight I put on during lockdown.'

'Oh, Lara.'

'Mum. I've got to go. Love to Bob, Nick – ' There are too many to name them all. 'And the others.'

'I will, but think about –' I cut her off and the screen freezes on her mid-sentence, mouth gaping, eyelids half-closed and I draw a stab of satisfaction at how much she would hate to see herself looking like that.

Jacob swoops in and gives me a peek on the cheek. 'Love you. Bye.'

'Love you, darling. Have a great —'

The front door slams behind him and the house is suddenly still and three times the size it felt half an hour ago. The dishwasher's stacked, the washing machine's already running and I'm dressed and ready to drop Zac off. Quite why Ben decided on today of all days to take him in, I don't know but typically he didn't bother asking me what I wanted. I still need to go to Asda and the school is on the way so he isn't helping if that's what he thinks he's doing. I feel a pang of irritation, bereavement almost at the loss of the handover. The usual thirty seconds that carries me through until pick up when I get to see Lenny again. The little hello, the throwaway comment, the bubble of laughter escaping too readily, the hair toss. And that's just Lenny. *Ha!*

'Sorry, old boy.' I say to Beasley who's pretending not to notice me pulling my jacket over my shoulders. 'Uncle Ben fucked off and left you this morning. He's a bit of a dick, isn't he? He's a bit of a twat. We don't like him, do we? No, we don't like him.' There's something therapeutic about talking to the dog but he won't be drawn into taking sides.

'That's right. Don't wake up on my account. You stay there. I'm going to leave him a note so he can deal with you when he gets back.'

I could take Beasley for a quick walk now and go to the supermarket later but like we're always saying to the kids – *how will they ever learn if we do everything for them?* I coerce the trolley out of the wide storage cupboard by the back door, pulling in frustration at the miscellaneous cables and extension leads that invariably wind their way around the wheels. My hands are jittery, my heart thumping with determination to be out of the house before Ben reappears. To not have to face him for a few hours. I drag the rucksack off the peg, grab my phone, keys and purse and shove them all inside the trolley in a way I'll regret when I have to take out everything I've already scanned to get to my credit card.

The door slams as I pull it behind me, harder than I meant to in a channel of cool autumn wind and I jump, nerves shot to pieces like I'm about to get caught breaking out of prison. Or an asylum in my case.

It's a few minutes after I turn the corner to avoid the school route before I can finally relax. It's nice to be out of the house on my own for the first time in over a week. To not have to constantly mutter, 'I don't know. We'll get there when we get there' or 'Sorry, but you have to do something other than stare at a screen all day.' And now I can take in the fresh air, squint at the bright clear sky and think without being interrupted, enjoy the silence.

'Lara. I thought it was you. How are things?' I whirl around abruptly, startled by the weight on my arm, the tug at my sleeve. Rattled suddenly by this woman with a scrunched, concerned face, flushed and overheating in an unflattering coat that looks to be made entirely out of beige cockapoos. A woman who's standing too close to me.

I step back and as the shock of being confronted dissolves I realise it's one of Jacob's old friend's mums. Not one of the Kingston Crew but part of the B Team. The people I'd turn to at the school gates when the friends I usually spoke to weren't there. She steps closer to me, reaching out her arm again and placing it awkwardly on top of mine.

'I keep meaning to text you. I've just been so busy. You know how life gets in the way...?' She smarts suddenly, self-consciously hyperaware. 'I mean... How are you all keeping up? Has your nephew settled in?'

'Zac?'

She nods her head vehemently, fear of me asking how she knows about him flickering across her thread-veined cheeks. How long she's known.

'He's fine. A little temperamental but we're all adjusting. You know how it is.'

'Of course. It's going to take time. It must be a godsend in a way. The distraction.'

She's talking as though picking up from the last conversation we had, as though we've been in touch in recent memory. But we haven't. This is all gossip she's heard on the grapevine – juicy titbits creeping tantalisingly from one house to the next until there are enough grapes for a vineyard. And yet still she didn't call.

'Well...'

'I can't imagine. It makes me want to cry just thinking about it. You're an angel to have taken him on, especially while you're dealing with your own grief.' Her voice croaks and her mouth contorts. Blood red capillaries suddenly stain the whites of her eyes and she brushes theatrically at the tears that have sprung up in tangible proof that she cares.

'Hmm. I didn't really have a choice if I'm honest, but anyway, nothing compares to losing your mother, does it?'

A shimmering teardrop falls and she smiles bravely, shaking her head so sorrowfully I don't know if I'm supposed to give her a hug.

'You're allowed to grieve too, Lara.'

I bite down on my cheek. 'Thank you.'

'I'm really sorry,' she says, shaking her head again, this time to clear the mask of sympathy she's assembled so convincingly. 'I have to go, but we should go out for a coffee some time. Catch up properly.' A streak of horror flashes across her face. 'Well, not catch up. Talk, if you need someone to talk to. I'm always here.'

She leans forwards, wrapping her arms around me stiffly and I stand, rooted to the spot staring at the wisps of white vapour forming overhead, my one free hand patting mechanically at her back. This woman who made herself a stranger, using that voice, looking at me like that.

She pulls away, lips pressed together, eyes still damp, coat charged with static that snaps as she slides her own hand down my arm and backs away dolefully and I continue to wait there, my heart in my throat, raucous buzzing filling my ears, long after she's gone.

Oh, God. Oh, God. For Christ's sake. The sky is starting to fall. The weight of the clouds gathering above my head is pressing down on me. My lungs are collapsing, every gulp I take raw and painful, the air too thick to draw enough of it in. I reel around on the trolley, bright spots flickering in front of my eyes, determined to get out of sight. One foot plants itself doggedly on the pavement leading the other, over and over, my thoughts on nothing else but getting home, on slamming the door behind me, turning the lock and sinking down onto the floor.

Beasley raises his head as if interrupted from a dream, lowers his chin onto the side of the bed and examines me as I collapse back against the kitchen cabinets and inhale, my chest rising and falling in noisy jagged motions that frighten even me. It's black, all black but for the translucent specks of light floating around like sticks thrown into a river. Sharon brushes against my thigh, butting her head into my knee with a maternal meow and as I lower my hand along length of her thick glossy coat, my sternum relaxes. My sobs subside.

Oh. I breathe. *Oh.* The blood drains out of my arms and I let them drop to my sides. *I need a drink, Sharon.*

Sharon is aware that I need a drink, she knows me better than I know myself. She also knows I finished off the last of the wine last night and that was the real reason I was so determined to go to the shops first thing. I wrench open a cupboard hoping desperately to find a forgotten bottle of gin in there. I'm sure we've got tonic in the fridge. Or soda at least but all I can find is that dusty almond liqueur and I don't know if I'll even be able to get it open, it's so old.

I hold it up to the light, stare through the amber tinted spirit, the glare reflecting off the glass. I can feel Beasley inspecting me and I turn to him. He sighs with an expression of absolute inevitability and without breaking eye contact, I twist the rusty lid. It clicks and turns without a hint of resistance and I hold it in my fingers, letting one hand drop back to the floor, raising the bottle to my lips. He blinks gravely and we stare at each other as the fiery liquid trickles down my throat leaving tracks like scorched earth that settle in a fermenting pool in my stomach. And then I drink some more.

It's Oscar who finds me five hours later. Oscar who shakes my shoulder and whispers, 'Mum' almost questioningly, inches from my face. Sharon who leaps up from my lap, her claws out, digging for purchase. Beasley who's done a dump in the utility room and me who will later find the message 'Can't. I'm on calls all day' scrawled under the one I left for Ben reminding him he still needed to take the dog out after he dropped Zac off.

'What time is it?' I gasp, the world snapping back into focus.

'Three fifteen.'

'Shit. Shit. Shit.' I scramble to my feet, grasping at the worktop, sending the empty bottle spiralling into the cupboards with a clang. 'Shit. Shit. Shit.'

'Mum?'

'I'm late. Sorry. I'm late.'

I clutch my head. Squeeze my eyes closed, the glint of the fading afternoon light too bright. My legs unsteady. I can barely see straight but somehow I weave my way to Park View on automatic pilot, ducking away from Lenny, avoiding his curious glance behind a pair of oversized sunglasses. Accepting Zac's summation that school was 'good' without further probing, letting him get on his tablet the minute we walk through the door. Tossing back two paracetamols and a pint of water. Rummaging through the freezer looking for oven chips and fish fingers, finding none and somehow putting together overdone pesto pasta without any cheese.

'Are you okay?' Jacob asks hesitantly placing his empty bowl on top of the dishwasher.

'Think I'm coming down with something.' I say, tired now but sober. Ish. The vein on my temple throbbing. My mouth dry.

'You don't look good.' He runs his eyes over my clammy skin, my slack chin, contemplating me. 'Why don't you see if a shower helps? Might make you feel better.'

I turn to him, every muscle in my body trembling and resistant. Aching and sore to the touch.

'Good idea.'

I make a feeble stab at a smile and he returns it with a look I've never seen before but he's right. As the hot steaming water cascades over me, massaging my crown, pummelling my shoulders, clearing my mind, I feel the knot in my stomach unclench, my ligaments loosen, the sense of dread hanging over me lift.

212

'Where are you off to?' Ben asks when I appear in my human form half an hour later. It's six thirty, my hair is deliberately styled instead of pulled back and a light trace of make-up tints my lips and accentuates my eyelashes.

'Just the park. Beasley hasn't been out all day.'

'But it's dark.'

'So?'

He grits his teeth and his jawbone rotates in small telling circles.

'Okay,' he says, all expression gone from his voice and I grab the lead.

The playing field is dimly lit and there are only a few other dog-walkers there, a handful of bright neon collars flashing in the darkness, tearing through the gloom. I strain my eyes towards the shadows, peering at silhouettes in the distance, my heart in my mouth and then sinking with the realisation that I'm too late. Then Beasley groans as two tiny paws gouge a strip of hair out of his back and a man sidles up besides me.

'You made it,' he says and I lean in towards him.

Fifteen

For Pete's sake. What time is it? Three twenty-three. Christ. How can I be awake? I'm exhausted.

No, don't get up, Sharon. I just want to lie here.

My head is throbbing again, my tongue swollen, throat parched and I could reach across to my bedside cabinet and take a long swig of the water I left there for this very reason but I'm hoping that if I lie still enough I might drop back off to sleep. Like that's ever happened and anyway now it's too late. My thoughts are starting to race. Unravel out of control like sheets of toilet paper streaming from a falling roll.

I shouldn't have gone last night.

But I'm glad I did.

I crossed a line I can't uncross.

But how could I not?

I could lose everything.

Or maybe it will make it better once and for all. He's good with kids. Obviously. How could they not love him? And he's going to love them. They're nice boys, if I do say so myself. Not Zac but, he, well, he won't be an issue anymore, will he? Still,

215

it's a lot to take on, even without a six-year-old – two teenagers. Or one and a tween.

Does he want that? He must want that. He knows what the deal is. I come as a package. Or maybe half a package. Maybe Ben will want to keep them half the time, joint custody. Could I live with that? It will mean having more free time with Lenny. But less time with Jake and Ozzie.

And you and Beasley. Would you guys be able to come too? I guess I could work that into the custody split if we do decide to share the kids.

But then how would Ben manage? He's inept. He'll forget to feed them. He's only got three signature dishes as it is. He can't just rotate them over and over until the end of time. Then again, the boys are older now. They could help out. There's no reason why they couldn't cook and keep on top of the housework. Not that they do now. No, he's going to want me to have them on weekdays and do all the mundane boring stuff like sorting out school and their clubs.

Shit, I'm going to have to start driving again – unless Lenny doesn't mind taking them, but that's probably asking too much. Especially at the start. I'm going to have to bite the bullet. Or wait… there are probably buses on that route. The boys are responsible enough to make their own way around. Or maybe Ben will want to carry on taking them. Actually he should take them, otherwise he'll just be getting them at the weekends and doing the fun stuff like bowling and swimming and McDonald's while I get stuck having to nag them to get ready for school and do their homework everyday. No, no. no. That's not going to work.

And poor Lenny. He might wish he hadn't signed up for that. It's one thing getting paid for teaching children but living with kids? That's a different kind of hell altogether. It would be even less amusing if you weren't biologically programmed to love them. Tolerate them, at least. And what if he wants his own family? We haven't even talked about it, but he's bound to. He's young, of course he's going to want his own. Oh my God. I'm not even sure I can anymore. I'd have certainly thought any eggs I've got left are well past their sell by date and then what? IVF? Surrogacy? Holy Moses. I thought I was done with all that.

Maybe he doesn't want kids. Not his own kids. Maybe that's why taking on mine at this age suits him. All the years he's spent teaching has probably knocked any romantic notions about how lovely they are out of his system. Although a tiny baby Lenny would be adorable. But I couldn't. I just couldn't. Unless we got extra help. Maybe that's the answer. Do it differently this time. Go back to work, make a success of the business and employ someone else to do the childcare like everyone else does. Or he could take a sabbatical. No, we'll need the money.

Oh, God, why can't I sleep? I'm so tired. I'm going to feel awful tomorrow.

Sharon. Stop scratching. You're making it worse.

I twist over onto my side. Squish the pillow up. Oh, my head. Why did I drink so much? It's no wonder I can't sleep. I missed half the day, although you'd think that would be counterbalanced by the alcohol poisoning. What was in that stuff? I need to rein it in now. I can't be doing that in front of Lenny. One last blow out. That was it. That was all I needed to get it out of my system and then tomorrow I'm going to give it a break. Today, in fact. It's already today and we still don't have any wine in so I'll have no excuse. I won't be able to just pop the bottle open because it's easier than turning on the tap.

Or because you're sitting in the sink, Sharon. I'm not blaming you, it's just that you do get in the way sometimes, you know you do. Don't be like that. It's not a criticism. I'm just saying, there have been times when I've been thirsty and it's been easier to pour myself a glass of wine than disturb you.

Anyway, it doesn't matter. I'm on a health kick now. For a week or so. Or tomorrow at least.

Oh, shut up, Ben! Why couldn't you have stayed in the study? I'm sure it must have been more comfortable for you too. You're always complaining I take all the covers, which is absolute rubbish. I'm not the one who wrestles the duvet up over my shoulders, nearly taking your head off in the process and don't pretend you don't know. You seem to think every move you make is as delicate as a butterfly. Well, here's news for you, buddy. Every time you flap your wings, it feels like a whacking great Tsunami slamming into me. How's that for talking about how I feel? Jesus Christ. If you only knew. For fuck's sake, stop snoring. Stop snoring! Stop snoring!

If people did this in the daytime, they'd be thrown under buses. Literally pushed in front of trains in the middle of their commute. Imagine that. Imagine someone making that sort of racket every time they breathed. It's completely unsociable and I'm supposed to take it every single night. This is how they torture people in some countries. Sleep deprivation. Terrorists probably get a better night's kip than me.

What if I blasted a horn in your ear for hours? Ran a model train track around your side of the bed all night? You'd have something to say about that, wouldn't you? Shuuuuut uuuuuuuup! Right, that's it.

I fling the duvet off. Grab my pillow. Sharon jumps back and gazes at me, one paw suspended, flecks of curious rebuke manifesting in her moonlit eyes.

I can't take it anymore. I'm going to the study. You're welcome to come, Sharon but I can't put up with this noise any longer. It's grotesque.

I stumble on my slippers as I stand, one foot tripping over the other and steady myself against the wall. God, I could do with a drink. That's probably all I need. Some hair of the dog, just to get through this hangover. Not that we've got any. Of all the times to run out. Maybe I should pick some up after the school run. It probably makes sense to cut down rather than go cold turkey. Cold turkey? That makes me sound like I've got a problem. I just need to slow down a little. Give my liver a break.

I stagger into the hallway and drag the spare blankets out of the cupboard, trailing them downstairs into Ben's office and absolutely nothing fills my ears. The glow from the street lamp outside the window lends a comforting cocoon-like feel to the room. I pull the sofa bed out and flake down onto it, the bare mattress scratching my skin.

Come on, Sharon. No purring. No, stop.

And with that I sink my head into the pillow, Lenny's kiss still tingling on my lips and sleep more soundly than I have for weeks.

Sixteen

The pesto from last night's pasta has dried onto the saucepan along with the crockery that didn't make it into the dishwasher, oily sheets of kitchen towel separating each bowl. I draw out the soiled makeshift napkins – bile green now – and drop them into the bin, supressing the urge to gag as a wave of basil and Parmesan hits me. The hairs in my nose stand on end and I stretch my neck back as far as it will go while running my stained fingers under the tap, massaging frothy washing up liquid into them. It's overpowering artificial lemon. Even worse.

'What happened to you last night?' Ben says. No hello. No perfunctory kiss.

'Couldn't sleep.' I tilt my head in his direction but don't turn around – instead reaching for the greasy dishes as if I was planning to do them all along.

'That was my fault, I suppose.'

I lift an eyebrow but that's the only rise he's going to get out of me. 'I put the bed away. It shouldn't affect you.'

'You needn't have bothered. I'm going in today.'

I twist around slightly and notice for the first time, his cycling gear. The ludicrous Lycra shorts and T-shirt he always wears when he rides to the office, his clothes rolled into a tube around the shower gel he keeps in his bag.

'Huh.'

'You okay to take Zac in?' he asks as though he's done it more than twice in his life.

I crush the scouring sponge with my fist, allowing the dirty water to run down the plughole before dropping it into the sink. The pan is draining on the side. 'Think I'll manage.'

'Okay then.' His voice tips up and then down emphatically, his attention purposefully focused as he fills a plastic cup with powered protein, a banana, peanut butter and cinnamon. He used to add a raw egg until I stopped buying them for him. He can replace his own if he insists on going through them so quickly. Bad enough I have to keep him in bananas, but at least brunch isn't ruined at the weekend if I don't realise we've run out.

'You look silly.' Zac says with a rare display of insight.

'Helps me go faster, buddy.'

'Think I'd rather go slow.'

'Ha! Cheeky sausage.' Ben ruffles Zac's hair – the messy blonde mane that looks so much like his own used to. Then without any warning he grinds his upturned cup down onto the blender and a hundred thousand shrill vibrations reverberate around my head. How long is this hangover going to last? I'm sure he's holding it down for longer than usual. Even Zac's put his hands either side of his face with a pained grimace not unlike the one I'm wearing myself.

'Sorry!' Ben cries, clearly not sorry at all. He unscrews the blades and downs the shake like a twenty-two year-old gym junkie. 'Want some?' He teases, waving the dregs under Zac's nose making him wince and jerk away.

'Urghh.'

Ben chortles to himself unbecomingly and messes Zac's hair up once more. 'Have a good day at school, little man. Love you lots.' Then to me. 'I'll be back about eight. Go ahead and eat without me if you're hungry.'

Why, thank you, my Lord. How very progressive of you. And there was me going to wait by the door with your slippers and pipe ready for when you walked in, I don't say. I don't have a chance. He's already headed out the back door and is striding down the garden in his cleats like a rugby player wearing heels on a stag do.

'See you then.' I do say under my breath, relieved that he's gone, despite the tingling absence of his goodbye kiss on my cheek. The one I didn't want anyway.

'Have you brushed your teeth yet, Zac?'

'Yes.'

'Go upstairs please.'

'I have.' He blows a stream of warm, sweet air in my face as I reach across to clear up his cereal bowl and my head recoils, my stomach churning.

'Alright.' *Jesus.* 'Shoes and coat on then. Let's try and get there on time for once.'

Bubbles of excitement are beginning to multiply in my chest despite the dull ache at the back of my eyes at the thought of having the house to myself when I get back home after drop off. A day off from that slightly oppressive feeling of being judged when Ben's 'hard at work' upstairs leading me to fill every moment while the boys are at school with mundane household tasks or admin for the business, extensive practical research, anything lest I be accused of relaxing while my husband's busy supporting us all. Of leading a cushy life. Not that he'd ever say it, but he'd think it and I won't give him the satisfaction. Not usually, but today, today I can do anything I like without listening for the click of the kitchen door. Without scrambling off the sofa and quickly returning to the laundry basket, chopping onions I've already chopped, tapping away furiously at some hastily opened spreadsheet. Today I might watch Netflix instead.

'Ready?'

Zac has emerged from the utility room wearing a thin body warmer with hundreds of pockets he could hide no end of emergency snacks and equipment in should he intend to get lost in a desert but is of little use on a chilly October school day. But what do I care? Kids never seem to feel the cold and this one's as insensitive as they come.

That kiss.

We walk quickly, neither of us in the mood to entertain the other with observations about the dew-covered cobwebs clinging to the iron fence surrounding the park. The puddles of urine

Beasley's keen to examine under every other lamppost or the stiff angry goose pimples scratching Zac under his flimsy top. I barely even notice when he wanders ahead through the school gates as I'm still tying the dog's lead up outside, my thoughts racing and reserved for someone else, the laughter playing on my lips concealed behind my facemask, eyes sparkling in anticipation as I'm caught up in the ebb and flow of the morning rush, sucked along with the current towards the classroom.

That kiss brushing my lips.

I hardly react when I catch sight of Zac climbing over the locked gate separating the contaminated modern world from the sanitised germ-free safe-zones. Instead I'm straining my neck trying to look through the windows, see past the low sun reflecting on the glass and then I spot Lenny and my heart skips a beat. Lenny, his back turned to the door and I take him in, drowning in him. Memorising every muscle and sinew outlined by his shirt, every fluid movement as he bends around and our eyes meet, the blood draining from my limbs as instant as the smile on his face and for a split second there's nothing and nobody else in the world. Just two ex-strangers with a secret simmering between us. Unspoken promises rich with unequivocal intent.

Our lips barely touching, the prickling urge to lean closer so delicious it hurts.

'Come on in then, Zac,' Mrs Haverstock sighs, opening the door and extending the tight grimace she's assembled to me. 'But from now on, wait behind the line with the others. You

225

know you're not allowed in the gate until I come and open it. If you could keep an eye on him, Mrs –'

'Oh! Sorry. Sorry. That was my fault. I wasn't concentrating.'

'It's for their own safety.' Zac darts under her arm and she continues to stare at me, steel haired and grim faced.

'Yes, I understand. Sorry.'

'They could fall and hurt themselves.'

Alright already. I just wanted another glimpse of Lenny before I left but sod that. I'll have to make do with seeing him at pick up. Maybe I'll need to hang around so he can tell me how dangerous Zac's behaviour is himself.

I step away reluctantly, a small sense of smug satisfaction at the sight of all the other mums competing for a second glance from their kid's hot teacher, knowing their efforts to attract his attention are in vain. I keep my head low, avoiding eye contact and make my way back to Beasley who is attempting to distance himself from the frenzied Jack Russell tied next to him with the same stoic concentration as one would a dishevelled man talking to himself at the bus stop. Although he could be so deaf now, he simply can't hear the little shit yapping like his foot's caught in a trap. My temples constrict as I approach, teeth grinding.

'Come on, old boy. Let's get you out of here.'

He staggers forlornly onto his feet possibly pleased to see me, though pleased might be a stretch. Relieved maybe. I'm light-headed with nervous adrenalin and the incessant barking, trembling and struggling with the leash, with the lack of oxygen

226

filtering through the mask. The memory of that kiss still tickling the corner of my mouth. My actions deliberately normal. It's fortunate that low-level incompetence has always been a strength of mine or I'd probably still be there.

'You know, what? Let's stop off quickly at the little shop on the way home. I need to pick up a few bits. I know. I know what I said. But this is the last time. I just need to knock this headache on the head. Ha! Anyway, we're having a lazy day today. Might as well enjoy it.'

The house is quiet when we get back, my tote bag clanking obviously as I place it on the ground. It's half past nine, which is ridiculously early and I would never, ever normally have a drink before midday but I know from experience that even a few sips of wine will do everything the Nurofen has so far failed to and if I wait until then I'll waste the whole morning feeling terrible and for what? So I pour myself a small glass of the cheapest Pinot Grigio I could find (so that it didn't look odd on the bank statement) and sure enough, within two glasses I feel so much better.

'I told you, didn't I?'

Beasley's clearly so disappointed with my behaviour, he can't even look at me.

'Don't be so judgy, Beastly. Today's an exception. I'll start the detox tomorrow. This was purely medicinal.'

He stumbles up to his feet, paws at the blanket in his bed like he's plumping up cushions and flops down with his back to me.

'Oh, forget it. You wouldn't understand.'

I slam the empty glass onto the worktop, resisting the instinct to refill it and stare down Sharon who is glaring at me either for waking her up or existing. It's still early – ten thirty. The fact I'm even considering having another is reflexive, that's all. My head is swimming now, but the niggling pain has gone. And this is just a one off while I sort myself out.

That kiss. The feel of his stubble against my cheek.

'I don't know why I'm trying to justify myself to you anyway. It's not like Elena couldn't put it away.'

We both could. All the way through university (mostly when we should have been at lectures), after work when we got our first real jobs, starting at six when we knocked off all the way through till sunrise. Weekend bar crawls followed by dancing until the clubs closed and back home for a nightcap. A midday fry-up to soak up the hangover and back down the pub again. It was normal. Everyone was doing it. There was nothing to be ashamed of.

'And this...?' I raise my glass again towards Beasley. 'This doesn't even come close to what your mum used to get up to. Remember when Jake and Ozzie were little?'

He probably can't. He was only a baby himself.

'We'd get through a bottle at lunchtime. Would have been more, I expect, if I hadn't been breastfeeding, but no one cares if you're drinking with someone. That's just being social. Sociable. But God forbid you drink alone.' I reach for the fridge door, not a hundred per cent certain I'm going to take the wine out again until I do. 'Anyone who drinks alone must have a problem.

228

Well, I've got a problem, alright. Several as it happens and one of them thinks he can keep blaming Covid for feeling like crap for weeks instead of admitting he's got old. Ha!'

I take a long swig from my Nutella tumbler (old habits) and toast the photo of Elena staring mockingly at me from across the room.

'Guess you won't have to worry about that, hey? Saved yourself a fortune on Botox, you jammy cow.'

There's a certain stage when I amuse myself when I'm drunk. As long as I'm in a jolly mood, I can really keep myself entertained. I sweep up to the mirrored sliding door next to her, stretch my crow's feet taut and examine the fine lines that have matured into canyons spreading across my face. Both eyes are sunken and tinged as though by nicotine, the shadows beneath them a permanent shade of lilac flanked by ruddy cheeks, note-worthy only because of the tangle of broken veins extending across them like frost creeping over glass. I trace each new wrinkle sceptically, rubbing tiny circles into my brow as if I can smooth them away. Pull the skin back towards my wiry, greying hairline, every pore accentuated, every blemish a scar. I look like a geriatric about to undergo laser eye surgery.

'Good God. What on earth does Lenny see in me?'

What on earth would any beautiful, healthy man in the prime of his life want with the old lady staring out from the mirror?

'When did this happen, Beasley?'

I trace the contours of my body, the curve of my breasts, still passable in an underwired bra, but marred by years of overexposure to sun and children, the cleavage creased and as firm as a week-old balloon. My fingers glide ruthlessly down to my stomach, lifting my shirt like an accident unfolding in slow-motion, probing the soft folds of flesh that have never recovered from the assault of pregnancy, the years of neglect, comfort eating, unused gym memberships. The lavender stretch marks that have faded and paled, blanched by time but still noticeable within a hotchpotch of new moles, some startling beetroot, others dark like freckles drawn by a child.

I twist my torso, squeeze my bum cheeks, release and lift them from their residence above my knees to where they should be, my legs instantly tighter, longer. I turn around slowly and observe myself again, this unhappy stranger I wouldn't think out of place drinking tea in a bingo hall.

The kiss flashes through me again. Drawing slowly, magnetically towards each other, every cell in my body alert, buzzing, aching to close the space between us. That sweet painful moment of anticipation, of longing. The soft touch of his lips against mine. Tantalisingly pulling away until I can't bear the agony and press into him hungrily, shrouded by darkness. Darkness.

And if I'm honest, I was probably still a little drunk, I was wearing lots of layers and while it felt like my whole body was on fire, it only really involved my face. He's seen that before, he knew what was coming, but now what? Much as my dusty old libido is screaming out to, it's impossible to even contemplate taking things further with Lenny. How can I possibly consider taking my clothes off in front of him, squashing this sagging meat against his firm chest, letting his eyes linger on my wobbly thighs, my deflated udders?

It's bad enough Ben has to put up with me, but at least he's partially responsible for my downfall. Besides, he doesn't have a choice. Didn't have a choice, when we still did that sort of thing. He had to take what he got and be grateful for it, but Lenny? Lenny could choose any woman he wanted and still put her to shame.

I sink my head back into my shoulders, my thoughts racing again, a horse galloping inside my ribcage playing the piano. Elena looks at me, young and shiny, forever trapped at twenty-five, green eyes flanked with gold, blonde highlights enhancing perfect cheekbones. Her polished smile. Bitch. I should find a more recent photo.

We'd both been shiny and new when we met. Fresh out of school, dipping our feet in the shallows of adulthood hoping we would swim, our fear of sinking disguised by youthful arrogance, the university halls a lifebuoy enabling us to tread water for a year. Ease the transition from childhood into what would surely be the foundation of many mistakes – good and bad, each of them leading to something unknown and untested. A future fuelled by the present, nourished by cheap beer and instant noodles. Chips and beans.

I was cripplingly shy, overwhelmed by the noise and vitality around me. The carefree confidence of my peers. The introductions I should make, the witty observations, all intelligent reflection stuck in my throat like dung beetles caught in quicksand, digging deeper the more they scrambled to get out. The more they struggled to be heard. Only Elena saw me, not as the apprehensive introvert the others soon learned to ignore, but the sepia version of myself I instantly became in the company of louder, funnier, undaunted people. Self-assured crowds.

And so she sought me out away from the chaos. In the quiet of the common room when everyone else had gone out. In the kitchen when all the others were still in bed. And she had no need to. She was far from lonely. She was effortlessly stylish and popular, people flocked around her like moths drawn to the light she emitted, the flame that burned within her. And as I basked in her glow, the rest of the students in the halls, in my lectures, in the bar, began to see me too.

We became inseparable. I idolised her but more than anything I became addicted the person I became when I was with her. The person we became. God, we were hilarious. I mean I'm not so sure anyone else thought so, but we could make each other laugh until tears were pouring down our faces, until our sides hurt and we could barely breathe. There was nothing in the world we couldn't make better by being there together and it wasn't all one big jolly. There were hard times, there were heartaches, there were many, many lapses in common sense after a night out and a few too many pints of John Smith, but there was never any judgement. She completed me, but not in a sexual way. She was the other battery in a pair without which nothing works – there were no flashing lights or loud noises. No music, no dancing, no fun.

When she introduced me to her brother – Ben – there was an instant spark of recognition, but as the first flush of excitement began to wane and I realised he had nothing of the infectious spirit of his sister, we had already settled into an affectionate relationship. Compatibility on a calmer scale. Steady and dependable. Love, but far from the symbiotic partnership I share with Elena. Used to share. But in the end it was what I loved most about her – her zest for life, her need to seize every moment, that got us here.

'Fuck you,' I sigh. 'Fuck you very much for leaving me to deal with all of this by myself. Not that you'd have been any real help. You'd have told me to stay with Ben no matter what, if it made life easier for you.' I accidently kick Beasley's bed. 'Sorry. Sorry, Beastly.'

My legs give way and I crumple heavily next to him, squishing him up and settling down on his blanket, my head resting on the wall, Sharon eyeing me jealously from the breakfast bar. An image of Lenny burned into my mind.

'What am I doing?'

My eyelids are leaden, limbs lethargic, the central heating too high and my breathing slow. I just need a minute. Just one minute. To sit here. Just until this feeling passes.

And so I don't watch Netflix after all, but I wake up before Jake and Oscar get home, before I have to pick Zac up. Too late to do anything about the untoned muscles on my flabby arse but with Ben out of the house, I'm still light with giddy relief like a kid playing truant. Overly happy after only a fleeting glance from Lenny at pick up, surrounded as he was by fans. Abnormally chatty when the boys come home and maybe still three sheets to the wind from earlier but a mother nonetheless – legal guardian to some. Still technically and morally responsible for not burning the house down or passing out on the sofa so with the sobering effect of trying to get Zac to leave me alone for three minutes in order to pretend he's not there, I pull myself together. Focus evangelically on making dinner despite my unreliable coordination, my jittery grip.

'Close your eyes,' he demands, back under my feet again.

'I told you. I can't. I'm cooking.'

'Just quickly.'

I groan inwardly, lower my knife and turn toward him, testy with impatience.

'Which hand is the ball in?'

'What ball?'

'This ball.'

'I can't see anything. You told me to close my eyes.'

'You can open them now.'

Zac is holding both hands out in front of me, his expression expectant, fists clenched and knuckles white with resolve. I shake my head irritably as Jake lets out a low evil laugh from across the room.

'It'll be your turn in a minute,' I say warningly.

'You don't know how to do it!' Zac protests. 'What hand?'

I tap the left grudgingly and he surreptitiously flings the ball behind him, revealing his empty upturned palm with exaggerated flourish.

'Oh, well done,' I say unenthusiastically, returning to my sweet potato with more interest than one might expect with regards to a vegetable.

'Lame,' Jacob whispers loudly enough to be heard in the next room.

'Wait! Check the other one,' Zac cries.

I sigh and tap the hand he's holding out expectantly in desperation to prove it's not there either 'Very good, Zac.'

'Do you know how I did it?'

'No.'

'I –'

I hold my own hand up like a lolly pop lady signalling to a Nissan Micra to slow down. 'A good magician never reveals his tricks.'

'I'll do it again.'

Zac scuttles off to retrieve his ball and Jacob mimes hysterical laughter.

'Why don't you practise on –' I start and Jake stops crowing abruptly, his mouth pursed like a goat's anus, his blunt forefinger slicing violently at his throat. '– Sharon. Look she's already trying to join in.'

'She's running off with the ball.'

'Let her play with it then.'

But he's got it back and remarkably she seems to enjoy guessing which hand he's hidden it in.

'Go on into the sitting room or I'll see how you do it.'

Zac bounces up from his knees the way only a six-year-old can. 'Come on, Sharon,' he calls, his voice higher and kinder than usual and even more remarkably she follows.

Jacob slumps back against the sofa, his thumb scrolling down his phone again.

'You could try being nicer.'

'It would only encourage him. What are you making?'

'Pasta.' That is to say, I'm making pasta for everyone else. I shall be having a salad every day until I lose the weight that's crept up on me over the years like ivy clinging to an old abandoned statue. It's all I can do. That and exercise fanatically, keep the lights off at all times and never fully remove my underwear if I can pull it to one side instead. It isn't ideal but I was reminded again at pickup that I can't keep living this way with Lenny so close, the both of us out of reach. All I wanted to do was run into his arms, rapidly spreading variant or not. Run and keep on running and I could tell without words that he was feeling the same. Overcome by frustrated longing. Hiding behind the façade of normality.

He tapped his watch as if to say *six o'clock* and my heart sank with the realisation Ben was out and I wouldn't be able to get away. Not in the middle of dinner and bath time. Pyjamas, bedtime stories and bed. Lights out by seven, never wavering from the routine or paying for it in the form of a tired, inflexible tyrant the next day. My stomach twisted at the thought of having to wait until morning but even that brief glimpse of him had me walking on air.

Hold it together, I tell myself taking a swig of wine to calm my nerves and another smiles bubbles out of me.

'Oh, Jake. Before I forget, I got a reminder about your school trip today.'

Jacob giggles suddenly, the lines around his eyes creasing, his nose crinkling. His head bows towards his mobile, the braces filling his mouth making him look both young and old at the same time.

'Jacob.'

He raises his head, the grin still etched on his face and stares blankly somewhere in my direction.

'Did you hear what I said?'

'Are you talking to me?' The smile fades into baffled confusion and he reluctantly drags out the AirPod he's wedged into his ear as though it might take the first three layers of skin off with it. It may well do, the way they're fused to him lately.

'No, I'm talking to Beasley.'

'Oh.'

Beasley's top lip shifts almost imperceptibly, but if he heard his name at all, he's decided to ignore it. Jacob goes to replace the ear bud.

'Wait. Of course, I'm talking to you. I said they've sent through the details about your residential trip. You're supposed to be off in two weeks' time and we don't have half the stuff you need. Have you even checked the list they gave you? There are about ninety things on it. Anyone would think you were taking a gap year. What do you need three pairs of shoes for?'

'Coz we're going to get wet probably.'

'Even so, three pairs is ludicrous. I wouldn't mind if you weren't going to outgrow them all before you've had a chance to even break them in. You're going to have to borrow a pair of your dad's.'

'We don't have the same size feet.'

Well, it's either his or mine and mine are pink and size 5.'

He gives me his best shrivelling stare and flutters his eyelashes sarcastically. 'You're so funny.' He leans back and flicks through his phone again. 'Anyway, it doesn't matter. I can't really be bothered to go now. It's going to be cold.'

'Oh really? You could have told me that before I paid eight hundred quid for it.'

'You can ask for it back.'

'No, I can't. It's non-refundable and anyway, it's going to be brilliant and all your friends are going, aren't they? Blimey, I'd go if I could.' That isn't remotely true. Six days hiking through rain and sleet, abseiling down cliffs and sleeping in a dorm room with five stinky teenagers is not my idea of a relaxing holiday. I would rather boil my eyeballs but there is no need to go into that. 'Why are you having second thoughts?'

'It's just a lot, that's all. Eight hundred pounds and then all that equipment. We can't really afford it.'

'Oh, Jacob. I'm just kidding about the money.' I put down my knife and stride across the room to hug him. He makes no attempt to make it easier for me by standing up but at least he doesn't pull away until I do. 'You're very considerate to think about it, but you deserve this and you're going to have a great time.'

He beams sweetly, slumping back onto the sofa and as I head back to the workbench I feel, rather than see him, reach for his AirPod again.

'Uh-uh. Up to your room please and let me know if anything still fits you. And by fits, I mean you can get it on. I'm less interested in how much of your ankles and wrists are on show.'

'Urghh.' He drops his head back like I've just ordered him clean the bathrooms with his toothbrush, groans, sighs, mutters… something, sighs again and wrenches himself up so despondently I have to wonder if it really is worth making him go at all.

'Atta boy. That's the spirit.' I just hope he doesn't try and walk the whole trip like that. He's going to need more than six days if he keeps that up.

'Close your eyes again!' Zac shrieks bursting back into the kitchen.

'I don't need to close my eyes. Just put your hands behind your back and then show me.'

'That's cheating.'

'How…?' I trail off incredulously, a light in the garden catching my eye as I look up.

Oh God, you're back early.

It's barely quarter to six and Ben is already lumbering up the garden with the bike, tinkering around in the garage, traipsing back down the path. I hear the door handle turn and stifle a grunt.

"Oh, look. Uncle Ben's home. You'll be able to show him your magic tricks instead.'

'Uncle Beeennnn!' he squeals as though he hasn't had human contact for weeks.

'Hi there, little man.' He gives Zac a peck on the top of his head and extracts his arms from around his waist, the thin clinging legs wrapped around his thighs dropping reluctantly to the floor. An affectionate smile gazing down at him. 'Where's Oscar?'

Upstairs trying to rebuild the confidence you shattered when you had a pop at him about his singing, I don't say. I just shrug because I can't be bothered to explain that we don't live in a castle, a theme park or a worm hole so if he's not downstairs, he's likely to be in his room.

'You're home early,' I say instead/ my eyes darting away from his as soon as he looks at me.

'Thought I'd get back and give you a hand.'

'What with? Everything's done. I was about to serve up for the boys.'

'Well, then. Maybe we could go upstairs and have a chat.'

'A chat?'

'A talk, you know.'

'Uncle Ben, I've got a magic trick.'

'Not now, buddy. Let me just have a quick word with Aunty Lara first, hey?'

'What do you mean – *a talk*?'

'You have to close your eyes.'

'Hang on two secs, Zaccy.'

What does he mean – a talk? *You patronising bell end.* 'Just let him show you his trick.'

Ben's face falls, the fake grin he's contrived drooping, the light behind his eyes snuffed out. *That didn't take long.*

'I really think we need to have a proper talk.'

'I tell you what.' I glance at the clock. It's five to six. Dinner's ready and Zac's pulling on Ben's arm.

'Why don't you talk to your nephew? And since you're back so early, you can serve this lot up. I need to take Beasley out.'

'What? Again. Why?'

'He's putting on weight. It's not good for his joints. He needs to keep mobile.'

'But –'

'You said you wanted to help.' I drop the spoon into the pasta sauce with a clatter.

Ben's lips are drawn tightly across his mouth as though he's scared of what he'll say if he opens them. Good, let him be. Let him be scared for a change, because I'm not. I'm done with all that. With tiptoeing around. With pretending we're something we're not. Pretending life's still the same, that nothing's changed. Bollocks to that. Everything's changed and nothing will ever be the same again. I'm going to see to it. I'm going out.

Seventeen

'Are you sure it's okay to come in?' Lenny asks and my eyes flit towards the street outlined over his shoulders as I step backwards, pulling the door open wider indicating he enter quickly. His foot crosses the threshold – over another line – and I realise I'm holding my breath. He glances at his watch. 'I've got forty-five minutes.'

'Hope you're a fast eater,' I say leading him into the kitchen.

A pot of soup is cooling on the side (Jerusalem artichoke, leek and thyme) next to a basket of freshly baked bread (out of a packet but I had to finish it off in the oven so…). Beasley lifts his head.

'There he is,' Lenny lopes across to his bed and bends down to pet him, his long body taking up more space than I'm used to. Filling the room. It's surreal to see him here in my house. In the place I've pictured him so many times, summoned him in my mind.

'Is it too early, do you think?' I hold two wine glasses up in the air, the stems crossing in one hand, a bottle of Chenin Blanc in the other. Lenny straightens up to his full height, snorting with laughter at the sight of me.

'I don't know about too early, but I'm not sure Mrs Haverstock will be too happy if she has to take over the class for me this afternoon,' he grins.

'Just a little one then,' I smirk back as the pale liquid glugs unseductively out of the bottle, swilling up the sides of the glass. I hold it out to him and he takes it from me, leaning forwards, his arm sliding across the back of my waist, gazing down at me.

'I can think of something else we can do,' he whispers, his voice low and there's a beat of silence in which we stare at each other, knowing that this is it. This is happening. The moment that will define the rest of my life is unfolding and I keep unwrapping it, layer by layer, every muscle in my body melting as I run my fingers down his arm, taking his hand in mine, guiding him back into the hallway and up the stairs (*Shoes!*).

Slowly at first, then more hurriedly the more conscious I become of his face trailing only inches from my rear end and quite honestly any sense of sensuality has worn off by the landing but we still have another flight to go. This is the point I always start to feel a bit puffed out too. I've brought the wine. I don't know why, seemed like a good idea but it's making me walk like I'm in an egg and spoon race.

'Sorry,' I grimace, turning apologetically. 'We're on the top floor.' I wince at the word 'we', immediately wanting to backtrack and clarify that I meant he and I, not Ben, although Ben and I obviously are too (or were. I'm still sleeping in the study).

In the end I say nothing, the flush on my cheeks no less due to the exercise as embarrassment. By the time we arrive at my bedroom it's with a sense of relief but the first thing I see is Sharon on the bed.

For goodness sake.

She stiffens and opens one eye, clearly affronted. Lenny makes his way across to her, recognition dancing in his eyes.

'Oh, hello there,' he cries delightedly, stroking her rounded back. 'You must be the famous Sharon I've heard so much about.'

She chirps, her eyes deliberately shut tight again.

'I'll get her out of here,' I blush. I'm not blushing about the cat. I am blushing about everything. The strangeness of this man being in my room, the reason why. The thought of the pasty folds of flesh about to be released from the one expensive set of lacy hardware I own, the one currently holding it all in place; the jiggling cellulite, the wobbling bat wings. *Oh, Christ. What am I doing?* 'Come on, Sharon.'

I slide my fingers under her and she hisses, curling into herself like a hedgehog but I persevere, pick her up, her pupils wide and indignant now, claws digging into the top of my shoulder as I carry her out and dump her outside the loo.

'Go on. Go downstairs.'

She glares as I close the door quietly behind her, her back arched, every hair standing on end.

'Aww. I feel bad now,' Lenny smiles and I almost say if you feel bad about the cat, you probably shouldn't meet my husband,

245

but somehow I hold it in, stand nervously with my back against the door, my heart in my throat, my legs trembling.

Lenny rises slowly and takes a step towards me, his arm stretched out inviting me into my own bed, pulling me closer, wrapping himself around me and then as his lips press down on mine, I forget everything else – just for a minute. As soon as he starts tugging my shirt loose from my jeans, I seize up again, suddenly out of my head and back in the room, very aware of myself, distracted by every imperfection hidden within the confines of my firm body-control polyester pants. He hesitates, questioning me with his eyes, staring into my soul, reassuring me.

'It's okay, we don't have to –' But as he pulls back, I realise there is nothing I've ever wanted more. I press his hand back against my side, allow his fingers to pull and probe beneath my reinforced shell. Lead him back onto the bed, both of us falling gently onto the soft, cool covers, the pillow billowing around the crook of my neck as he feels his way around, smoothly unzipping my jeans, peeling down the waistband. His eyes never leaving mine.

The only noise is the sound of our breathing, heavy with desire. And Sharon scratching the carpet outside.

I close my eyes, sink back into the pillow, allow one arm to rest against my forehead, the other on Lenny's shoulder as he works my trousers down my hips. My entire body is electric, fully charged. God, he's having trouble getting them over my backside.

246

Just give them a good yank.

It's no good. I knew skinny jeans were a bad idea. I reach down and wrench them over my buttocks, wriggling them down past my thighs, both of us giggling as our eyes meet again, clumsy and sixteen again. Sliding them inside out when they get stuck on my ankles, finally tossing them aside. Tittering self-consciously as he runs the back of his finger down the inside of my thigh, shrinking away from his touch. He looks up reassuringly, a tiny shake of his head.

'It's okay.'

And so I relax into it, forget about the pattern of thin translucent scars criss-crossing my loose skin and focus on the light sensation of his hair brushing over every raw nerve ending, as sensitive as fresh sunburn. On the rasp of incessant scratching still audible through the door.

'Oh, God. I'm sorry.' I sit up. 'She's going to wreck the carpet.'

'Let her in,' Lenny says, slanting aside.

I leap up, self-conscious again and regrettably angled like the fat kid in a ballet class as I arabesque ungainly between the bed and the door. Sharon shoots in like I might change my mind any minute pausing only to sniff my jeans with unnecessary distain as she circles the floor.

'Sorry about that.'

'That's okay,' Lenny murmurs. 'Where were we?'

I stretch my T-shirt over my bum and settle back down again, legs astride as he kneels between them and sweeps his own shirt

247

over his head, his chest smooth, every muscle toned and I can't help but reach out to touch him. Sharon jumps up on the bed.

Ignore her.

She sticks a foot out in the air and starts licking it. The whole mattress vibrates.

Don't think about it.

I turn my head and she pauses, staring at me, her tongue sticking out.

Oh, for crying out loud.

Lenny starts to laugh.

'I'm so sorry,' I wail.

'It's okay.' He's grinning now, making his way up the length of my body, lying down besides me. 'We can just lie here.'

But we don't just lie there. Instead, he lifts my top up past my pants, trailing his finger along the soft skin leading from my belly button down to the elastic. And then Sharon starts purring loudly and completely unnecessarily. It's very intrusive. Lenny reaches out and scratches the side of her face.

I swear to God, Sharon... but the moment's lost.

He slides back down against me. 'We've got plenty of time,' he says. 'I'm not in any rush. Are you?'

'I thought you had to get back to school.'

'I mean...' he props himself up on one elbow and runs his fingernail across my waist. 'In general. I'm in this for the long run. If you are too.'

I curl my fingers around his hair, twisting his tight springy dreads. 'Me too,' I whisper, my voice hoarse with emotion.

'Well, good then.' His eyes are the colour of treacle, rich and warm and I could fall into them every day for the rest of my life. All I want to do is lie here in his arms, the sound of his heart beating in my ears like the ocean, the rhythmic rise and fall of his chest, the tide drawn to the moon. I hardly dare to break the spell but I have to say it.

'But you know there's more to this than just me though, right?'

'You mean the kids?'

I nod.

'I know and I don't want to put you under any pressure you're not ready for. But if you're asking whether I understand that things are complicated, that you come as a package, then I do.' He fixates on me. 'I like packages.'

'I might need a bit of time. Before I can introduce you...'

'Listen,' his knuckles graze my cheek as he skims the back of his hand lightly against it. 'I want you. I haven't felt this way in, I don't know– I don't think I've ever felt this way. You're funny and smart and interesting. And sexy as hell, of course. I'd have put that first but I didn't want you to think I was shallow.'

'You can be shallow. Be as shallow as you like.'

He laughs softly again, his fingers tracing the curve of my collarbone, his thigh resting on my leg. 'And I understand that you are also... a mother. And a bloody good one, I'll bet and I would never do anything to jeopardise that. Your relationship with your boys... I'll never come between you.'

I trace the shape of his nose tenderly. 'Jacob will be fine. Oscar might need a while to get his head around it. He's the more sensitive out of the two. I think his hormones are starting to kick in.'

'And Zac? What will he make of it, do you think?'

'Well, he thinks you're great, but…it hardly matters really. He's Ben's nephew.'

Lenny reaches across me to the bedside table. Passes me a glass of wine and I bolster myself up, take a sip of it, pass it back to him. He adjusts the cushions, sits up and I rest my head on his stomach as he refills the glass from the bottle.

'So what happened to Zac's father, if you don't mind me asking? Is he out of the picture?'

Is it weird that we're having a normal conversation, but in bed? In my bed. 'Never been in the picture. Elena always said it was a one night stand –'

'Oh wow. So she's never even known –'

'Apparently not. I always thought there was more to it, but –' Sharon traipses across the duvet to have a closer look at whatever we're drinking.

'Married man, you mean?'

'Could have been. Or just someone she didn't want to keep around when she found out she was pregnant.

'Or who didn't want to be around.'

My fingers linger on the downy hair leading up from his waistband to his belly button. 'Maybe, but to be honest, I'm probably getting carried away. I mean, I'd have known if she was seeing someone. She was my best friend. We talked about everything. It's just that part of me wants there to be a father so he can step in a bit. You know. Take on some of the burden. I know that's an awful thing to say.'

Lenny shrugs, tops up the glass, hands it to me. 'Well, there definitely is a father. That much is undeniable. And if it was a one-night stand, there's nothing to say he wouldn't actually be pleased to find out he was a dad. I know I would. It would be weird at first, of course, but –'

'Really? Christ, I'd have thought it would be anyone's worst nightmare. Especially if Zac turned up on your doorstep. Imagine that. Holy hell.' I grimace at the thought of it. 'Anyway, there's no point getting myself worked up about it. There's no way to track him down even if he was interested in stepping up.'

Sharon has climbed onto the pillow next to me and is kneading it like she's making the sexiest bread on earth. It's almost perverse. It's most definitely more fun that kneading bread should be.

'You never know. I did a DNA test once...' Then at my inquiring knee-jerk response 'Just one of those cheap ones off the Internet that gives you a breakdown of your heritage, you know, like you're 16% African, 12% Scandinavian...'

'Right...?' I think I read an article about that the other day.

'I was curious about my ancestry, that's all. My mum's mum was Jamaican and her dad was Chinese, which is quite an unusual mix, but I didn't know anything about the other side of my family other than they're all White British. Typical sort of English stereotype.'

Oh, Sharon, please stop jiggling. Can't you go and clean yourself somewhere else? 'And were there any surprises?'

'Only that I'm two per cent Neanderthal, which I'll be honest, I didn't even realise was an actual thing –'

'Aren't they cavemen?' I start to laugh and the cat looks up sharply, both legs prostrate, her round furry belly bulging.

'No, see, no. That's where people get it wrong. Us poor bloody Neanderthals have a bad rep –' He takes the wine from me, swigs a little.

'Is that why your arms are slightly too long and drag on the ground?'

His arms are perfect.

'No! Oi! That's very offensive. We're misunderstood, that's all. It simply means more of my ancestors originate from the Neanderthal Valley than you'd typically get in England. It's quite normal in Germany.'

'Oh, is it?'

'Apparently.'

'Your head is quite large now that I think about it.' I say running my hand down the side of it.

'Stop.' He pulls me towards him, my body jerking in spasms as he tickles me, short sharp spurts of laughter bursting out of my chest, as liberated and carefree as a child. 'This is why I never tell anyone. All it means...' One long finger pokes playfully into my side one last time. 'All it means, is that lots of my dad's side were German originally. And Irish.'

'Which is fascinating stuff,' I chuckle (never chuckle naked), wiping the tears from my aching cheeks, composing myself. 'But I'm not sure –'

'You could do a DNA test on Zac –'

'To track down a bunch of cavemen…?' I take the wine back, pleased with myself.

'No, sorry. I'm not explaining this very well. I did the test and they give you a breakdown of whatever, but they also match you to anyone else you're related to who's done a test too. I'm always getting emails from them saying they've identified my third cousin so-and-so from America –'

'Oh gosh. That is amazing.' I'm listening now. I lift my head up, take a sip.

'Not really. I can't be bothered with any of that. If they ever turn up with a brother or something I might look him up, but I never even get around to seeing my first cousins and I grew up with them. What I mean is, if you do Zac's DNA they might be able to tell you if anyone else that he's related to has done the same test and then you might be able to track the father down through them. I don't know, it's a long shot…'

"It's better than nothing.'

'The question is, do you really want to open that can of worms? You might get more than you'd bargained for.'

'I've already got more than I bargained for. Much more and quite honestly, even if I just got one day less a week, that would be life changing at this stage.'

'Well, mull it over with Ben then.' And at the thought of his face if I told him any of that, my heart sinks.

Still what does it matter in the long run if I'm planning to leave? I'll be shot of him anyway. Let Ben worry about finding Irish Neanderthals to look after him.

'Listen,' Lenny glances at his watch. 'I've really got to go. This has been... nice.'

He lifts himself off the bed, pulling his shirt over his head in one smooth motion, leaning back towards me, one knee resting on the bed, kissing me goodbye as a thousand butterflies take to flight.

'Don't get up. You look beautiful lying there, your hair all tousled like that.'

What's he mean tousled? Oh, Christ. I bet it looks shit.

'I'll see myself out.' And with that he backs out of the room, soundlessly closing the door on his way out.

Oh, Sharon. What have I done? It's awful I know, but I can't stop smiling. I pour the last of the wine into the glass. *Give me a minute. I need to let this all sink in. You were no help, by the way. I'm not letting you in here again if you're going to do that, mood killer. No wonder Ben and I never used to let you up here at night.*

My throat tightens at the thought of my husband, at the thought of spending another moment with him, living this lie, bending the truth until such a time as I can leave him. Line my ducks in a row and escape this sham of a marriage. I knock the wine back, hold it in my mouth, savour the sensation of the alcohol numbing my tongue and swallow, my head falling back against the pillow, my eyes heavy, emotions drained.

Just give me a minute, Sharon, I whisper.

'What the actual fuck!?"

Ben is standing in the doorway. I shoot up, my eyes bulging, head whirling, disorientated. The room's dark, the curtains still wide open.

'What's going on?' I feel around for my trousers, for anything that shouldn't be there.

'You tell me,' he snarls, slamming his hand against the light switch.

'I –'

'Really?' He strides towards me and snatches the wine bottle off the duvet, brandishing it in his fist, his eyes flashing with fury. 'Twenty-six missed calls. That's how many you've got. On your phone. Downstairs.'

'What?' I'm looking around, taking this all in. I don't understand.

'You forgot to pick up Zac. *Forgot.*' He snorts staring down at the empty bottle. Shaking his head. 'They had to get me out of a meeting with a client. Do you know how long I've been trying to finalise that deal? I had to get Oscar to go to the school and get him.'

'Why didn't he just wake me?'

'He didn't know where you were. Don't suppose he imagined you were up here passed out in bed.' His tone is incandescent. I scoot to the edge of the mattress, my hands feeling desperately around on the floor for something to cover myself with.

'I normally hear him come in,' I protest.

'Normally? How often do you do this?'

'You know what I mean. He's so loud.'

He is so loud. He's been quieter since Ben had a go at him. It was bad enough at the time but now look what's happened. Ben picks up my jeans and flings them at me.

'Let's not pretend this is his fault.'

'I'm not...'

'You know what? Just stay up here. The kids shouldn't see you like this. I'll sort out dinner and walk the dog. You just nurse your hangover. Try to pull yourself together like the rest of us have.'

And with that he turns and walks out, Sharon hot on his heels meowing in concern and I stand at the side of the bed, one foot in my trouser leg, my reflection pale and ghostly in the wardrobe mirror and I don't recognise myself anymore.

Eighteen

It's been quieter around the house since Jake went off on his residential trip. Quieter and there's more food in the fridge. I don't know why I insisted on him going. He was quite happy not to. Must have been the need to enforce some sort of normality, I suppose. Keep up the veneer of everything being how it should be. That we're a normal family doing normal things. That he's the same as all the other kids. Nothing to see here. Move on.

But I miss him. I could never have imagined how much. His presence, his occasional wisdom, his big booming laugh. He'd know what to say, not that I could have this conversation with him. Not that I can ever tell him what I've done, but still just having him here, nearby, saying nothing at all would be better than him being so completely out of reach.

Oh, Jake, I weep banging my head against the back of the toilet door where I've hidden myself for a few minutes' peace. *Maybe I made a mistake making you go. Should I come up with an excuse to get you back? Would you want me to? If only I could talk to you. Everything always feels better when you're around.*

'Aunty Lara.' The door thumps jolting my neck forwards, pounding in my ears. 'How long are you going to be?'

I close my eyes and groan. Tear off a strip of toilet roll and wipe the long strings of mucus rolling onto my lip from my nose, shards of paper disintegrating in my hand, the clear sticky dregs of it on my fingers.

'What do you want, Zac?'

'I can do it now,' he announces, his mouth mushed up against the door. 'Can I show you?'

I take a deep jagged breath and sigh. 'In a minute.'

'Okay. I'll wait here.'

Lovely. Yes, please. If you could. I roll onto my knees, grab the sink and pull myself to my feet, disgusted by the sight of my face in the mirror, eyes puffy, skin blotchy and no more familiar to me than an inconsequential aquaintance, half-forgotten and half-remembered, but with no idea why. I run the tap, rinse the transparent fluid from my fingers, lower my head into the cold water. Numb my senses.

'Aunty Lara?'

For the love of Lucifer. 'I'm coming, Zac. Good God.' I take a last look at myself. *What a catch. No wonder Lenny's gunning to throw the rest of his life away just to be with me. Oh, Lenny. What are we going to do?*

'Aunty Lara.'

Kerrrriiiiiiiiiiisssssssstttttttt. 'Yes.' I wrest the door open. Bowl past him into the kitchen.

'Ewww. You look funny.'

258

'I've got a cold. What's your excuse?'

'Hey?'

'Nothing. Come on. Get on with it then if you want to show me. I've still got lots to do here and I have to leave in half an hour.'

Where the bloody hell is Oscar anyway? I thought he said he was going to quit drama club last week. He should be home by now, keeping Zac busy.

'Pick a hand.'

Not this one again. I grit my teeth and tap his clenched fist a tiny bit more firmly than I mean to but a lot less firmly than I could. He makes a terrible job of switching whatever he's got in there from that hand to the other, twists it over and opens it triumphantly.

'Wrong.'

'Very good.'

I turn my attention to the two tagines simmering away on the hob. I have fifteen minutes tops to finish them off. It was all supposed to be ready an hour ago but I can't seem to get them right. I added more seasoning and spices to the chicken but that only made it worse so then I tried balancing it out with more apricots, but it still tastes bitter. It wouldn't be such a big deal except I got this anniversary booking on the back of Stella's fortieth so Arabella knows exactly what it's supposed to taste like.

Maybe I'm over thinking it. She's clearly not a great cook. The whole reason she wants it delivered so early is so that she can pretend she made the whole meal while her husband was at work. Could it be that's how they've kept their marriage alive? Lying intermittently. Hiding the ugly truth. I'd better be careful I don't prolong mine.

Eurghh, it tastes too grainy now. The cumin hasn't had a chance to infuse. I need some apple puree to pull it together but there's no time to make it. Maple syrup! That will do.

'Now choose the other one.'

'Oh, Zac. I don't have time for this right now. I have to get the food done. Go and find Sharon. She's always impressed by your tricks.'

Plus she needs cheering up. She's not pleased to have been banned from the kitchen again.

'I'll be quick. Choose the other one.'

Arghhhhhhh. 'The other one then.'

'Ta-dahhh.'

Twelve minutes to go. Jesus. Maybe it just needs a little longer to sit. I'll leave it for now. Get everything else ready. Oh, for God's sake. Why won't the lentils soften? They're supposed to practically disintegrate not taste like gravel.

Boil the kettle. They shouldn't need more than ten minutes as long as I add more water. Get the couscous out the fridge so it has a chance to warm up to room temperature. Wait. Might as well have a quick top up while I've got the door open.

'Why are you putting that in a mug?'

Zac's right. It's five thirty. I could probably swap over to a wine glass now.

260

'Just saving on washing up.'

'I know another trick with cups.'

I'll bet you do. I add some boiling water to the harissa, squash, lentil, chickpea bloody-who-cares-anyway. *Just cook!*

'Lucas showed me yesterday.'

Bloody Lucas. I ramp the heat up. 'How do you know this Lucas anyway? He's not from your class, is he?' There can't be anyone left in gold class who'll still play with him.

'He goes to breakfast club.'

'What's that mean?'

'Breakfast Club. It's where they give you jam sandwiches before school.'

'What's that –' *Shit.* It's all sticking to the bottom of the pan.

'What are jam sandwiches?' Zac asks like I'm a moron and he's the culinary chef.

'No.' *For God's sake.* The lentils are burnt. 'I just asked you how you know this kid who keeps showing you magic tricks, that's all.'

'From breakfast club.'

'Fine.' Whatever. I don't even care. It's earth shattering enough that he's made a friend. Maybe he'll stop insisting on following me about so much if he can suck someone else's energy dry. Talking of which, where the hell is Oscar?

'So, you take these three cups. Look at me.'

'No, Zac. Enough. I have to concentrate on this.'

'Just look at me.'

'No!'

261

'I put the coin under this one. Look. Aunty Lara. Look. I put the coin under this one.'

Arghhhhhhhhhhhhhhhhhhhhhhhhhhhhhhhhhhhhhhhhhhhhhhhhhhhh hhhhhhhhh.

'No wait –' He fumbles and drops to the floor, scrambling about, grasping at the pound as it rolls in an arc just out of his reach. Beasley lifts his head as though he might be up for the challenge.

'Grab it quickly,' I cry and Zac stamps his foot down, bringing the coin to a rattling halt. 'Right, that's enough. Put it away now. Or go and practise in the other room, I don't care. I just need to finish this.'

The chicken tastes too sweet now. I've put too much maple syrup in it. *Fuck itttt.* The back door slams and the scuffle of shoes being kicked across the utility room, the thump of a bag being dropped onto the floor instead of hung on the peg makes my heart soar.

'Oh, listen. Oscar's back.' *Thank God.* 'You can show him instead. Oscaaar.'

Oscar shuffles into the kitchen, his back stooped, tie dishevelled, his pocket torn.

'Oh, for goodness sake. What have you done now?'

'Nothing.'

'What do you mean nothing? You've ripped your blazer.' I nearly fling the serving spoon at his head in irritation. He doesn't answer me. 'I really don't need this right now, Oscar. You have to take better care of your things.'

'Can I show you my new trick?'

'No.' Oscar glowers at Zac, swiping him aside, his face grim, an aura of resentment seeping out of him like dry ice from an aeroplane.

'Yes, actually,' I bark, wincing at my own outburst. Even Beasley jumps and he's half deaf. 'You're late coming back from school. You've got a massive strop on and instead of apologising, you've landed me even more work to do. I've got enough on my plate trying to get this order out for tonight without having to sew that bloody thing up before tomorrow. The least you can do is spend some time with your cousin to help me out.'

'I don't want to.'

'I don't care what you want, Oscar. Take that look off your face and keep Zac busy until I tell you otherwise.'

'That's not fair.'

'Now.'

Zac doesn't really look like he wants to be kept busy anymore, not by Oscar at any rate, but it's not up to him either.

'Go on, the pair of you. Until you can learn to be civil.'

I drain my wine mug and return Oscar's glare, though perhaps without quite the same conviction. Our eyes lock and for a moment I contemplate how his can look both so dead and animated with sheer distain at the same time. The hormones are certainly taking effect. How long have I got of this to look forward to? Six, maybe seven years? Twelve or thirteen if I'm to put up with Zac for that long too. What a treat.

If you think you can out-hate me, you've got another think coming, I don't say. Instead I summon a voice so low and non-negotiable a wounded animal would sound more approachable. 'I said now.'

'God.' He breaks away and flounces towards the kitchen door as Zac gawks on warily, weighing up the least awful of his options and ultimately choosing to shuffle out reluctantly behind Oscar. Or at least choosing to get out of my way.

I turn back to the mess I've made on the hob – the over-seasoned chicken, the burnt lentils – and scream silently, my nails digging into my palms, the muscles either side of my throat stretched to breaking point.

It will have to do. There's nothing I can add to pull it back. It's five thirty-seven and I have to drop it all round to Arabella's house by six o'clock before her husband gets home from the office.

Shit, shit, shit. I lift my mug to my mouth and finding it empty, slam it down on the counter. It'll be alright. No one else ever seems to notice when food's crap anyway. Why else would they keep going back to those pubs and restaurants I refuse to eat in anymore? I just have to brazen it out. Disguise what I can with coriander and parsley. She'll be on the champagne by now, I expect. She won't care.

I grab a couple of foil containers from the bottom drawer, scoop the chicken into one and the veggies in the other, my hands shaking with adrenaline, the sauce spilling over the sides. It's five forty-four now. *Time to go. Don't think about it.*

I'm antsy with nerves by the time I get there, two minutes early and it's only as I'm pressing the buzzer that I remember I've left the couscous in the fridge. I scream silently again and that's the face Arabella's confronted with when she flings the door open, sober as a judge and delighted to see me. Or at least she would have been if I weren't mid-wail and ready to drill myself into the ground.

'I'm so sorry,' I gush, handing the bag over. 'I need to pop back and get something.'

'Oh,' she says, on the verge of adding 'that's alright,' but apparently it's not. 'Nothing important, I hope.'

'Just an accompaniment.' *Not really an accompaniment so much as an integral part of the meal.* 'I won't be long. Five mins.' I span my fingers out and shove them in her face for emphasis. Again not appreciated. 'Maybe less.' There is no way it's going to be less than five minutes. It took me thirteen to get here. 'Don't take the lids off just yet to keep the heat in.'

'Okay then,' she says with masterful composure, clearly torn between polite restraint and being totally hacked off that I'm ruining the evening she had planned. 'You will be quick though, won't you? Hugo's due back in fifteen minutes. I'd really love to have it out of the containers before then or he'll twig that it's not all my handiwork. I know it's cheeky…'

'Not cheeky at all.' *Shiiiiiiitttt.* I've reduced my five fingers to one now and accompanied it with a disarming grin I manage to maintain all the way backwards down the path.

Shut the door. Shut the door.

She eases it closed dubiously, her own smile fractious now and I grab my phone out of my pocket.

Pick up. Pick up.

If I can get Oscar to quickly run down to the kitchen, get the couscous out of the fridge, pop it in a bag and ride down on his bike to meet me, there is a slim chance in hell I will be able to get it to her before old Hoodwinked Hu gets home. Of course, this is going to entail some serious explaining – to Oscar, not Arabella.

Pick up, pick up.

I'm not sure he even knows where the fridge is and if I can direct him to it I'm going to need him to identify the only silver box in it on the middle shelf right at eye level. This could take forever. I keep moving.

Pick up.

Answer phone. I dial again, a little more desperation in my step now. If I can get him to the fridge, that still leaves the problem of finding a bag.

Pick up, pick up.

There are a few plastic ones under the sink (that's 10p down the drain) but he'll have to move the cleaning caddy to get to them. He'll never understand what a cleaning caddy is – *pick up* – which leaves the cotton tote bags (*damn it* – maybe I can ask for it back) but they're in a bag marked *Bags* at the bottom of the coat cupboard. He'll never find them.

Shit, pick up. Answer phone. *Oh, Christ.*

I'm breaking into a sweat. An actual sweat caused by sprinting (stumbling with a sense of urgency) in a thick woollen coat in the middle of a crisis on an early November evening with all the layers that entails. I loosen the scarf around my neck.

Oh my god. I could call Ben. He wouldn't be able to find the bags but he could probably work out where the couscous was, but he's not speaking to me and I can't let him know I've screwed up so he has to rescue me. Not again.

Pick up, Oscar!

Where, where, where is Jacob when I need him? He'd be glued to his phone and I can't keep him out the fridge. On the bright side, he'd have probably eaten the bloody couscous by now. The only person I could actually rely on to do this for me without messing it up or denying it's anywhere to be found is Lenny and this is probably not the way to break the news to everyone – *Hi. Lara's bit on the side here. Just need to pick something up for her. I know, what is she like?*

Oh, pick up your phone, Oscar! I do not believe for a second you're still playing with Zac or doing your homework. You had better not be ignoring me.

Arghhhhhh! It's ten past six. I can see the house. If I don't collapse and die before I get there, I might just be able to bike it back on time. As long as Ben's pumped up the wheels for me recently. He might not have, what with –

Right. I'm in. Twelve minutes past six. Don't get distracted. Just grab it.

I just grab it, grab a bag from under the sink while I'm at it. Scuttle out to the garage, wishing too late that I'd downed a glass of water and left my coat. No time. It's fine. I can make it even on two flat tyres if needs be, as long as I don't stop for anything.

For the love of God!

Oscar's chained his bloody bike up to mine.

'Oscarrrrrr!!!!' I might almost never use it but what a stupid thing to do. I bet this is Ben's way of foiling any thieves that break into the garage. *Because they'd never dare to steal two bikes, would they? Mary, Mother of Christ!* 'Oscarrrrr!!!!'

I'm going to kill him. I am actually going to kill that boy. And he can bloody well take the couscous round to Arabella's for me now.

You little…

I can't even think of a suitable insult, I'm too busy storming up to his room, fired up by indignation, outrage beating a path in front of me as I mount each stair like I'm tearing through it with a sledgehammer.

I swear to God, if I get a bad review because of this…

I burst onto the landing, catatonic and wholly unprepared to find Jacob's bedroom door ajar, muffled grunting radiating through the gap. His feet on the desk, his dexterous fingers pummelling the Xbox controller, the shock of seeing him so unexpected my stomach lurches. I grab the banister to steady myself, the anger draining out of me and I reach out to the door, hesitantly pushing it back towards the blurry racing cars,

268

towards my son who shouldn't be there but as my vision swims into focus, I realise it's not him.

'Oscar! What are you doing in here?'

He wrenches the headphones off, spins around and stares at me with flared eyes, guilt stinging his cheeks like a slap.

'Nothing.'

I suck the air out of the room, try to still my heartbeat. Let my irritation settle.

'Did Jacob say you could use his stuff?'

'Yes.'

'Really?'

He pulls the headphones off slowly, his mouth working.

'You can't use someone's things without their permission. You know that.'

'He wouldn't mind.'

'Oh, wouldn't he?' My mouth is set in a sneer but I can't help it. 'You can't just take advantage of him not being here, Oscar. What if Zac used your things without asking?'

He rotates on the chair ready to pounce. 'He's always taking my things.'

'Well, quite, and you don't like it, do you?' I have my hands on my hips, the infuriation on my face a match for his.

'It's not the same.'

'Ozzie. Turn it off right now and don't let me catch you in here again.'

He flings the controller down on the desk. 'It's not fair. I just want a bit of privacy. Why does Zac have to sleep in my room? He's so annoying.'

This again. '*Enough.* We've been over it a million times. I apologise for the inconvenience but this is just the way it has to be. None of us likes it, believe me. Do you think I want him here? News flash. I don't. This affects me more than anyone. At least you haven't had to put your whole life on hold.' I hear the floorboards creak before I see the small figure flash by in the hallway. Feel the walls shake as the door slams in the next room, flinch at the sound of something smashing on the floor. 'Oh, great.'

Oscar glares at me, tears the headphones from his neck, throws them down on Jacob's chair and barrels past me muttering under his breath. His bedroom door slams again and suddenly Megan Trainor's blasting through the walls. I blink away the sting from my eyes and stare unseeingly at the screen.

'Nice one.'

Of course, now you appear. 'Oh God. Not now, Ben.' I turn around slowly, my arms limp, my fury spent, skin crawling at the sight of him languishing in the doorway, cocky and self-composed.

'No, really. I thought you handled that really well. It's got to be a new record even for you, two down in less than a minute.'

Oh, fuck off. 'You can talk.'

He stands taller at that, lowers his arms from the doorframe and cocks his head innocently. 'I can talk?'

270

'You're the one who shamed Oscar so badly he's barely sung a note since. Barely spoken at all actually.'

Ben's jaw drops open theatrically, his wrist bent in protest against his chest. 'Are you joking? You think Oscar's been quiet lately because of me?'

'Oh, don't look so surprised. You broke his spirit and then you have the gall to criticise me.'

'Broke his spirit?' He steps towards me, his words so steeped in contempt, I can hardly make them out. 'You are actually unbelievable, do you know that? Yes, I got stressed and took it out on him but I apologised straight afterwards so don't worry about my relationship with him. Worry about your own. '

'Don't try and turn this around. Oscar and I are fine.'

'Really? Oscar's fine, is he? His usual cheerful, happy-go-lucky self?'

'Well, he…'

'He – he's what? Having a hard time at school. Been bullied ever since he gave that performance? Needs a mother who isn't drunk half the time.'

'What? He – I – I'm not and he's not being bullied.' *Is he?* 'He'd have said something.'

'He has said something, you just don't listen anymore. You're so full of hate and resentment. And booze. Look at you. You're tanked up already. I can smell the alcohol on your breath from here.'

'Oh, for God's sake. It's six o'clock. I'm a grown up. I'm allowed a drink once in a while to help me cope with the shit I have to put up with looking after your nephew.'

He throws his hands up in the air. 'Of course! It's Zac's fault. Of course it is. Nothing to do with the Chardonnay bottles spilling out of the recycling bin.'

'I don't drink Chardonnay.' As far as comebacks go, that isn't my finest.

Ben shakes his head, his eyes narrowing with disgust. 'Oh, it can't be that then! It really must be down to how focused you are on Zac. On complaining about Zac, I should say.'

I've never seen him so angry. His lips curl and his eyes flash.

'Well, I get it. I get it. You hate him. You've sacrificed everything all over again to bring him up. It's all you. It's all about you. And Jacob of course. God forbid anyone love him as much as you do.' He hones in on me. 'Well, you've got another son, one who needs you and it's time to get your head out of your arse and be his mother because you're not the only one who's suffering here. We've all got our shit to deal with but he shouldn't have to deal with his alone.'

Time stands still and he stares at me shaking as I stare back stunned and then slip past him without a word. I head straight into the bathroom, lock the door behind me and crumple to the floor waiting for the tears to hit me but they don't. Instead waves of shame overwhelm me, wave after wave as the realisation of what I've missed winds me. The mood swings, the silence, the introspection. I've been selfish and self-obsessed while Oscar's been hurting.

The boys' bedroom door handle squeaks and the music gets louder before it's replaced by Ben's reassuring voice cajoling Zac into going downstairs to play a game, give Oscar some space. Footsteps drum down the stairs followed by a void in the commotion and I slowly raise myself from the floor. Lean back against the wall composing my thoughts and then turn the lock, my fingers stilted with numb exhaustion, my mind weighed down by guilt.

Oscar doesn't answer when I rap softly on the door and when I peer in and whisper his name he stiffens, refusing to look at me. I tread carefully across the carpet avoiding the scattered fragments of the Lego Ninjago dojo Zac worked so painstakingly on and ease myself down onto the bed next to Oscar.

'I'm sorry,' I say knowing it will never be enough. He doesn't answer. Instead he turns his head away.

'I'm sorry, Oscar. I overreacted back there. I shouldn't have got mad like that.'

'You're always mad.'

'No, I… that's not –'

He pulls away from me but I snatch his hand back. Rest it on his leg, resolutely massaging the tension out of his knuckles with my thumb. 'You're right. I've been very stressed about… stuff. It's nothing you've done and I shouldn't have taken it out on you. I really am very sorry.'

He looks down at our hands, loosely entwined on his lap. 'S'alright.'

'Daddy told me you've been getting bullied at school.'

He presses his lips together and when he finally speaks his voice is gruff as though he's on the brink of shattering into pieces. 'So you know then.'

'That you're having a hard time...?'

'That I'm gay.' He turns away again sharply, his muscles clenched as he goes to withdraw his hand, but I squeeze it tight.

'Oh, darling. I've always known you're gay.'

He freezes again, his breathing quick and shallow. I smile and rub back and forth between the thin bones on top of his hand.

'I tried to bring it up a few times but you never took the bait and I didn't want to force it, not if you weren't experiencing those sorts of feelings yet.'

He looks at me. Cautiously. Fleetingly.

'But we've always done our best to be inclusive when we talk about your future girlfriends or *boyfriends*, your *husband* or wife. We've always made it clear that being gay is completely fine, completely normal, so that when you started having feelings for... anyone, boy or girl, you'd know that there was nothing to worry about.'

He doesn't say anything but his body begins to relax.

'We just didn't want to put a label on you before you'd even had a chance to work it out for yourself, but there's absolutely

274

nothing wrong with anything you're feeling and it's nobody's business but your own.'

He turns to me at this point and makes eye contact for the first time. 'But they won't stop going on about it at school. Asking me all the time if I'm gay.'

'And what do you say?'

'Well, if it's my friends I say I don't know but if it's just some random I say no.'

'Okay, well, that's up to you, but you don't have anything to be ashamed of. You're only twelve though. I'll bet no one else is going about telling all and sundry who they fancy, if they even fancy anyone yet. You're still very young to be thinking about that, unless... Is there anyone in particular...that you like? Has there ever been?'

'No. no. There isn't any*one*. I just always knew. I don't know how. I just knew I preferred boys.' He pauses and gives me a slow sideways glance. 'How did you know I was gay?'

I can't help but crease up. 'Oh, Oscar. I'm sorry to say it, but you are the archetypal stereotype of a gay man. It's like you were made for a sitcom and some lazy scriptwriter threw every so-called gay trait at you so there'd be no ambiguity – *No backstory. Just make him sing musicals and raid his mum's make-up drawer every episode.*

'Not that that's always a sign. You do get some camp straight men and I'm sure there are loads of boys up and down the country who've put Arianna Grande perfume at the top of

275

their Christmas list, but you're hardly in the closet.' I nudge him playfully and a tepid smile breaks through his clouded face.

'I mean we've had to keep an open mind in case we were wrong, but my God, what a waste of glitter that would have been. Imagine if you'd had to come out as straight. We'd have been so disappointed.'

He laughs.

'Look, I'm not going to pretend it's always going to be easy. Some people are going to give you a hard time, but who cares what they think because they're dicks. If you get picked on for being different to some small-minded, ignorant bully, thank heavens for that. They're only targeting you because you're not like them. I'd disown you if you were.'

He shrugs and shakes his head, stammering all at the same time. 'I don't want them to like me or anything. I just want them to stop going on about it.'

'I know, darling.' I fold my arm around him now and he moulds into my side, his head resting under my chin as I cling on to the last traces of my little boy before he becomes a man. As I steel him against the pain and confusion that is his now that he's leaving his childhood behind. 'Have you spoken to anyone else about it?'

'Just Jake ages ago when this all started happening. Back when I first joined Deer Hill.'

'And what did he say?'

'To ignore them because they're dickheads.'

'There you go. See.'

'I just wish they'd leave me alone though. They won't let it go.'

'I'm sorry, darling. I haven't been there for you. I've been so caught up in my own stuff –'

'And with Zac and Jacob.'

'You're right. There's no excuse for it. But I need you to know that you are perfect. You are funny and confident, absolutely gorgeous and I'm not just saying that because I'm your mother.'

He blushes and looks down at our interlaced hands with a smirk.

'Everybody knows it. You're in all the top sets, you work hard, you've got a great set of friends, a family who loves and supports you. There's absolutely nothing I would change about you. Except for your horrible lack of hygiene and general untidiness. I mean, for goodness sake. Every gay man I've ever met has been immaculate so if you're going to conform so spectacularly to type, that's something you need to work on.'

He giggles but I can't shake the guilt I feel for not realising there was something up with him earlier. I've been so wrapped up in myself lately I haven't noticed the change in him. I let the ball drop when I should have been providing him with positive role models to aspire to. People to talk to like the gay dads we used to hang out with when we lived in London. And the lesbian couple. There was a wider mix of people there, more diversity, less 2.4 kids conformity.

It was inevitable that we'd see less of them when we moved out, but Elena would still invite them over when we popped around. It wasn't Oscar's fault that after the accident there were too many memories. That it hurt too much to be around them and so I hadn't been in touch. It simply wasn't good enough.

'Listen, you don't need to 'confess' anything to anyone until you're ready – just know that both Daddy and I know exactly who you are and we love and support you. We always have and we always will.'

He leans against me and I hold him as tightly as I've ever held anything in my life, my arms aching at the thought of letting go. My baby. Facing the unknown. He was so brave. I'd always taken it for granted that he knew he was perfect and that everything he felt was completely normal. Nothing to worry about but he was going to go through things I would never really be able to understand and all I could do was be there for him. Be his mother and keep him safe. Because that's what mothers do. They keep their babies safe. And with that, I don't know why but an image of his bicycle linked to mine flashes through my head.

"Oh, shit. The couscous!'

Nineteen

Right. It's eleven thirty. The potatoes are parboiled, the parsnips and purple carrots are peeled and glazed in honey with a sprinkling of rosemary ready to be popped in the oven in forty-five minutes. The chicken is already infusing gently with the lemon and garlic I stuck up its backside earlier and it should be ready in time for Ben's parents to turn up at midday, have their usual cup of tea and moan about the traffic, say something inane about the food smelling good, offer up an empty threat to help they know will be turned down and be sitting at the table by one. Again.

We've seen more of them this year than in the rest of our marriage put together. It's like they think they can fill the Elena-shaped hole in our lives with themselves when if they really wanted to help they could take Zac away for the weekend, or, I don't know, hire a caravan in the holidays, book a trip to Spain.

Hell, it's not like they live in the middle of nowhere. They could take him back to their house, it would still be something different for him to do. An escape to the coast. Call me crazy, but they could let the other two join them as well if they really wanted to do something nice, but no, they'd rather come up to us every other weekend so they can feel like they're making an effort while actually not putting any effort in at all. The sooner this is all over the better.

I was telling Lenny only yesterday, I can't do this for very much longer. It's not just the deceit. It's spinning my marriage out when I know it's going to end soon. I'm not sure what I'm waiting for. The kids will come with me, at least half of the time anyway. And Beasley and Sharon, although I haven't mentioned that to Lenny yet. I guess it depends on how big his place is. It'll take a while before Ben and I can sell this house and split the equity so I might have to play it by ear. Find a way to visit Lenny, weigh up the situation. It's just a pain he lives a drive away. I don't really want to get him to pick me up and chauffer me about. He thinks I'm stronger and more independent than that. I am more independent than that, I just can't get an Uber without it showing up on the credit card, I can't get any cash without asking Ben for it and Lenny's flat is nowhere near any bus routes.

I could drive myself of course, but then again, it's still relatively early days. I probably shouldn't freak him out by moving too fast. We haven't even had sex yet. There's a high chance he'll take one look at this body and run for the hills anyway no matter what he says about curves being sexy.

'Oh, I nearly forgot the gravy.'

Onions, oil, stock, corn flour, bay leaf, sugar, red wine. One for me, one for the pot. One for me again. It is nearly lunchtime and I am cooking after all, only now I'll bet my teeth have gone black. What do they say about getting rid of red wine stains? White wine. That's better.

'What do you think, Sharon? Nope, you won't like it, I promise you. Take your paw out. Oh, Sharon. What are you going to make of all of this, I wonder?'

I hope he's got a garden. I should probably find out. Don't want to look like I'm probing too much, although of course I need to probe. I've got to know what I'm getting myself into. It's not like I can wing it. I'm not twenty-one anymore, fresh out of university, content to put up with any old mould infested rat hole as long as I can call it my own. Even with Lenny there, that might be a push. With an extra five of us, not counting Zac, it'll be more than a push. It'll be a squeeze too.

I almost cackle at my own whimsy but it's no laughing matter. Maybe we could rent something in the short term. Let his out and get something bigger for ourselves. Use the money I make from this place as a deposit on a three-bed semi when the sale goes through. A three-bed would do. That's one room each for the boys. For my boys.

Lenny made a joke about the DNA test again so I know that Zac living with us is also on his mind. And the truth is, I have thought about it. I've done the research and I know exactly which company I'd use – one that's not so cheap they barely give you any information nor one that practically promises to trace back to the colour of the sheets your great-great-grandmother gave birth on – for a price.

This one is mid-range and offers the usual genetic breakdown but more importantly they put you in touch with any relations who have also taken the test. I mean it's a stab in the dark, but all I need is one close contact out of all the thousands of people who've been using these services. One close contact who can potentially point me in the right direction towards a man, probably in his forties now, likely to be living or who used to live in London, no doubt fairly good looking (knowing Elena, but then she was quite possibly drunk on the night in question and her tastes did veer towards the eclectic at the best of times). Better leave that one for now.

But then again, I've got the same issue with the credit card. I can't use it without Ben getting pinged a huge glaring notification of my betrayal – and he would see it as a betrayal, even if in the long run it would be nice for Zac to know who his father is, to form a relationship with him. I'm not suggesting they'd move in together straight away. I'm not naive and truth be told, he hasn't actually done anything too outrageously offensive lately. If he wasn't there all the time getting under my feet, asking questions, followed by follow up questions it would almost be tolerable. But he is always there. Making too much noise, too much mess. Making me think about him when I should be thinking about me. I deserve to be able to think about me. I refuse to feel guilty about that. I've put my time in. It's someone else's turn now. Like his father's. Or his grandparents'. *Now that's an idea.*

'Good grief. I've run out of wine again. I'd better not have more than one glass before everyone gets here. One more glass after this, I mean.'

I took a bottle of Pinot to the park a couple of nights ago. That was fun, getting drunk under the stars. We felt like a couple of teenagers. It's a good job no one could see us giggling away in the dark, Beasley and Coco sitting intertwined at our feet. Not in an affectionate way, I should probably note. Coco wouldn't stop running around in circles until she'd tangled herself so tightly to Beasley they were forced to lie down next to each other and be quiet. I did wonder at one point if they were both asphyxiated but I think in retrospect they were trying to conserve their heat. That is the one downside of these clandestine outdoor hook ups. They might be hopelessly romantic and as sexy as hell but sweet Jesus, it gets cold as soon as the sun goes down. That's why I brought the wine last time but a hot toddy would have made it more bearable.

I swear to God, there is no one else on earth I would happily hang out in those sorts of temperatures for. Certainly not the kids, although I have hung out plenty in that playground with them in all sorts of weather but until now, happily was not an adjective I could have associated with it.

Even so, it would be nice to find somewhere with a fireplace and a bar where we could go without drawing attention to ourselves, but who am I kidding? This is Kingston. Ben would hear what I was up to before I even got a round in. Before Lenny got a round in, that is. I wouldn't be able to use the bloody credit card, would I? What I should have been doing all these years is syphoning off my loose change and putting it aside. All those five and ten ps, the occasional pound coin. I could have had a small nest egg by now, although knowing Zac he'd have found it and made it all disappear.

What I need is an excuse to have a night away. 'A weekend with the girls', not that there are any girls any more. I can't remember when I last saw anyone from the old crowd. It was after the funeral that was for sure. After Zac came to live here and suddenly all I ever got were excuses not to come over, not to meet up, not to put anyone in the awkward position of having to chose between dealing with death or endlessly skirting around the issue. Was it the excuses or the overly sincere concern when it did come that was most upsetting? I can't remember to be honest. It's all a bit of a blur that period of my life.

Ultimately, the accident finished what lockdown had started. The spiralling demise of friendships that were built on circumstance and the fact that our children went to the same school. It was all superficial and transient in the end. A lesson not to bother going down that route again.

'This gravy tastes rubbish.'

It needs more sugar or something. Or maybe I've got Covid. Isn't that one of the symptoms, losing your sense of taste or is it smell? I should probably do a test. Actually, I should definitely do a test. Even Ben's parents wouldn't come if I actually had it, would they? For all their talk about herd immunity and booster jabs, it would be reckless, not to mention I'm only halfway through lunch and there's no way Ben will be able to work out how to shove the veg in the oven or baste the chicken again in an hour. Even if they escape the virus, there's a high chance they'll end up with salmonella. This could be just what I need.

God, is it supposed to be this painful? Five times round each nostril, then stick it in here for…thirty seconds. Ohh, my eyes are still watering.

'Don't look at me like that, Sharon. It's not like I want to do it. No, it's not food. Get back.'

Should I feel this excited? I don't feel any worse than usual. My head hurts and I'm a shade woozy, but that could be lack of sleep. Oh, damn it. What's it mean when there's only one line on the C? For God's sake. What do I have to do? Go out and lick lampposts? I thought I was going to be able to go back to bed then. Well, the study.

Talking of which, where is Ben? And why am I the one cooking and cleaning when it's his parents who are about to land on us?

'Oh no, the bathrooms.'

I haven't done them for a few days and Sylvia always makes a point of using all of them while she's here. What on earth is that about? Ours is still okay but the boys' one is already a crime scene. There's nothing less rewarding than polishing that thing until it gleams only for them to immediately wee everywhere but inside the bowl. Someone had literally sprayed the whole wall up to shoulder height this morning. Shoulder height! How is that physically possible? What are they doing? For my own peace of mind, I've got to assume it's incidental rather than deliberate, although I wouldn't put anything past Zac.

I'd better put the parsnips and carrots in now and go and wipe it down before I forget or Sylvia will take it as an open invitation to comment on how busy I must be. In they go.

'Make sure I remember to take them out five minutes early though, Sharon.' Wait. Is it forty-five minutes they need or twenty-five? My mind's gone completely blank. 'Don't sniff the spuds, Sharon. The spuds! It's the potatoes that need to go in now. Well done, love. That could have been a disaster. No, you're not getting any treats. Those big eyes won't help you. Save them for your dad. You're getting too chubby. I don't know who's worse, you or Beasley.'

Beasley lifts his head optimistically. I knew he was only pretending to ignore me. The toilets!

'Stop distracting me, you two. What was that?'

Oh, Ben's back. With the boys. I didn't realise they'd all gone out. And look at the state of them. There can't be any mud left in Richmond Park, assuming that's where they've been. Oscar's entire back is covered and Zac appears to have taken a roll in a puddle.

Thanks a lot, Ben. I'll add that to my list. I'm never going to get a chance to do the loos now.

'We're back!' Oscar beams straggling filthy footprints into the house.

'Shoes!'

'We went all the way past Isabella Plantation to Pen Ponds and then up to Sheen Gate.'

'Take your clothes off in the utility room, please. Leave them in the laundry basket.'

'And we bumped into Melissa.'

'Zac. Zac. Don't come out here until you've taken your tracksuit bottoms off. They're caked in mud.'

'That's not mud.'

Oh. How does he still have the capacity to disgust me? You would think I'd be used to it by now. 'Put them straight into the machine then.' I'm not touching that. "What was it? Deer, fox, dog, rabbit?'

'I dunno. It was brown.'

'I can see it's brown. Oh, for goodness sake. Just leave it there. I might have to give it a soak first.' There's no point putting a wash on right now. Jacob's due home from his trip in a few hours and I expect he'll turn up looking just as crusty as this lot only he'll have a whole week's worth of dirt with him too.

'Did you hear me? I said I saw Melissa.'

'Yes, I heard you. That's nice.'

'Can I meet up with her this afternoon?'

'No. Nanna and Grandpa are coming.'

'Not again.' His whole body goes limp with disappointment. "Why do they have to come here all the time?'

'Shhh. Your dad's coming.'

He groans and rolls his eyes, his shoulders slumped practically all the way down to his elbows.

287

'How are you getting on, Zac?'

'Good.'

'Come on out then. Wait, you're getting mud everywhere. Where's it coming from. Oh God, your hair. Go and get in the shower.'

'I'm having a shower first!'

'One of you go and have a bloody shower then! Your grandparents are due any minute.'

Ben peers into the kitchen with the kind of expression he normally uses on traffic wardens and people who don't clean up after their dogs.

'All okay?'

'It was before you lot dragged half the park in here.'

'Sorry. Just trying to give you a break from the kids. Should have realised it would only piss you off somehow.'

'Well,' I bustle self-righteously. 'I might have enjoyed it if you'd told me. I didn't realise they were gone.'

'No.' He glances towards my wine glass and slowly pulls off his cycling gear. 'Just leave this. I'll wash all our stuff later.'

As if. Oh, for pity's sake. There's the door.

'I'll get it,' Ben says without a trace of emotion and I brace myself for the ensuing round of effusive hugging and exuberant exclamations that would seem less out of place had we all been shipwrecked on different islands for years.

'Something smells good in here,' Sylvia cries, striding into the kitchen. *Tick.* She's already swapped her shoes for the slippers she leaves in the cupboard by the front door.

Make yourself at home.

'Sorry we're late. Traffic was bad.' *Tick.* Martin doesn't leave his slippers here. He has a pair of giant crocs that look like hacked up strips of car tyres instead. 'Is that chicken in there? Thank god. I thought you were going to do nut roast or something awful. Bad enough Elena was a bloody carrot-cruncher without you getting in on the act.'

'Oh, Martin. Come here, Lara. We both did a test before we came up. It's safe to give us a hug.'

It may be safe. I just don't want to. And I can't make any dubious claims about my own health with my negative test result screaming at them from the worktop. Why didn't I throw it away? Sylvia takes me into her arms and squeezes me too tightly and for too long.

'We've done one too, Mum. All clear.'

Obviously, Ben.

My mother-in-law pulls away with a tweak to my cheek that feels more determined than affectionate and I'm almost certain leaves a mark. Then she leverages a bag-for-life between Sharon and the chopping board, methodically piling packets of Jaffa cakes and readymade apple crumble onto the cooling rack I'm going to need to rest the roasting tin on when it comes out of the oven, spitting oil and buckling dangerously.

'Oh, you shouldn't have,' I say, equally methodically unpicking her pile and creating another on the breakfast bar where there's less chance of it injuring me. Sharon wastes no time getting in the bag and then together they are whisked out to the hall.

'I know how those boys love their treats,' Sylvia grins returning empty-handed. 'Now, what can I do?' *Tick.*

'Nothing at all.' *Except get out of the way.*

'Well, if you're sure. I must pop to the loo.' *You do that. Be sure to grab a hazmat suit on your way up.*

There's a good fifteen minutes between Ben going up to change and the boys coming back down when I'm stuck on my own with my in-laws and I not only get to finish off lunch but also make two cups of tea – twice – because they only had one this morning in anticipation of a long drive. And it was a good job they restrained themselves or they'd have struggled to get through those road works. When are they going to finish anyway? It does seem like they've been at it for years which is hardly surprising given you never see anyone actually working on those damn things.

So not only did the fifty-mile an hour restriction hold them up but it was also inadvertently responsible for me forgetting to take the root veg out in time. The purple carrots were already deceptively dark but there is no disguising the smoke billowing out of the oven or the twig-like texture of the cinder blocks fused to the tin. Still, it's nothing a little gravy won't be able to fix even if Beasley is turning his nose up at them and he's partial to eating his own poop. I take out a few more wine glasses and fill them. As long as everyone catches up with me, no one will even notice.

'Lunch is ready!' I bellow up the stairs, frightening poor Sharon who is still curled up next to an old receipt and Martin's heartburn medication.

It's a good job you brought that today.

'Euwww,' Zac cries as he bundles over to the table, his fingers pinched around his nostrils, the other arm chopping through the smoky air. At least everyone else has the manners just to blink furiously as they take their seats.

'It's not that bad,' I bristle, smothering his plate with gravy.

'Ughhh.'

'Zac,' Ben chides. 'That's no way to talk about food. Especially not when someone's gone to the trouble of making it for you.' That's me. I'm the someone.

'It tastes disgusting.'

'Don't talk about Mummy's cooking like that,' Oscar joins in delightedly, taking a mouthful. 'Urghhh.'

'Boys!'

It is disgusting. I've used salt instead of sugar in the gravy. A tablespoon of it, plus the teaspoon the recipe called for. It tastes like the sludge that gets between your toes at the bottom of the ocean (*Zac's use of similes has really improved this year, thanks Lenny*) and it's fortunate that Ben is on hand to scrape it off our plates and boil up some Bisto, earning him shared credit for the rest of the meal.

I open another bottle of wine to settle my nerves before I say something I might regret. I need to eat something soon. I'm shaking so much I'm struggling to pour it into the glass.

'And how are things going with the business then, Lara?' Sylvia asks, her eyebrows poised in interest, her fork poised more warily over the roast.

'Oh, quite well, Sylvia, thank you. Some weeks are busier than others but I've been easing myself into it gently, getting my head around it all. You know,' I giggle. I don't know why I giggle. 'It's not easy while the kids are still little but still, if I can build a reputation now, by the time they leave home in another fifteen years, I might actually be able to make a go of it.' *Or by the time I leave which will hopefully be quite soon.*

'So you're still getting orders then...' She tapers off as though privately debating whether to press this course of conversation. As though she's already had it before but not with me.

'Slowly, but surely. It's hard to fit everything in what with having so much to deal with –' I glance at Zac and mutter into my glass '– pretty much by myself.'

'There are some other issues,' Ben says in an undertone that makes me want to take another swig of wine and put it down at the same time. I catch the tail end of a look pass between my in-laws and feel the colour rise instantly on my face.

'Well, it's not like I've been marketing it at all. Everything I've done has been through word of mouth, which is about all I can take on right now. Once Zac's a bit older –'

'Ben said something about the cat's hair getting in the food.'

One complaint. There was one complaint about Sharon and that was Arabella who wouldn't have said anything at all if I

292

hadn't shown her up in front of her husband, as if he wouldn't have realised she didn't cook that damn meal. What did she think was going to happen the next day when she served him up an M&S meal for two in a microwave dish? She couldn't even make her own couscous.

'I'm not sure that –'

'I have noticed that myself,' observes Martin, the downward turn of his mouth suggesting he isn't Shazza's biggest fan.

'It's because she licks the food out of the saucepan,' Zac pipes up, inviting a round of horrified gasps and overreactions. Oscar makes the most of the opportunity to dig him with his elbow but again, I'd like to point out that was one time. That I know of.

What is wrong with these people? The only reason she's up on the worktops at all is to avoid Beasley, who, let's face it, shouldn't even be here. You'd think someone would be grateful, but no. All anyone can do is complain about the shoddy standard of their free meals. The ones I spend hours slaving over while they sit around drinking tea and boring us all with stories about strangers no one's ever heard of.

'That's not quite –'

'I think the main thing to remember,' Ben interjects hastily to move the subject along. 'Is that even though the timing and conditions aren't perfect, Mummy – Aunty Lara – is having a go at something a lot of people would be too scared to even try. I hope you learn a thing or two from her, boys. Never let anything stand in the way of doing something that you want.'

I do take a drink now. My hands are trembling and the glass tips unsteadily as I clip it on the side of my plate. I can't meet anyone's eyes but Sylvia is nodding and Martin looks bored rather than disgusted. The heat on my cheeks is still creeping up from my neck. I need to get out of this jumper. I need to get away from this man. From the constant fluctuations of love and hate that rise like bile in my throat whenever I'm with him, complicating everything, tarnishing the simplicity of my plan to move on, to make a new life with someone who wants to know me for who I am now, not who I once was.

To think I won't have to sit here with these people for too much longer. How many more meals will I have to endure? How many more tedious discussions? I feel a buzz of excitement at the thought of never having to see them again. Of breaking this endless cycle of monotony.

'I was never any good at anything,' Sylvia says.

Well, that's honest.

'Not like your Mummy – Aunty Lara.'

Okay. No need to make me feel bad for the honest comment.

'Oh, I don't know, love,' Martin bellows, stabbing a shard of parsnip towards her. 'Think even you could give Lara a run for her money with these. Only joking, Lara. I'm used to my food being chargrilled to a crisp, isn't that right, Sylvia?'

I am not going to miss you.

'Oh, Martin.' Sylvia shakes her head and then shakes it more emphatically covering her glass as I go to refill it.

Oh well. More for me.

294

'You know what you'd be good at, Zacster,' Ben says. 'Putting out fires. All that sliding down poles and climbing ladders. That wouldn't be bad, hey? Getting paid for doing what you love best.'

Zac seizes an imaginary hose and shoots us down with it. I hope to God there's some training involved if he does decide to go ahead with it as a career.

'What *do* you want to be when you grow up, Zaccy?' Sylvia asks.

'Oscar.'

'You want to be Oscar?' Ben's dad laughs at his own joke. He's certainly on form today.

'Yes.'

'Why?' Bemusement takes over Martin's face, the complaints about the substandard cooking temporarily postponed in favour of sneering at my child.

'Because he's good at singing and dancing and he's going to teach me.'

'I am not,' Oscar protests, upsetting his glass.

'Oscar. Be nice. Your cousin's giving you a compliment,' Sylvia murmurs indulgently, her eyes half-moons of pride. 'What do you say?'

Oscar stares at the puddle of water trimming his plate begrudgingly and mumbles 'Thanks.'

'And I'm going to be famous too and get rich and buy a big house with two swimming pools – one inside and one outside and a rollercoaster.'

'You only want to be famous because I'm going to be.'

Ben chuckles. 'You're going to have to do more than sing in the shower then, mate. We can't have people queuing up for concerts outside the bathroom.'

'He doesn't only sing in the shower,' Zac butts in outraged at the suggestion and he's quite right. Oscar's back to singing everywhere and he still has no volume control. 'He's got a really good voice. He can sing anything. He won the Models'

'MODHOs.'

'He's getting a bit old for all of that, isn't he?' Martin scoffs pointing a cauliflower cheese floret at Oscar for emphasis. (Cooked to perfection, but will anyone remember that? Of course not, after Ben came blazing to the rescue with his pot of Bisto.) 'People are going to start getting ideas about you, son.'

I'm on the verge of blazing to the rescue with the Bisto myself (by pouring it down Martin's midriff) when Oscar replies, his voice calm, his head high – 'Then they'd be right, Grandpa.'

There's no time to get the camera out to capture the look on Martin's face but it's both puce and grey like he's been holding his breath all his life.

'Goodness,' Sylvia says. 'Are we talking about...? You're a bit young to be making decisions like that, aren't you, Oscar?'

'It's not a decision.' I say, somehow, even though my jaw is clenched. 'It's not a choice and it's not a stage.'

'Oh no, of course not. I just mean –'

'I blame the schools.' Martin states as though we're discussing low literacy rates. 'We didn't have gays when I was young. No one ever even thought about it.'

'I'm sure there probably were gay people, Dad. They just might not have mentioned it for fear of being prosecuted at the time.'

'Nonsense. It's the education system and the media that's caused this. Gay this, gay that. It's everywhere you look. Making kids think it's normal –'

'It is normal,' I snarl. Oscar's back is as straight as a rod but his shoulders are wilting.

'Let's change the subject,' Sylvia simpers.

'What subject?' Zac says.

'The subject of me being gay,' Oscar announces, the trace of a tremor in his otherwise defiant voice.

'It's the fashion these days, Zac,' Martin jeers. 'All the kids are doing it.'

'Martin. Not at the table.'

'Well, that's what it is, isn't it? This season's latest fad and we're all supposed to think it's bloody marvellous.'

'Oscar having the confidence to be true to himself is bloody marvellous,' I retort. 'He's perfect and we wouldn't change a thing about him. What does it matter who he loves, as long as he's happy?' My eyes are burning into my father-in-law but he juts his chin out and stands his ground.

'Take a walk through Ham Woods at night, Lara and tell me if what they're doing in there is love.'

'That's enough, Dad.' The tension in the room is audible. For a moment, no one speaks and then Zac shoves a roast potato in his mouth and decides to show us what it looks like half-chewed.

'My teacher says the colours of a rainbow are different types of love and the more colours a rainbow has, the more beautiful it is.'

'I hope that's not your science teacher, Zac.'

'And also you can't see a rainbow if you don't open your eyes and that's a shame because you'd be missing out on something good. Look.' He screws his whole face up. 'See. It's all dark. There's no Oscar anymore.'

'Thank you, Zaccy,' Ben says evenly. 'That's a nice way of looking at it.'

'Politically correct new age mumbo jumbo is what it is.'

'Oh shut up, Martin.' Sylvia cries. 'He's here and he's queer. Get used to it. He. Is. Here.'

The table falls silent again and Martin's mouth droops, his fork suspended mid-jab and in the second or two that passes, the universe shifts.

'You're right, Sylvia. He is here. You are here, Oscar and that's all that matters. We still have you and there's nothing in the world we would ever change about you.

'There,' Sylvia says definitively. 'That just leaves us to decide who's having ice cream or custard with their apple pie.'

Zac cries 'I'm having both' and for once, I don't mind if he does.

'Shh, everyone.' Oscar cries excitedly, recovered now, his eyes full of expectant awe.

Sharon has crept back into the kitchen to comfort whoever is on the receiving end of this latest conflict, but instead of seeking out Oscar she's made her way over to Beasley and is covertly sniffing his nose while he sleeps. It's the closest she's ever gotten to him and the delighted ensemble falls into a state of trancelike wonder, mouths gaping, splayed fingers frozen in glee, waiting to see what will happen next. All except for me. I have my hand on my chest and a lone tear sliding down my cheek because Sharon's not the only one who's realised Beasley's not going to wake up. Not this time.

Twenty

It's strange going out for a walk without stopping to sniff every tree, pick up every stick. It's even stranger not having anyone to talk to but I needn't worry. Kay catches me on my way back home across the park, the facemask I've kept on as a barrier clearly limited in its power to repel. I ping the elastic off my ear, shove the mask in my pocket. Settle into character.

'No dog today,' she beams happily.

'No, he died yesterday.'

'Oh.'

This poor woman. I honestly don't know why she talks to me.

'So sorry about that.'

'It's okay. He was old.'

She bears down on her bottom lip sympathetically, her eyebrows burrowing towards each other. 'Still though. So sad.'

'Yup. It was sudden so that's one thing. No long drawn out illness or operations. Saved us a fortune.'

'Ahhh. Good.' I don't know what the etiquette is in Japan when discussing bereavement but I suspect it's to move the subject along quickly in much the same way as over here but I plough on regardless. Can't seem to stop myself.

'The worst thing was working out what to do with the body. I mean, at least if he'd been put down, the vets would've sorted it out for us.'

'Ahh.' Her eyes are wider than they were a few moments ago and she seems to be in more of a hurry.

'But when it happens at home, you're like – eek. What do we do now? It's not like a gold fish. You can't just flush him down the drain or make use of the self-cleaning function on the oven – you know, the one that burns everything to ashes. Not when there's still an apple pie that needs heating up for dessert.'

'No.' You never do hear about that famous Japanese dry wit, do you?

'I'm just kidding. He was too big for it anyway. I did check.'

'So...' Kay seems to sense she's supposed to be involved in this conversation. 'What did you do?'

'Buried him in the end. In a blanket. Couldn't find an Amazon box big enough and now I'm wishing we'd used a different one because it went really nicely with the curtains in the sitting room.' I really should stop drinking before midday.

'Ahhhh.'

'Thought about taking him to Ham Woods but the last thing you'd want is for a fox to dig him up and drag him out onto the street. Imagine finding that spread across your driveway. It's bad enough they go through the food compost bin. Besides we figured there's probably some ancient bylaw decreeing burying him on public land is treason against the crown. Knowing our luck we'd get slapped with a fine of thirty sheep or something.'

302

'Ahh.'

It must feel like it's taking her longer to get home today for some reason.

'We tucked him in the back garden in the end, by the hydrangea bush, which is poisonous to dogs but I don't suppose it matters now. I mean, there's still the issue with the foxes, of course...'

'Yes.' Kay looks like she's discovered an unexploded World War II grenade in her grandad's garage. People always get so awkward talking about death.

I glance down at my feet and then instinctively across the grass with a sudden jolt of anxiety before remembering Beasley's not there and a sob that I disguise as a cough erupts out of me.

It was awful, just awful taking in the sight of him lying there yesterday, still and lifeless, Sharon kneading her paw on his leg, trying to nudge him awake. The moment of eager anticipation that turned like milk left in the sun as the sinking realisation dawned one by one around the room.

Ben bolted into action, directing his mum to get the kids upstairs but she and Martin were rooted to their chairs, the buzzing in their ears almost audible. And I – I don't know what I did but all of a sudden Oscar was bustling Zac past me, around the table, taking him up to their room, his voice sweet and calm, the picture of control, Zac's own face incomprehensible.

Sylvia rose a few inches before her legs buckled beneath her and she collapsed back down heavily into Martin who put his

303

arm around her, resting her head against his shoulder, the light drained from his eyes.

'Lara.' Ben barked as though he'd been calling me for some time and I found myself rocking on the balls of my feet, jumping up and heading towards him, my arms already reaching to pick Beasley up, will the life back into him, keep him warm. Sharon mewed around us, tangling herself among our legs as we stroked his soft back, kissed his sweet head for the last time and covered him with his blanket.

'What do we do?' Ben murmured, looking at me for the first time in weeks.

'I don't know,' I whispered, my voice breaking, eyes filling with tears. 'Call the vet, I suppose. I don't know.'

The vet said we could take him in to be cremated for £125, which seemed like good value, but when we went to say goodbye, we found we couldn't. It was too clinical, handing him over to a stranger. Imagining him all alone.

'Let's bury him here,' I said, the urge to protect him, to keep him near still governing me and Ben nodded slowly turning to his mum and dad.

'You okay?' he asked and they both nodded grimly.

'Sorry, love –'

'It's okay.'

'I'll be glad when this year is over.' Sylvia's voice was craggy, her mouth quivering on the verge of a breath that would sound inhuman when she finally took it. Martin squeezed her shoulder and began to rise out of his chair.

'Let me give you a hand.'

'It's alright, Dad. You look after Mum. Lara and I can see to this.'

Beasley's blanket was too small to wrap him in and I glided mechanically to the sitting room, stripping a fleece off the sofa and returning with it clutched to my chest as if to keep the pain from spilling out of me, contain the horrible, dull, stabbing ache.

'No, really,' Martin said, extracting himself from Sylvia's grip. 'This is too much to ask of you, Lara. If you could stay here and look after Sylvia, Ben and I will call you over when it's time.'

I handed the blanket over soundlessly, relief trickling through me as he and Ben pulled their coats on and headed outside to the shed. Sylvia and I watched in silence as they took turns smashing the shovel into the solid, resistant ground. Father and son, stood together, staring into a hole once again. I was sober by then, far too sober for that and I reached for the wine to top up my glass.

'Go on then,' Sylvia said. 'I'll have one of those. Actually, have you got anything stronger?'

My default response was denial, but one look at my mother-in-law's face made me get up and walk to the laundry basket, rummage through the dirty washing and reappear brandishing what was left of a litre of vodka.

'Don't want Zac getting hold of it,' I said and her focus faded away like she wasn't particularly interested one way or another.

'I know he was just a dog –'

'He was never just a dog, Sylvia,' I said and we sat in silence again, the food abandoned on our plates congealing, until Ben and Martin trudged back into the house. Zac and Oscar came down and said their last goodbyes to Beasley but by then he was cold and stiff. An imposter we rigidly tiptoed around as Sharon, drawn to the drama once again, sniffed the crust of the overturned earth outside. And then we stood at his graveside and sobbed, every last one of us.

'I'm sorry for you,' Kay says, nodding sympathetically, her little crooked teeth almost too contrived to take seriously.

'Oh, don't be. He was just a dog. Not even my dog, come to that. It's for the best really. He was only going to become more of a nuisance the older he got.'

'Ahh, okay.' The sides of Kay's mouth rise dubiously into a hesitant smile that she's not fully ready to commit to.

'Anyway, enough about my crappy weekend. How was yours?' I say lightly, grinning back at her.

'Ahh, good. Paul is away on business again so it was quiet. He has lots of business trips these days but I get to spend more time with Theodore. It's nice sometimes when it's just us.'

Sounds like he's having an affair. Talking of which, it's going to be harder to get away and meet Lenny now without my furry alibi backing me up.

'That's nice.'

I can hardly bear to think of seeing Coco without Beasley. She isn't going to understand where he's gone. I haven't even told Lenny he's died yet. Didn't want to do it over text but I couldn't get out to see him last night.

'Yes, he is a little nervous at the moment about all the changes so it was good to spend time together. Make him feel better.'

'That's good.'

I could have probably come up with an excuse to get out but Jacob got back from his school trip in the late afternoon, tired, grubby and bearing a drenched, musty rucksack spilling over with putrid, damp clothes. I'll never know if I'd have got more out of him other than 'It was good' if he hadn't come home to find Beasley dead and already buried before he had a chance to say goodbye.

His face crumpled like a little child upon hearing the news, his high spirits instantly deflated but he understood we couldn't wait for him to get back. It was already dark and his grandparents' need for closure was greater than his own but even so, it was a shock. He was nothing more than a baby when Elena brought Beasley home from some dodgy breeder in Camden. I say breeder. He was her dealer too but Jacob being born had brought out a need in her for more than a gentle comedown after a night out. It wasn't quite like having a new-born, but it wasn't far off and the two of them basically grew up together. We all did. Kay is staring at me expectantly, her big brown eyes inquiring. 'Sorry. What are you asking me?'

'If you know Ms Collins, the new teacher.'

'Ms Collins.' Doesn't ring a bell, but then I don't remember anyone if they didn't teach Jacob or Oscar. I shake my head slowly, allowing the name to ruminate. 'Don't think so. Who is she?'

'Their new teacher.'

'Whose?'

Kay laughs gaily as though I'm winding her up. 'Zac and Theodore. It's all in the email. Oh, sorry. Maybe you didn't see because of... Ms Collins will be covering for Mr Matthews when his wife has the baby.'

The blood drains out of my face, my next step falls short. 'What do you mean? Mr Matthews isn't married or... or –'

'Partner, I mean. Girlfriend.'

'Who are you talking about? You can't mean Lenny.'

'Lenny? No. Mr Matthews. Zac's teacher.' Her smile is dissolving and there's a look in her eyes that suggests if she had a panic button she'd be edging towards it right now. 'He has two weeks of paternity leave, maybe more. Any time now. So I wonder if you know the lady replacing him. Theodore is worried about getting to know someone new. Are you okay?'

I can't breath. I am tearing through the emails on my phone looking for the one marked *for the attention of Gold Class Parents and Carers*. My thumb shakes as I press down, almost sending it to trash and as the writing appears on the screen I skim read it, too jittery to take it all in. The words *paternity leave – and his partner – capable hands – Mr Matthews – two weeks – Ms Collins* jump out of the page. My stomach clenches and a surge of vomit rises up my throat as if I've been punched, the bitter taste of bile lingering in my mouth after I've swallowed it back down. Kay stares at me, alarmed by my panicked expression, the ashen pallor I can feel mushrooming over me as my heart gallops, threatening to burst out of my chest.

'What is it?' she persists.

'I... I ...'

'Come sit down.'

She leads me to a bench, assimilating the weight my legs are too unstable to support. And then I tell her. Everything. Hysterical, irrepressible confessions pour out of me in ugly, agonising spasms and throughout it all she sits stock still, her hand suspended on my trembling thigh, her mouth agog, taking it in. Digesting the details. Absorbing our betrayal. His betrayal of me. My betrayal of everyone. And when it's over, when I'm spent, she guides me back to my house, steers me to the sofa and pours me a drink.

Twenty-One

'Get up. It's been two days.' Ben whisks the curtains open and daylight floods in, burning my eyes. 'Zac's headmistress wants to see us.'

'What?' I sit up, my eyelids scrunched tight, a streak of drool sliding back towards my ear.

'You need a shower.' Ben flings my covers aside and drapes them back across the sofa bed.

'What…what's going on?'

'We have to be at the school by 10.30.'

I press the heels of my hands into my eyeballs, grinding them back and forth, rubbing them into focus. 'Can't you go?'

'She wants to see both of us. Wouldn't say what it's about. We need to leave in twenty minutes.'

'Where's Zac?'

'For God's sake, Lara,' Ben shakes his head at me in disgust. 'Go and get ready, can you?'

He strides out of the study and stomps down the stairs with the words 'don't fall back to sleep' cutting through me and I peer bleary-eyed down at myself, my crumpled T-shirt and jeans. The one sock hanging halfway off my foot. It hurts to move. My head is pounding and my throat parched, my mouth a sewer that's run dry. Every part of me stings as I ease myself up, one palm seeking out my temple, the other reaching for the wall as I stumble towards the bathroom, haltingly at first, the churning in my stomach holding me back, then propelling me forwards to contain the vomit that spews out of me, over and over until there's nothing left. Just wrung out emotions and disbelief.

What day did he say it was?

I can remember coming home on Monday. Kay sitting me down, asking if I wanted tea. I didn't. She poured me a glass of wine when I asked her to. I told her to leave the bottle. She wanted to know if she should stay. I said no. Said I needed to be alone. She hesitated then, torn between looking after me and getting as far away as possible. In the end, she chose to leave like they always do.

I didn't know what to do with the information she'd given me, how to adjust to the new canvas of my life, peeling already and stained with deceit. I found myself laughing at the irony of my indignation, my outrage at Lenny's treachery.

Once a cheater, always a cheater only who was cheating on whom? The deception ran so deep I couldn't work out which parts of it I had a right to feel misled about. Which bits were real, which bits an illusion I'd willed into reality. Convinced myself were true, were more serious than he'd intended.

Was I a fling? Did I really misread what we had between us? How was our relationship everything I ever wanted and at the

same time a fabrication built on lies? Should I text my
congratulations?

I crunch over the sink, a wave of nausea flowing over me, but there's nothing left in my stomach. I am completely empty inside. I turn the shower on and step into it, allowing the water to pummel my scalp, clear my mind. I'm all out of tears.

Ben said it had been two days. I don't remember that. I remember picking Zac up from school, but I don't know how I managed to move my body back down the road, up to the school gates. How I locked eyes with Lenny outside the classroom as the kids filed out, his smile smugly content, no hint of remorse or shame clouding his expression. As far as the world was concerned he was just another happy expectant father fielding well wishes. Revelling in the attention. I barely recognised him and he made no attempt at acknowledging me. I didn't know that man at all and the blood in my veins ran cold.

There was no confrontation – not then. Maybe there had been later. I only remember walking home, Zac dragging his feet, ripping leaves off all the bushes lining the pavement, scattering them on the ground like a trail of breadcrumbs.

'Don't do that,' I said but he only pulled at them more.

I remember pouring myself a glass of water when we got home, my hands so shaky most of it spilled onto my chin. I was ravenous and violently nauseous at the same time, hollow but overflowing with fury. Too ready to snap at Zac when he interrupted the uncontrollable stream of accusations hurtling through my thoughts. Too wounded to tend to his wounds.

I remember going through the laundry basket, searching for the unopened bottle of vodka I'd hidden there, coming out and finding Zac had gouged a huge groove into the dining table with a knife. I remember Ben thundering downstairs as I was telling him off. He said I was over-reacting. I said I was reacting exactly the way that I should. Said Zac was a monster. A savage stray who spoilt everything. And then I don't remember anything after that.

By the time I get dressed and head downstairs, Ben is standing in the hallway, his shoes and coat on, his face obstinately dour. We set off in a sullen temper, each of us stewing in resentment towards the other, our voices clipped, our conversation stilted. An overriding sense of dread and inhibition taints what was once an insignificant route to an unexceptional destination.

When we arrive, I hover in the background and let Ben do the talking, sign us in, respond to the receptionist's judgemental scrutiny with a nod. She takes us through to the headteacher's office like disobedient schoolchildren and my discomfort turns to umbrage at the way we're being treated, at the lack of empathy for Zac. For what he's been through. Only I have earned the right to be cross with him and yes, he can be difficult and disruptive. Destructive even, but he is braver than anyone I've ever met. I hadn't even realised how settled he'd become until Beasley died, knocking him sideways, setting everything back.

How dare you look at us like we're bad people? We're all here clinging on by a thread. Doing our best. Trying to get through each day. Whatever he's done now, he's done with good reason.

She pushes the door inwards, holding it open with one arm and ushers us in. I resist the instinct to thank her and glare witheringly as I shuffle in behind Ben.

'Ahh, Mr and Mrs Harrison,' Mrs Wilson declares staidly, looking up briefly from her computer screen and for a moment I wonder if she's expecting me to curtsy.

A movement in the corner catches my eye and as I glance instinctively towards it, my heart stops. The strength dissipates from my legs.

'Take a seat, please.' She indicates towards the two chairs in front of us and the tension in the room is instantly magnified. Ben and I lower ourselves down obediently and Lenny makes his way across to the desk. He doesn't sit and he doesn't look directly at me. His mouth is drawn in a hard line, his nostrils flared and he's jangling the change in his trouser pockets in a failed attempt to disguise his nerves.

'I'm sorry to have to bring you in under these circumstances,' she continues without inviting us to take our coats off. Without a single word of greeting. 'But we take all allegations made against our staff very seriously.'

Ben's neck twitches from one direction to the other. 'I'm sorry, are we not here about something Zac's done?'

Mrs Wilson smiles at him brusquely, yet to meet my uncomprehending gaze. 'I'm afraid not, Mr Harrison. As you may or may not be aware, there is a rumour circulating regarding the nature of your wife's relationship with Mr Matthews.'

Ben freezes, his lips parted prematurely in defence of his nephew, now hanging open, his eyes unblinking. Lenny steals a glance at me, his grave face flushed, his dark pupils skittering between my husband and me.

'I don't...' Ben begins, the rest of the sentence failing to follow.

'If I am to understand correctly, the rumour in question was started by you, Mrs Harrison.'

I try to speak but the words are suspended in the vast cavern inside me, drowned out by the deafening heartbeat drumming in my ears, thundering as relentlessly as the squall of a storm.

'Now, obviously, I have spoken at length with Mr Matthews regarding the accusations laboured against him but it would be improper not to offer you the opportunity to present your own side of the story. If indeed, it is just a story.'

Why are you talking like a barrister on the telly? This whole situation is surreal. The room is starting to spin.

Ben leans forward and says, 'I think there's been some sort of misunderstanding' and Mrs Wilson replies, 'I certainly hope so, Mr Harrison. We do, however, have unequivocal first-hand parent testimony stating that Mrs Harrison has made certain claims about Mr Matthews, which are jeopardous to both his career and his personal life. So my question, Mrs Harrison, is are

316

you, or have you ever, engaged in a sexual relationship with any member of the Park View faculty.'

"No. I –' I gasp for air. *What is happening? What's going on? Why is everyone looking at me like this? Lenny, say something. Do something.*

Ben stiffens at her unflinching vulgarity and Lenny bows his head, his eyes downcast, refusing to meet my silent beseeching cries.

'Mrs Harrison.' The headteacher's thorny voice snaps through my confusion like an elastic band, stretched taut and released for maximum impact. 'Have you, in fact, had any contact with Mr Matthews beyond that of a professional nature besides a handful of incidences during which you apparently discussed alternative diets and... your pets?'

I still can't speak. I feel like I'm watching the whole scene play out from afar, witnessing somebody else's life unravel. She raises an eyebrow. Looks back towards her screen as though she needs prompting. As if the details aren't emblazoned into the forefront of her mind.

'There's been a suggestion that the two of you became close during dog walks...' Her voice rises as if she's asking a question rather than stating a fact.

'But I don't have a dog,' Lenny blurts out, interrupting her sanctimonious spiel. 'I've never had one.'

My eyes widen. I start to object. *What are you talking about? Why are you doing this?*

'And if, if I did – which I don't – I live a half hour's drive away. Why would I come back here to walk it.'

To see me I almost cry but I don't. I don't understand what's happening.

'But Coco –' I whisper instead.

'What's cocoa?' he cries and my bewilderment crystallises.

The air hisses out of my chest but Ben places his hand on my arm and says, 'It's the name of her business. It's a new venture. She's been under a lot of pressure.'

'That's understandable, Mr Harrison and please believe me when I say that we are all very sympathetic to your situation. However,' Mrs Wilson continues, casting doubt on her sincerity. 'This sort of gossip – malicious or otherwise – paints the school in a very unfavourable light. Not to mention the extremely awkward position Mr Matthews has found himself in.'

'No pun intended.' *Oh my God. I said that aloud.*

All three of them stare at me, dripping with repulsion and loathing. Suspicion and doubt. The old woman blinks slowly and turns back to Ben to deliver both her verdict and judgement.

'The events of the last year have obviously taken their toll on everyone concerned which is why the school has decided not to take this matter further on the understanding that Mrs Harrison will no longer be allowed to enter the grounds.' Her expression hardens. 'Is that going to be a problem?'

Ben coughs. 'Not at all. I've already taken over drop off in the mornings and Zac's been going to Breakfast Club on the days I go into the office.'

What?

'And pickup?'

'I can move my afternoon meetings around. I'll make sure I can get him.'

'We offer wrap around care until five thirty if you are unable to attend any earlier.'

'Thank you, we'll – I'll sort that out.'

What is going on? What are you all talking about? My head is swimming. I can't focus any more.

'I promise you it won't be an issue.'

'Well,' Mrs Wilson places her hands on the desk and starts to stand. 'I hope we can put this matter behind us –'

'I'm quite certain –' My husband leaps to his feet.

'Please note, however, that should further allegations come to light, we will have no choice but to involve the police.'

'Of course,' Ben splutters, gripping my arm, urging me up from the chair where my thighs are cemented, escorting me to the door. I squint back at Lenny, indignity blurring my vision, confusion rocking my judgement, but he bites down and refuses to look at me.

Ben tightens his hold on my elbow and leads me, tripping and scrambling, back down the corridor, through the front office, past the unsmiling receptionist, ignoring her demands to sign out. We burst out of the doorway like terrified toddlers shooting out of a water slide, disorientated by the unseasonable sunshine, blinded and caught off guard by its light.

'Well, that wasn't humiliating at all,' Ben sneers, dropping my arm and picking up the pace. 'What? Nothing to say for yourself? No, please. Don't apologise.'

I scuttle after him into the park. "Ben wait. We need to talk about this.'

He stops and turns, his palms facing towards me. 'So talk, Lara. Talk. Go ahead for fuck's sake. Tell me what is going on with you. Please explain. I've been asking you for months.'

'I just…'

'What? What the fuck was that about? An affair? Christ. When? Tell me, I'd love to know.'

'I…'

'I what, Lara? What? Why would you tell people that? The poor guy's having a baby any day.'

And at that the indignation I've been holding in spews out of me. 'What do you mean poor guy? Why the hell would you take his word over mine?'

'Oh, let it go. Let it go, Lara. What the fuck is wrong with you? Jesus Christ, what I wouldn't give to have you back in the sort of shape it would take for you to have an affair. You're either pissed or passed out upstairs these days. There hasn't been anything in between for so long I'm beginning to forget what you're like when you're sober.'

'How dare you –'

'No.' He rounds on me, pulling himself up to his full height, filling my personal space. 'How dare you? I know things are hard. I know things are never going to be the same again, but you have people depending on you.'

My anger flairs and my fists thump against his chest. 'You bastard. Don't even think about undermining me as a parent, especially not to that entitled brat. I've put my whole life on hold to bring him up.'

Ben throws his head back. 'Oh, here we go again. Your whole life. Ha,' he snorts. 'He's lucky if you remember to pick him up after school and you haven't taken him in weeks. It's a bloody miracle if I can even get in the study before ten o'clock with you in there sleeping off your hangover and what? You think I'm fooled by those glasses of water you won't let out of your sight? Those empty bottles you hide around the house?'

That's not – I'm not – what's going on? Nothing makes any sense. My mind is whirling, grasping at the fragments of memories, disorganised flashbacks flitting haphazardly through it. I'm dizzy with conflicting images, blinded by the incandescent rage dictating every move I make.

"Maybe I wouldn't need any of that if I didn't have to put up with Zac and all the shit you let him get away with. The bad behaviour, the constant fighting with Oscar, the toxicity –'

'So let him move into Jacob's room. Give them both some space.'

'You are not touching that fucking room.'

Ben sighs, the fight draining out of him but I stand defiant, more angry than ever. He takes hold of my upper arms, squeezes them firmly and swallows.

321

'Honey. I know it's been less than a year and it will take forever but we can't go on like this. I loved him as much as you but we have to accept that he's gone.'

'No, we don't. I will never accept that.'

'And you have to stop blaming Zac for surviving.'

'Why? Why the hell should I? It should have been him in that car, that ancient piece of shit. If he hadn't insisted on coming with Oscar... And I knew. I knew it was a mistake but Elena always gave in to him. It was just supposed to be a nice day out, that's all, but she had to be the cool one. The fun one. God forbid she put her foot down for once.'

'It wasn't her fault, Lara. It all happened too quickly. She didn't have time to react.'

'Why not? I saw it. I had time to react. I put the fucking brakes on. I saved her child. Why the fuck couldn't she save mine?'

And I saw it playing again and again in my head. Elena and Jacob in the car ahead, Oscar, Zac and Beasley in with me. The low evening sun shining through the windscreen, the smell of salt in our hair. The Peugeot veering in recklessly from the outside lane, cutting across the traffic, indicating towards the exit. Elena's arms waving up in the air, goofing around again, singing at the top of her voice, Jacob shaking his head, peering at her sideways through the gaps in his fingers.

Me on the horn. Me on the horn watching helplessly as Elena failed to slow, failed to notice the Peugeot at all until it smashed into the side of her car sending it spinning, spinning into the back of the lorry that lay ahead, crushing it, crushing them. Crushing him.

And I see his face, turned towards me now, eyes open staring straight at me and the blood trickles down his nose. And so I scream. I scream. I scream and no matter how hard Ben holds me against him I can't stop. I can't because it's not real. It can't be but no amount of noise will block it out. And he's sobbing too. The two of us locked together in a bubble, our own island of pain. But I don't want it. He can keep it. I want it all back to the way it used to be.

'He's gone, Lara,' Ben murmurs pulling me off him, wiping the tears from my face. 'We have to let him go.'

But I don't want to let him go. I don't want to move on. I refuse to live in a world without Jacob in it. I want Zac gone and I want my son back.

I want my son back.

I want my son back.

I want my son back.

Twenty-Two

Our new potted tree is squished in the corner next to the armchair and the sweet smell of pine penetrates the whole ground floor of the house. Beautiful, shiny wrapping paper has been replaced this year by the brown paper bags our online shop was delivered in making the piles of presents look like recycling waste, but not to worry. The hideous handmade ornaments adorning every surface lend the room enough Christmas spirit for a hundred Santa's grottos.

'Think we've probably got enough garlands for now, Zac,' I call out from the kitchen.

'Just one more.'

Oh, whatever. It's keeping him busy and anyway, Shazza's already ripped three of them to pieces. I weigh up the time it will take me to pick up the shredded paper scraps she'll scatter everywhere against the few minutes of tranquillity Zac decorating the place in tat will award me and on balance, it's worth it.

I've already prepped the veg for tomorrow and I only have three more orders to complete before six o'clock when I said I'd drop them off – in the car. There are too many different addresses to even contemplate walking and driving's been fine lately. I just had to throw myself back into it and it really was like riding a bicycle. Well, it wasn't. It was considerably more comfortable than that, especially in December. I have a laugh at my own expense and double-check my recipe.

I've put together a seasonal menu of side dishes in addition to the hors d'oeuvres I was planning on offering this year. Ben's idea and it was a good one. I've had so many requests I can hardly keep up with them all. He's regretting suggesting it now. Keeps coming down and checking I'm not giving all the root veg mash away. The roasted crumb-coated Brussels sprouts, the spiced cabbage, the potatoes dauphinoise. The creamed spinach. It's certainly true what they say about the way to a man's heart.

I decant the last of the garlic and lemon-marinated green beans into a foil container and the sound of my mum and Oscar practicing for their seasonal duet filters down through the floorboards, inexplicably stirring me.

This will be the second Christmas she's missed, but she's determined not to let another opportunity to shine in the spotlight pass by, her protégé at her side, on an iPad, nine thousand miles away. It couldn't be better. I can even adjust the volume if she has too much sherry and Ben says he's ordered a life-size cardboard cut-out of himself so he can pace around in the other room muttering under his breath when she starts singing.

'Aunty Lara.'

'Yes, Zac.'

'Can I show you a magic trick?' Zac stares up at me with big blue saucers for eyes.

'Of course you can.' I put the spoon down, brush my hands against the front of my apron, turn my attention to him.

He beams up at me brandishing a gold coin he cups and hides. 'Which hand?'

'That one.' I tap the left and he seamlessly slides the coin up his sleeve, presenting me with an empty palm. If I hadn't sat with him through thousands of YouTube videos I wouldn't have known how he did it. I tap his right hand. 'Well, it has to be in here then. What?!?'

He grins triumphantly. 'Tricked you.'

'I hope you're going to put on a show for us tomorrow. Nanna and Grandad will love that.'

'They've already seen all my tricks.'

'Well, fingers crossed Santa thinks you've been a good boy this year. You never know what he might bring you.' I bend down, pull him towards me and kiss the top of his head. 'Oops.'

There's a clang as the coin drops onto the floor, bouncing off the floorboards and rolling on its side in undulating circles Sharon finds irresistible. We fall about laughing.

'Not again,' Zac groans delightedly, scrambling to the floor. Sharon pounces on the coin like it's a wayward mouse and immediately loses interest but I smile dotingly as he spins it for her again. The kitchen door handle clicks and a draft of cool air rushes in from the hall.

'Just checking you're not giving my dinner away,' Ben grumbles light-heartedly, pulling up behind me and wrapping his arms around my waist.

'I'm not giving anything away,' I tease. 'This lot's paying for Christmas.'

'My sugar mummy.' He nuzzles into my neck and I jerk away giggling.

'You need a shave, Mr Harrison.' His chin tickles but I curve my head around to kiss him.

'Ughh,' Zac cries.

Ben squeezes me tighter and gazes deeply into my eyes. 'Merry Christmas, Mrs Harrison.'

'Morning, Lara.'

Oh, for goodness sake. Leave me alone. You're always interrupting.

'Time for your pills.'

It's the irritating, fat woman this time. The skinny one must have finished her shift. Good. This one's easier to distract with biscuits and I've got a whole tin of them this time.

'No, thank you.'

It was worth a try. She wheels her trolley up to the bed, picks up a small plastic pot and arranges her face in a patronising cloak of encouragement.

'I know it's hard, but the sooner you respond to the medication the sooner you get to leave. Let's get you feeling better. Clear your head.'

I do feel better. I'm exactly where I want to be. At home with my family.

She passes me the rattling pot of multi-coloured pills and a cup of water.

'Gingersnap?' I offer, nodding towards the metal tin on the bedside cabinet.

'I shouldn't,' she sighs longingly. 'If I take one from every patient I'll be needing a gurney to wheel me off the ward.' Her double chin jiggles merrily as she laughs.

'One won't hurt,' I urge and she wiggles her shoulders in surrender.

'Don't go telling my daughters I've gone and caved in. I'm supposed to be on a diet,' she grins wickedly.

How would I tell your daughters, you fool?

She prises the lid off the tin and helps herself to a handful of biscuits, all without taking her beady eyes off me. I throw my head back and upturn the pot into my mouth, chugging the water with a splutter as it hits the back of my throat. Swallowing strenuously, coughing and stretching my lips open wide, presenting the vacated cavity for her examination. She pats my hand, scattering crumbs on the bedclothes.

'There. That wasn't so hard,' she says and I pull together a feeble smile, allow her to wallow in self-satisfaction as she waddles back to her trolley and retreats behind the curtain.

'Mrs Davies! How are you this morning? Looking very festive in your Christmas hat. Ha ha ha. Ohh, mince pies? You know, I shouldn't...'

I pour the pills out from my sleeve and drop them soundlessly into the scum-coated dregs of tepid tea I've been saving since breakfast. The surface breaks into creamy rings as I grind my spoon down and stir it around the mug, the chalky pressure at the bottom gradually lessening. When all resistance has dissolved, I place it back on the side, close my eyes and lean back against the pillow.

Ben kisses my lips and twists me gently towards him, taking me in his arms and rocking me lovingly.

'Get a room,' Oscar cries, sauntering into the kitchen, the hours and hours he's spent watching American sitcoms finally paying off and Zac guffaws like a donkey with its head in a beehive. 'Cool Christmas decorations, Zaccy. Did you make them yourself?'

Zac beams with pride. 'Yes. Want to make some?'

'Sure.' Oscar lets himself be led into the sitting room, turning only to look back at us and smile.

'Thank you,' I mouth and he shrugs graciously, glowing with pleasure.

There's a knock at the back door and I pull myself out of Ben's arms with a rueful groan.

'That boy,' I sigh, making my way to the utility room. 'How many times did I tell you to take your keys?'

I hold the door wide and the winter chill sends a shiver through me.

'What's the point? You were all in,' Jacob objects, stomping his feet against the mat. Dropping his bag on the ground.

'Oi, grab him,' I yell, scrambling to shut the utility room door but I'm too slow.

'Not so fast,' Ben cries, dragging Beasley back inside. 'We need to clean this mud off first. Good grief. Where did you take him?'

'You're welcome,' Jacob smirks, brushing past us as I rub down Beasley's paws with a damp cloth. 'Ohhh, something smells good.'

Ben and I stare at each other, our eyes wide with panic.

'Don't you dare…!' we shout in unison, our alarm dissolving into laughter.

'Some things never change,' Ben murmurs affectionately and a warm sensation swaddles me like a tender hug, wrapping me tight and keeping me safe.

I walk back into the kitchen and feel myself drowning in love for my three beautiful boys playing nicely together, for our crazy fur babies glaring at each other, for Ben, for all of them. So I pour a glass of mulled wine and treat myself to a minute to enjoy it because there's nowhere I'd rather be than right here, right now.

Printed in Great Britain
by Amazon

87003624R00188